For members of a police K9 Unit, partnership is everything—in work and in love.

LOVE AT FIRST NIGHT . . .

Shuttled between her alcoholic parents and foster homes that separated her from her beloved younger brother, Steven, it's no wonder Tish Beck is a woman with trust issues. To avoid getting hurt—or hurting someone else—she's kept her romantic life commitment-free, and that's fine by her. Until she meets exasperatingly hot, funny, smart-ass K9 officer Jeffrey Pearl, and stupidly spends the night with him . . .

Currently single and content, Jeff's always got his canine bestie, Rio, by his side, and loads of human friends. He enjoys the occasional close encounter, but hasn't been tempted into anything serious. Until Tish. He's inexplicably head over heels. Too bad she's determined to keep him at arm's length. But when Tish's brother winds up in jail—again—Jeff's glad to be the man Tish turns to for help. And with Steven back on the scene, she'll need it. Soon Tish will have to open her eyes—and her heart—to love, and realize where, and with whom, her safety truly lies . . .

Books by Dorothy F. Shaw

Arizona K9
Avoiding the Badge
Redeeming the Badge
Trusting the Badge

Published by Kensington Publishing Corporation

Trusting the Badge

Arizona K9

Dorothy F. Shaw

LYRICAL PRESS
Kensington Publishing Corp.
www.kensingtonbooks.com

LYRICAL PRESS BOOKS are published by
Kensington Publishing Corp.
119 West 40th Street
New York, NY 10018

All Kensington titles, imprints, and distributed lines are available at special quantity discounts for bulk purchases for sales promotion, premiums, fund-raising, educational, or institutional use.

Special book excerpts or customized printings can also be created to fit specific needs. For details, write or phone the office of the Kensington Sales Manager: Kensington Publishing Corp., 119 West 40th Street, New York, NY 10018. Attn. Sales Department. Phone: 1-800-221-2647.

Lyrical Press and Lyrical Press logo Reg. U.S. Pat. & TM Off.

First Electronic Edition: June 2021
eISBN-13: 978-1-5161-0678-3
eISBN-10: 1-5161-0678-4

First Print Edition: June 2021
ISBN-13: 978-1-5161-0681-3
ISBN-10: 1-5161-0681-4

Printed in the United States of America

This book is dedicated to the men and women who have lost their lives to drugs or alcohol abuse. May you rest in peace. And may those who loved you find peace in their hearts and minds.

To the men and women who have found recovery in AA, CA, NA, HA, and Al-Anon—keep coming back. It works if you work it!

Acknowledgments

A big shout-out and thank you to the following awesome men in law enforcement for their dedication and service to the community, as well as their help with this book. Officer Matthew Warbington and my wonderful adopted dad, retired Connecticut State Trooper, Sergeant Robert Gawe.

Author Sidda Lee Rain...as always, you rock. I adore you and all that you do. I hope I always know you.

Last but not least, to my Night Writers group on Facebook. To those who wrote with me night after night, thank you. As usual, I could not have finished this book without you.

Playlist

Bon Jovi—"Lay Your Hands on Me"
Lady Antebellum—"You Look Good"
Sara Evans—"Alone"
Trace Adkins—"This Ain't No Love Song"
Kenny Chesney (feat. Grace Potter)—"You and Tequila"
Tim McGraw—"It's Your World"

Chapter 1

Tish Beck stared at the text message from the most annoying man on the planet.

Do Not Reply: *Hayy, girl. Hayyyy. Wait... Hay is for horses, right? Yep, at least that's what I've been taught. Anyhoo, how's it going, mami? Figured I'd check in on you. You heading home from LA tonight?*

God help her, she was *not* going to answer him. And not just because that was what she labeled him in her contacts.

Mami... Annoyance bounced around her brain.

He *loved* to call her that.

And she *hated* it.

Tish hit the side button, closing down the screen, and turned the phone over on her lap. Exhaling a long breath, she looked out the small oval airplane window at the ground crew loading luggage into the underbelly of the plane. Absently, she tapped her nail on the back of the phone case. Tish blew out another breath and swiped a stray hair away from her eyes.

Nope, for sure not answering him because....Jeff Pearl was the most obnoxious man she'd ever met.

Definitely a clear reason to not answer the text, but if she needed another, all she had to do was think about the designation she'd given him—the "deadly good-looking, goofy asshole" designation.

What made all this worse was he'd gotten under her skin like a nasty splinter forever ago, and Tish had yet to dig him out.

He'd text her again before he went to bed, just to say good night. He'd text her a "good morning" tomorrow. And then he'd text during his dinner break at work, or if he wasn't on duty, he'd text anyway, just to "check in" with her.

It wasn't stalking, per se, not in the real sense of the word anyway or the kind that was a crime. Annoying? One hundred percent yes. But that was it. The only silver lining was, apparently, she'd gotten under his skin too.

Except it was more than obvious he was *not* willing to dig her out. In fact, as far as she could tell, he wanted to do some digging in—more digging in, that is.

Tish closed her eyes, and immediately, as if always cued up and ready to go, the memory played...

* * * *

Outside the Whiskey Barrel, with her back pressed against the wall, Tish Beck gazed up at him. And what a beautiful sight he was. He'd rested one hand on the bricks above her head and hooked the pointer finger on his other in the belt loop of her jeans. Aside from that, he hadn't touched her...yet. At least not touched her in the way he was looking like he wanted to touch her.

She hadn't touched him yet either. Her palms were pressed firmly against the wall she was backed up to, but God help her, her entire body buzzed in anticipation of what the expression in his pretty brown eyes was promising. Even so, the excitement pumping through her veins was a shock. Jeff Pearl was not the type of man she would've chosen for herself in the past.

He was too goofy.

Too good-looking.

Too...everything.

His gaze settled on her lips before moving—oh so slowly—to her eyes. "So, we doing this?"

Tish's breath caught at the raspy sound of his voice. The heat from his body so close to hers felt wayyyy *too good. And for the love of all things holy, he smelled incredible. Jesus, she needed to get a leash on herself. Tish ran her tongue over her bottom lip. "Doing what?"*

He grinned, the corners of his eyes crinkling in reaction. "All right, mami."

Mami...

She had no idea why he called her that. Most of the time, it was annoying. Except the way he said it this time, the raspy low tone had a knot of arousal tightening in her stomach in a way she'd never thought possible. Jeff let go of her belt loop and ran the flat of his palm up her side, breaking contact long enough to frame her jaw in his big hand between thumb and forefinger.

Christ, she was going to spontaneously combu—
Jeff tipped his head to the side and kissed her.
No preamble. No little strokes. No teasing, coaxing, nothing timid about it. This annoying god of a man kissed her, his tongue immediately in her mouth, tangling with hers and...
Yeah, wow...just, wow.
Unable to keep her hands to herself any longer, she slipped her palms up his sides, relishing the feel of tight male body beneath his T-shirt. Tish's entire body lit up like a Roman candle. Hot tingles spread from her tummy to between her legs, and a moan escaped. Shit, she was so screwed. Totally done for.
Jeff broke the kiss and pulled back. He let out a sigh and stroked the pad of his thumb over her bottom lip, trailed it down her chin and continued down her neck. "Yeah, mami, we're doing this."
She swallowed, nodding her head. "Yeah, we are."

* * * *

Tish snapped open her eyes, drew in a harsh breath, and crossed her legs. She swallowed a groan at the wetness she felt... *Damn.*

One night—for God's sake!

And that was all it took.

After months of him annoying her and teasing her and flirting with her, she'd given in. Blame the booze, right? It was the only way to justify her actions, to herself anyway. One drink too many, though not enough to be intoxicated, of course. Just enough to lower her guard.

End result? One night together that had rocked her world in a way nothing else ever had. Jeff was still in hot pursuit, and she couldn't get away fast enough.

No one knew about it either. Not even her best friend, Rayna. And to Tish's knowledge, Jeff hadn't told anyone. Specifically, Derek—Rayna's man.

Yes, the sex had been off the charts.

Yes, when he'd kissed her, the world fell away...like it did in romance novels.

Yes, when she fell asleep in his arms, she felt safe...for the first time in, like, ever.

And that was precisely why she would not, could not, go back.

Jeffrey Shawn Pearl was a goofy asshole, who was deadly good-looking, but more than all of that, he felt like home. Tish wasn't emotionally equipped to handle all he represented, or more, give him what she was sure he'd want from her.

She had too many other things to worry about. Okay, maybe not too many. Perhaps just a few. But they were big things. Getting her credit cards paid down. Making more money was definitely at the top of the list. Shit, getting some money back in her savings could go a long way.

But really, at the end of the day, her biggest priority was taking care of her younger brother, Steven. Making sure he was okay was a hell of a lot more important than Tish having some satisfying fling with some goofy asshole. Hell, for that matter, Steven was more important than *any* of Tish's needs. The top of the list was reserved for Steven and always had been.

With the childhood they'd suffered through? Saddled with two alcoholic, addict, abusive and neglectful parents...they'd both needed to be taken care of. With Steven being younger, his care and protection was a job Tish had taken on before she'd even entered kindergarten, and she was only a mere two years older than him.

It had been harder to take care of him after they'd eventually been taken away from their parents and put in foster care—especially after they'd been separated a few times.

People talked about having baggage from growing up in a dysfunctional home. Please, their stuff didn't even compare. Tish and Steven had baggage in spades. How could they not?

But as far as Tish was concerned, she was doing just fine. She'd survived and persevered.

Sure, things had been dysfunctional, extremely so, but that didn't have to define a person.

Her father died in prison, and she had no idea where her mother ended up, but she assumed she was dead too. Despite all that, the future was a person's God-given right to fuck up or make a success.

Her parents had fucked theirs up.

Tish was on the success path, but sadly, Steven was on the same road their parents had been on.

Shifting in her seat, her text chime rang again. *Seriously?* Tish rolled her eyes, debating whether or not to even look. Could be Steven, though. She hadn't heard from him in weeks, and he hadn't returned any of her calls or texts. Half the time when he went off-grid on her, she had no clue if he had picked up and moved out of state or if he was living on the streets in their own city or if he was dead. The not knowing and the fear that plagued her—especially the thought of death—was unbearable.

Grabbing the phone, she swiped the screen. Tish's heart sank. *Damn. Not Steven...*

Jerry Hamilton: *Hey gorgeous. You want to grab a drink this weekend?*

After letting out a sigh, she hit the back arrow to exit the message, then swiped to delete. Sorry, Jerry. Not interested. One drink was enough, especially since his one drink really meant six Budweisers over two, maybe three hours. The beer breath was outstanding! Not.

Besides, even if she were interested in seeing Jerry again, it didn't matter because she already had dinner plans tomorrow night with the very good-looking, fully self-supporting Chad Williams. A coworker she didn't know well had introduced them a few weeks ago at a vendor mingling event her bosses were having, and she'd given Chad her number.

Why not, right? She was single, after all, and planned to stay that way.

Tish glanced up and eyed the older woman heading down the aisle, her eyes pinned to Tish's row. As expected, the evening flight was always full, and Tish was about to get her row buddy.

The woman set her bag down on the end seat. "Is this spot open?"

Tish smiled. "It's all yours."

There was gray present in her short, light brown hair, but in a way that made it look like silver highlights were expertly added and perfectly styled. Nice. Makeup done to perfection. Jewelry, which was obviously high dollar. Assuming she was someone's grandmother, she was definitely not a typical one.

This was the kind of woman whose grandkids called her "GG" because "Grandma" just sounded too much like an old lady in orthopedic shoes and support hose. Tish shook her head and chuckled. Totally the kind of grandmother she hoped to be someday.

Returning her attention back to her phone, she scrolled and came to a few unread messages from earlier in the day. Tish rolled her eyes.

Cole Prince: *Hey sweetness, hit me up if you want to check out downtown Gilbert tonight. I'm meeting some buddies down there.*

Once more, Tish hit the back arrow and deleted the message. Cole was sweet but too young, and she wasn't in the mood for him and his boys, though downtown Gilbert would probably be hopping tonight.

The phone dinged in her hand. Tish smiled.

Rayna Michaels: *Did you board the flight?*

Tish Beck: *Yup. Sitting in my seat now. Taking off in about fifteen min I'm guessing. How about I text you when I get home?*

Rayna Michaels: *Sounds good, honey.*

The endearing response from her best friend went straight to Tish's heart. Rayna was so different, and in all the best ways, since she and Derek got together a little over a year ago.

Tish Beck: *You and Derek going out tonight?*

Rayna Michaels: *Nope. We have Megan this weekend.*

Tish Beck: *Gotcha. I'll text later. Say hi to Derek for me. Love you.*

Tish set her phone back down in her lap. She was not going to read Jeff's message again. She should just delete it like she did all the others, but she couldn't bring herself to do that. It just felt so...final. Annoyed with herself, she put her phone in airplane mode and shoved it into the seat-back pocket.

Sitting back, she crossed her legs, brushed some lint off her thigh, and glanced over at the woman again. She was putting on a fresh coat of lipstick. Her nails were nicely manicured, a little long, and filed into ovals. Tish smiled. She smelled good too.

The flight was short to Arizona, true, but at least her copilot was more livable than most. "Maybe we'll get lucky, and the middle seat will stay open."

"Let's hope so." The lady recapped the lipstick. "I've got a bit of luck that follows me around." She winked and put the tube away in her purse.

Tish chuckled. "I could use a little luck for sure."

The urge to go back into her phone was making her skin itch. Instead of giving in, she grabbed the drink menu out of the seat-back pocket in front of her. About ten minutes passed, and the announcements started. The boarding door closed, and low and behold, the middle seat was still empty.

Tish glanced at the older woman. "Looks like your luck paid out today."

"Looks that way." The woman smiled.

The flight attendants started their routine statements and rundown of the rules. Tish flew so much she could practically recite them for the crew. Bending forward, she pulled her purse onto her lap. "I've got an extra drink ticket. Can I get you a drink too?"

The woman's eyes went wide. "That sounds nice. I'd love a drink, thank you."

"Great!" Tish pulled out two tickets and shoved her purse back under the seat.

The woman leaned toward Tish. "It's a metaphor for life, you know."

"What is?"

"The oxygen mask."

Tish tipped her head to the side and felt her brows pull together. "I'm sorry?"

The woman nodded, her expression soft but her gaze sharp as a tack. "You know how they tell us we're supposed to put our own mask on first before assisting others."

"Right."

"It's a metaphor for living. Basically, we need to take care of ourselves first. If we don't do that, we are no good to anyone else. Can't give away what you don't have, you know?"

"I guess that's true." Tish shrugged. "Never really thought about it."

The woman leaned back as much as the seat allowed and closed her eyes. "Not many do, sweetheart."

Tish shook her head and let out a soft laugh. And this was what it felt like to get grandmothered.

Anxious for something other than air masks and Jeff Pearl's texts to occupy her mind, she pulled out the in-flight magazine. It was looking like it was going to be a relatively quiet flight. One with the middle seat still open. Not a bad deal.

* * * *

Jeff checked his phone again. No reply from Tish. Not that he expected one; she usually didn't answer him. But sometimes he got lucky and she did, so a guy had to try, right? Sure, one might consider his pining a tad pathetic...though he preferred to think of it as wooing. Didn't matter. Not like anyone knew about it anyway.

Shoving his cell in the running sleeve strapped to his bicep, he turned his music up, attached Rio's leash to his harness, and walked out of his house. "Come on, partner. Time for some cardio."

Five, maybe six miles today. He needed the stress release for sure. The workweek had been grueling, and although today was his second day off in his normal four-on, three-off work schedule, he'd been busy all of yesterday with K9 training.

At the end of his driveway, Jeff took a moment to stretch before bouncing on his toes to loosen things up. "You ready?"

Rio jumped to all fours from his sitting position and let out a half bark, half chuff, and then a sneeze.

Jeff chuckled. "Me too. Lead the way, partner."

Rio set out down the sidewalk, and Jeff followed, staying a couple feet behind the dog. Their pace was evenly matched, and they were in total sync.

That was how it'd been between Jeff and Rio from the minute the animal had been assigned to him as his K9 partner. It was as if they shared a brain.

As they rounded the corner in his neighborhood heading for the greenbelt about a half a mile down, the next song came up. The intense drumbeat of Bon Jovi's "Lay Your Hands On Me" came through the phone's speaker, not as loud as Jeff would've preferred, but he'd take it.

Oh, yeah. Good tune. He should text Tish later with a link to the song. Jeff could think of a million awesome ways he'd lay his hands on her...again. That was if she ever gave him another shot. The woman was stubborn and had an ironclad will. But he wasn't giving up.

Jeff had decided a little over a year ago, when they'd met, that she was it for him. His end all, be all. His bee's knees. The greatest thing since sliced bread. Really, he could go on and on.

Never in his life had anyone ever matched him in shit for shit, like she had. Plus, she took zero crap from him or anyone. Smart as a whip. Feisty as a wild stallion. Bitchy, moody, and flat-out fucking gorgeous.

God, he loved every part of it, every part of her.

The more she shot him down, the more he wanted her. It was fucked up, but it wasn't a case of wanting what he couldn't have. Jeff had no issue finding dates or one-night stands if he wanted. Word on the street was he was a hell of a man-whore, but really...who listened to rumors? Not him, that was for damn sure.

All joking and rumor aside, Jeff wasn't opposed to relationships at all, and he didn't have commitment issues. Not that he knew of anyway. No matter what any past flings might think either. He just hadn't found the right fit for him.

But then there was Patrice Beck.

Patrice...such an awesome, unique name. Elegant was what he'd thought of the first time he'd heard it. Shame she never went by her full name, preferred to be called Tish. He doubted she was aware that he knew her full name.

Lucky for him, her bestie, Rayna, had let Tish's full name slip one day, and Jeff had never forgotten.

Jeff cleared his throat and rounded another corner, heading deeper into his neighborhood. Tish was the picture of elegance and beauty, as far as he was concerned. Ice-blue eyes—the color so pristine a person could get lost in them, drown in them even. Dimples in both cheeks when she smiled.

Fuck, gorgeous.

Long, thick, dark brown hair. When he'd met her, it was just below her shoulders, but a year later, it was close to the middle of her back. The woman had amazing hair. Like, shampoo commercial perfect hair. And then her lips. God. Damn. Jeff wiped his mouth with the sweatband on his wrist. Tish's lips were so full, they were almost puffy. Suckable and perfect for nibbling on.

He knew this because she'd let him. That one night, six months ago, she'd let him kiss her and do a whole lot of other things to her too. The memory was so fresh, so vivid, it was as if it'd just happened.

* * * *

Jeff broke the kiss and pulled back. He let out a sigh and stroked the pad of his thumb over her bottom lip, then trailed it down her chin and continued down her neck. "Yeah, mami, we're doing this."

She swallowed, nodding her head. "Yeah, we are."

Jeff practically had to bite his tongue to keep from shouting "'BOUT TIME, WOMAN!" but he managed to get his smart-ass-self under control. There was no way he was going to do a damn thing to jeopardize this shot with her.

He had one chance to show her they were meant for each other. No way he was fucking this up.

Leaning in to her once more, he flicked his tongue out, tasting the edge of her top lip.

She let out a shaky little moan, and the desire she'd been stoking inside him for months unfurled like a hungry tiger.

Dropping his hand to cradle her waist, he moved so his lips were at her ear, the strands of her thick, pretty, brown hair tickling his face and nose. He drew in her intoxicating scent and knew he'd never forget this moment, this time, for the rest of his life.

"Your place or mine, mami? Your choice."

Her fingers flexed against his sides, and she cleared her throat. "Yours."

"You got it." Jeff stepped back and extended his hand.

* * * *

Yeah, she liked things on her terms. Liked making the rules, calling the shots, being in control. Not in a femdom kind of way, more in a control freak, don't trust anyone kind of way. Blame it on the cop in him, or just plain old sixth sense, from day one, Jeff hadn't missed the fact that she had issues.

He had no idea the whats or whys behind said issues, and maybe someday he would. Maybe she'd volunteer the info. Either way, it wasn't a deal-breaker for him, because who didn't have baggage? Himself included.

Jeff rounded the back end of his large neighborhood and caught the winding dirt path along the Eastern Canal. It was a beautiful fall day in Arizona. The sun was hot, but the air temp was still cool, balancing things out. Snowbirds' and golfers' paradise for sure.

As he approached the crossing at one of the main roads, Jeff glanced down at Rio. "You need some water, young man? I know I do."

Coming to a stop, Jeff squatted down and poured water from his CamelBak mouth valve into his palm, and Rio lapped up the cool liquid. When the dog had enough, Jeff took a few pulls on the valve for himself. "Good deal. Let's keep moving, my man. Don't want our muscles to cool down. Right?"

Rio shook himself out, grumble chuffed, and resumed panting.

Jeff gave Rio's side a gentle pat. "You're good, partner. You got this. Let's get these last three miles."

The crosswalk light changed, and Rio leaped forward, taking Jeff with him. Jeff laughed. "Go easy, stud. There's no *fraulein* doggies around here to impress, you know."

Jeff chuckled at his own joke. Whatever. Not like Rio was going to laugh. Besides, he needed to distract himself somehow. Spending the entire run thinking about Tish (again) was not healthy.

He had to draw a line somewhere.

Chapter 2

"I can already tell we have incredible chemistry."

With a mouthful of salad, Tish started to laugh and then did her best to not choke on the lettuce. She glanced at Chad across the table and—wait a second. His expression was serious, with a hint of bedroom eyes mixed in.

Oh, wow. She thought he was kidding. Oookay then. Clearly, he was picking up on something she was not. And never would.

Mainly because he chewed with his mouth open. No amount of good-looking or self-supporting could ever cover that up.

Picking up her napkin, she wiped her mouth and chewed a little more before swallowing. Contemplating her reply, she palmed up her wineglass, swirled the gorgeous burgundy fluid, and took a healthy sip. Swallowed that down and cleared her throat. "Sorry, I was mid-chew. You were saying?"

"No problem." He smiled. "I was just saying I could tell we have incredible chemistry."

Jesus, take the wheel. "Really?" Tish set her glass down. "How so?"

"Well, for one, you're totally hot."

"Mmhmm." Tish nodded. "Thanks." She lifted her glass again. "Is there more?"

He shrugged and leaned back in his seat. "I can just tell. Trust me."

Yeah, no. "Hmm. You know, I think you're nice. And this—" Tish's phone rang from her clutch. "Sorry, one second."

He nodded. "Sure."

Tish pulled her phone out and checked the caller ID. Not Steven. *Damn.* It was Rayna, and well, call her an asshole, but Tish was for sure going to take the call and thus invoke her get-out-of-jail-free card. "Chad, I'm so sorry. I don't want to be rude, but I need to take this. It's important."

"Of course." He furrowed his brow as if truly concerned for her. "I hope everything is okay."

She nodded, pressing her lips together. *Okay, dude. Sure. Let's go with that.* In one motion, Tish got to her feet, swiped the screen, put the phone to her ear, and stepped away from the table. "This is Tish."

"Why hello, my dear, Tish. This is Rayna."

Tish grinned and moved to the ladies' room. "Thank you for calling me. Did you have some sort of sixth sense going on? Telepathic premonition?"

"Do telepaths have premonitions?"

"I don't know. You tell me." Tish laughed. "Doesn't matter, because you just saved me from the date from hell."

Rayna gasped. "You're on a date? Why didn't you tell me? With who?"

Tish waved her hand as if her best friend could see her. "No one you know, and no one that matters. What's up? You need something?"

"Well, as it turns out, Megan is having a sleepover at her friend's house, so we're off duty. We're going down to Dry Desert Brewery for an impromptu meetup, then probably over to the Whiskey. I was hoping you'd come meet us. But if you're busy—"

"I assume king goofball is going to be there?" Tish crossed one arm under her breast and rested the elbow of her other on her hand.

Rayna giggled. "Yes, of course."

"Compared to this fool, Jeff will be a picnic. At least he's entertaining and doesn't chew with his mouth open."

"Ew, gross. The guy chews with his mouth open?"

"Yes, I can't look anymore, and the noises are just—"

"Wait, did you just compliment Jeff?" Rayna giggled. "You did!"

"Whatever. Don't read anything into it. Sir Chews Aloud would make anyone look good."

Rayna burst into laughter. Tish couldn't help but laugh too, then got back on track. "Okay, okay, so when are you guys going? Because I hope it's now so I can go break the news to Chad Charleston Chews."

Rayna cracked up again. "We're heading there in thirty or so."

Tish leaned forward and checked her mascara in the mirror. "Perfect. If I get there first, I'll grab a table. How many?"

"Six of us, I think? Maybe eight. Better get eight just in case."

"See you soon, and wish me luck."

"Yay! Good luck!"

Tish disconnected the call and got ready to give a performance, win the Oscar, and get the hell out of Dodge.

Before she left the bathroom, she ordered a Lyft via the app on her phone, and then headed back to the table. Chad looked up, smiling from ear to ear at her as she approached.

When she reached the table, Tish smiled but furrowed her brow. "Sorry about that."

"Everything okay?"

"Yes. I mean, no, well...nothing life-threatening, of course." She picked up her small purse. "I hate to do this, truly. My friend—that was her just now—well, she's having a bit of an emotional crisis. Really bad breakup. Anyway, she's a little hysterical. I really should go to her."

Chad stood. "Oh, wow. Sorry. Yes, of course." He started patting his pants pocket. "Let me get the check, and I'll drive you."

"No, no. No need." She held out a hand to stop him. "I can take a Lyft. Already have one on the way, actually. I just feel so bad leaving in the middle of a date." She let out a nervous chuckle. Oscar-worthy for sure. "I mean, who does that, right? Can I get a rain check, maybe?" She shrugged one shoulder. "I can at least try and make it up to you. I was really enjoying this." She glanced down at the table, trying her best to look genuinely disappointed.

"Oh, uh, yeah, of course. I'd love that. But..." He frowned. "Are you sure you don't want me to drive you? I would feel better if—"

"Nope. Truly, I'm good. How about we split the check, though?" God, she was almost feeling bad now. Almost. The least she could do was not stick him with the whole bill.

"Tish, please, no." He placed his hand on his chest and shook his head. "I wouldn't hear of it. Please, go take care of your friend. Text me later. Let me know how she is." He bent toward her and gave her a soft peck on the cheek.

Don't think about the chewing... Tish smiled as he pulled away. "Thank you. That's so nice of you." She glanced down at her phone. "And look at that, my Lyft is here." She waved. "Thanks again, Chad."

Feeling like an ass, though only a little, Tish walked through the restaurant and out the door. As Tish stepped outside to meet the Lyft pulling in, she noticed another couple off to the side. They were caught in an embrace, kissing. It was sweet and soft and...

Wow.

Tish stood, awestruck, watching the couple. The man broke the kiss and gently brushed a strand of hair out of the woman's eye. She smiled and rubbed her nose over his. God, the way he was looking at the woman. Plain as the light of day, the man was completely in love with her.

Sadness hit Tish hard and fast, like a punch in the gut, and she nearly gasped. What would it be like to have that? To feel that? Was that kind of bond possible with someone? Anyone?

And really, did she want it, or even deserve it? Could she ever trust it?

The sound of the car pulling up in front of her forced her attention away from the couple. Tish drew in a deep breath, opened the back door of the small four-door, and slid inside. "Perfect timing. Thanks."

"No problem." The driver put the car in gear. "Dry Desert Brewery?"

"Yep." Instead of looking back at the couple, she focused on her phone. She didn't need to see more of what she didn't want anyway. Instead, she sent her brother a text, hoping he'd reply.

Tish Beck: *Worried, please check in and let me know if you're okay. Love you.*

She watched as the "delivered" status showed on her screen. At least his phone was still active.

It wasn't a response like she wanted, but at least it was something.

* * * *

Sitting at a table in the back of the Dry Desert Brewery, Jeff bounced his heel under the table while nervous energy bounced around his insides like a damn glow-in-the-dark Super Ball.

He was keeping his eye on the door, though trying—and probably failing—to look like he was watching the game highlights on the big screens mounted over the bar. Any minute, she was going to walk through that door, and just like the first time, and every time since, he'd lose his breath at the sight of her.

Derek nudged his shoulder. "Chill, Nelly. She's coming."

Yep, failing. Not taking his eyes from the screen, he lifted his beer, took a swig, and swallowed. Stalling because he was not going down without a fight. "Who?"

Derek chuckled. "You know who."

Rayna turned toward both of them, an amused look on her face. "Why do you call him Nelly? And why does he call you Shirley? I know you told me this, but I don't remember."

Derek scratched his chin. "Come on, you just like the story."

"Go on." She grinned.

"Fine." Derek motioned to Jeff with his thumb. "Mr. Nervous Nelly over there earned that one when you and me were first dating. I think it was the second double 'date' we went on with him and Tish, and he was as nervous as a schoolgirl. Nervous Nelly fit, and so it remains."

"Oh, that's right." Rayna pulled her hair over one shoulder and nodded. "I remember now."

Derek chuckled. "Uh-huh." Then he nudged Jeff in the shoulder again. "Well, he's nervous now too. He always is when he's going to see Tish."

"Look, Shirley." Jeff slid his chair back a bit and stuck his chest out. "I know I'm awesome, and the sheer electric energy that flows off me in waves, completely natural of course, is hard to absorb all at once. I get it. I do. But"—he raised a hand—"that does not translate to me being nervous. So you, sir, are mistaken."

Derek shook his head and picked up his beer. "Still full of himself, but also in denial. Again."

"Doc, ignore him. He has no idea what he's saying. Plus, I call him Shirley because, really, look at his eyes. They scream Shirley to me. Don't they?"

Rayna grinned and looked at her man. "Ya know, they kind of do."

"Whatever." Derek laughed and took a swig of beer.

Jeff grinned, scooted his chair back in place, and glanced toward the entran—

There she was, the most beautiful woman he'd ever seen, ever touched. He lost his breath...

She wore a pair of dark, skintight jeans. A pair of gray, chunky-heeled ankle boots with an open toe. Yes, he noticed shoes, especially on Tish. An oversized cream-colored knit sweater, half tucked in the front, hanging off one shoulder, exposing her collarbone and creamy skin. Her hair was perfect, all thick and wavy. Her makeup light and flawless, and her lips... *Fuuuuck. Kill. Me. Now.* Her lips, painted a dark matte burgundy, were just unfuckingbelievably sexy.

"Yay!" Rayna hopped up and ran to meet Tish halfway, and they embraced. Which was good. It gave Jeff time to remind himself to breathe.

"Easy, Nelly."

"Yeah, yeah. You just do you, Shirley." Jeff pressed his lips together and shook his head, unable to take his eyes off Tish as she approached the table. He'd left her alone today and hadn't texted. Not even a good morning one. Mostly because he knew he'd see her tonight—or hoped anyway—so he was saving it all up.

Which meant this could go awesome or go really, *really* bad.

He stood when she got to the table. "Your highness, so nice of you to grace us." He bowed and motioned to the chair to his right, between him and Derek.

She snorted and rounded the table, taking the seat he offered. "Be careful. If you annoy me tonight, I might order your head to be taken."

"The pleasure would be all mine." Jeff sat.

"You are a sick, sick man." Tish set her small wallet-sized purse on the table. "What're we drinking tonight?"

"Whatever you want, mami."

Derek looked over. "I already got my Yuengling while we wait for everyone to arrive."

"Heather and Rob coming?" Tish grabbed the menu.

"Yes. And you look like you need a shot. Let's go get one?" Rayna stood. Derek grinned up at his girl. "There's my wild ginger!"

Right then, the waitress walked over. "Hey, guys, ladies. You want another round?"

"Hey, beautiful." Jeff leaned forward, resting his forearms on the table. "These two awesomesauce ladies would like a shot of Patrón."

"Why is saying please so hard for you?" Tish nudged him in the side and then rolled her eyes. "Jesus."

He bent to her ear. "Sorry, mami." He looked back at the waitress. "Pretty please? With salt and lime on top?" He grinned.

"You seriously need home training." Tish leaned forward and directed her attention to the waitress. "Please ignore him. We're going to wait for now, but Rayna and I are going to come up to the bar to do a shot there. Girl time."

The waitress laughed. "Sounds good to me. Give me a wave when everyone else gets here."

"Let's go, Rayna." Tish stood, rounded Jeff and the table, and made her way to the bar.

Derek tugged at Rayna's arm before she stepped away. "Hey, give me a kiss before you run off."

"Of course." She let out a little giggle, bent, and gave him a soft peck. Derek caressed her cheek and let her go.

Jeff couldn't help but smile. He loved seeing how happy Rayna made his bestie. She was good to him and good *for* him. They made an awesome couple.

If only...

"You trying to annoy her already? Why do you do that?" Derek leaned back in his chair.

Jeff watched Tish at the bar with Rayna and shrugged. "What can I say? It's our way. No need to read into it."

"You know she tells Rayna everything, right?"

"No doubt. They're besties, like us. I tell you everything too." Jeff winked. "Your point?"

"My point is, Rayna then tells me."

"Again I ask, your point?"

Derek groaned. "Fine, play hard to get. Point is, Nelly, I know you text that woman daily. I know you love to pull her pigtails. I know you get some sort of fucked-up kick out of getting her riled up. What I don't know is why don't you just tell her how you feel?"

Jeff knew what Derek's point was, but he wasn't going to give his best friend an inch, and for good reason. Jeff knew for a fact Tish hadn't told Rayna about the night they'd hooked up.

If she had, Rayna would have told Derek, and Derek would've come right to Jeff. That was how the couple game worked. Especially when they were all BFFs.

The brutal truth of it was, if Tish didn't tell Rayna, then she likely regretted that night to the point she was willing to take it to her grave. That was more than Jeff could face, let alone accept.

Especially when he knew, deep down in the depths of his dark, smart-ass soul, that it'd been the best night of his life. Hers too. At least, that was what he felt between them that night.

So if she actually regretted it...then how could he be so off base?

Jeff focused on Tish across the bar as she threw her head back, downing the shot of tequila, and then set the glass down beside Rayna's on the bar top. As always, she captivated him, but she also frustrated the ever-loving hell out of him. That was much of where the teasing stemmed from.

He knew they were meant to be, though. Had to be, and she knew it too, even if she wouldn't admit it to him or herself.

There was just no other possibility, and no, not because he was an egotistical asshole who thought he was God's gift or something. Yes, he was guilty of that kind of thinking in the past, but this was different.

Tish was different.

The whole damn situation between them was one hundred percent different.

Jeff ran his palm along the back of his neck. "There's nothing there, man. Nothing going on other than me teasing." He hated lying to his best friend, but technically, it wasn't exactly a lie. Sadly, there really was *nothing* going on.

Whether or not he'd give his left nut to have something, anything, going on between him and Tish was irrelevant. Derek didn't need to know that. "I mean, yeah, don't get me wrong, she's hot. We all know this. It'd be a lot of fun to mess around, a little slap and tickle, right? But...we're all friends, and that just wouldn't be a good idea. It would make things awkward." He palmed his near-empty glass of beer. "Of course, I ain't gonna lie, Shirley. When that woman is pissed off or agitated, she is off the charts hot. That alone is worth yanking her chain anytime I get the chance." He pursed his lips and shrugged before downing the last of his beer.

Derek laughed and shook his head. "Okay, brother. If you say so. Here they come, so I guess, game on?"

"Game on for sure."

Tish locked eyes with Jeff as she approached their table. When she got close enough, she licked her lips and pushed the hair off her shoulder. Tequila on deck, and she was taunting him. AKA, trying to fucking kill him.

Jeff gave her a minute to get settled before setting things in motion. "Feel better?"

"Who said I felt bad?" She pushed the sleeves of her sweater up.

"Psshaw. You don't give me enough credit." He leaned back, balancing his chair on its two back legs. "I know when my mami isn't feeling up to par."

"Hmm. Highly doubtful." She brushed a lock of hair out of her eyes. "By the way, what, no texts for me today? Did you finally find some other girl to harass?"

Jeff gasped and pressed his palm to his chest. "You wound me. I'm an officer of the law. I would never harass anyone. But wait. Are you saying you consider yourself a girl and not a woman? That's so surprising. I never would've guessed that."

Tish rolled her eyes. "Wounded, my ass. Whatever you say, Jeffrey."

Jeff lowered his voice. "Your ass? Mmm, yes. I've seen it, it's not wounded though. Not at all." He bent closer to her and winked. "On the contrary, it's quite amazing."

She locked eyes with him, lips pursed. There were only a few inches separating them. Seconds passed, a conversation happening but no words being exchanged. She was remembering, as was he.

God, what he wouldn't give for just one more night...

* * * *

Tish could not look away from Jeff's deep-brown eyes. He had that same look in them he always had when he looked at her, and time froze, and the world around them disappeared.

A silent promise.

A desperate plea.

A longing she felt vibrating off him, penetrating deep inside her bones. Jesus, he was a beautiful man. And yes, he knew what her ass looked *and* felt like. A shiver rippled down Tish's spine at the memory of how he'd touched her, the things he'd done to her that one night.

Swallowing, she pushed the memory as far away as she could, considering he was sitting right beside her, his cologne blanketing her senses like some sort of drug. "Leave my ass out of this."

The words she spoke were a bare thread of a whisper, but he'd heard her. She was sure of it. Jeff Pearl wanted her. Badly. And when she spoke, when she said anything at all, he listened—even if he pretended like he wasn't.

For the love of God, what girl wouldn't find that appealing? Especially coming from a man who looked like Jeff did. Yes, he was goofy and a smart-ass, completely obnoxious and sometimes an arrogant asshole, but he was also super intelligent, witty, and funny as hell. And lest she forget, good in bed.

The whole damn deadly package, really. That said, it made perfect sense that she was attracted to him—biology and all that stuff.

The corner of his sassy mouth twitched. "Whatever makes you happy, mami."

If he only knew.

"Hey!"

Tish glanced over and saw Rob as he waved to them from the entrance and made his way, Heather in tow, to their table. Grateful for the disruption and distraction, Tish glanced around the bar to see if she could spy the waitress. It was getting warm in there, and she was getting thirsty.

"Rhonda! You made it." Jeff grinned. "Hey, have I told you lovebirds how adorable you are together? It's like a match made in heaven, for realsies."

"God help me." Tish rolled her eyes. "For realsies? How many slaps to the back of the head are you going to earn tonight?"

"Ay, mami." Jeff raised a brow and rubbed the back of his head as if she had, in fact, slapped him there. She was certainly willing. "You know I secretly love it when you're mean to me."

"It's not a secret if you tell everyone, Jeffrey." Ugh, enough of this. Tish stood, leaned toward Heather, and hugged her across the table. "Good to see you, gorgeous. You too, Rob."

Heather shook her head. "You two are funny."

"That's one way of putting it." Rob laughed.

Sure, laugh it up. Tish was sure all this cat-and-mouse bullshit in front of everyone was totally freaking hilarious. She took her seat and managed not to scowl. Everyone thought she and Jeff were "funny." They also thought, or assumed, they were sleeping together.

"First round is on me." Jeff slapped his hand down on the table, and Tish jumped.

Rob grinned. "Best idea you've had yet."

Jeff looked at her and bent to her ear. "You okay, mami?"

"I'm fine. Just stop slapping the table."

He straightened in his seat. "You got it."

"Hello, my favorite couple. Tell me again, why aren't we at the Whiskey Barrel instead?" Heather said.

Rayna smiled. "Hi to you too. We can head over there in a little bit if you want. Just figured since it's still early, we'd be able to have better conversation here."

Derek nodded. "Basically, you can't hear yourself think with the band they got playing over there tonight."

"Got it. Good thinking." Heather took a seat. "I should text Kim and let her know we're here."

"Already took care of it." Jeff slid a menu to Rob, who'd sat beside Heather.

Huh? Shock spread through Tish's veins. "Took care of what?"

Damn, her tone sounded far too frustrated. And sure enough, Jeff caught it loud and clear. His brows rose. "I texted Kim. Let her know where we are."

Easy, girl. She did not need to be going all batshit crazy jealous. Breathe. In and out, in and out. Calm, even tone. Besides, he couldn't really be interested in Kim, could he?

Sure, the woman was gorgeous, and guys usually stopped in their tracks when they saw her the first time, but he and Derek had known Kim forever, so it wasn't like there was a "thing," though there could've been a "thing" at some point, and how would Tish even know that? *Fuck...* "I wasn't aware you had her number." She looked away and shrugged, trying to act like all was well in the world, especially with her. She reached for the menu. "Anyway, I need something different tonight. I want to check what guest beers they have on tap."

Jeff frowned but then smoothed his features and slid a little closer to her. "Is there a problem, mami? You jealous?"

Ignore him. Ignore how good he smells too. Tish focused on the beer list, though she had no idea what any of the words said. "Stop calling me that."

His chest brushed against her arm. "Only when you stop pretending to hate it."

Enough. She was going to do something stupid if he didn't let up. She needed to get things under control.

Tish rolled her eyes and looked back at him. "First, I'm not jealous *or* pretending. You're completely delusional." She poked him in the chest. "Second, my palm is itching to knock you in the back of your head for annoying me."

Jeff looked down at her finger against his chest and popped both brows, the corner of his mouth arching into a grin. But he said nothing. Tish rolled her eyes once more and looked away. She actually did want to slap him.

Goddammit. She was totally at risk of losing the "fend off Jeff Pearl" battle tonight. There were far too many things rattling her. Too many things causing her guard to drop. Between not being able to reach her brother, too many bills to pay and not enough income, and then not hearing from Jeff, even though that was *supposed* to be a good thing...and then that *damn* couple she saw when leaving that horrible date tonight...

"You know, anytime you want to talk about it, we can." He spoke the words in a low tone...so no one else could hear.

Fuck it. Tish looked at him. "Why didn't you text me today?"

Rayna blurted a laugh.

Tish and Jeff looked their way. Rayna had her hand covering her mouth as if trying to stop herself. But Heather and Derek were laughing out loud, holding back nothing.

"Ahem, what's got everyone giggling like a gaggle of girls over there?" Jeff leaned forward, which caused him to press harder against Tish's arm.

Oh, God. His body merely pressed against her arm, he felt like heaven on a stick. The tingles spreading from her arm to between her legs were enough to make her cross her legs to keep from squirming. He needed to stop. Like right now. "Gaggle?" Tish laughed, trying to act contrary to how she felt.

She wiggled her shoulder, trying to get him to back off. Of course, he wasn't budging. And trying to do more was only going to look like she was being a bitch, so she let it go.

Ignore him. So what, right? He was touching her arm. Big deal. Tish drew in a deep breath and blew it out slow and easy. She could handle this. Maybe...

* * * *

Oh yeah, he was definitely getting to her. Tish was agitated for sure, but he could tell she was also fighting the attraction to him. Truth be told, he wasn't sure what it was exactly that kept her holding back. She'd stumped him thus far, but no matter what, he was not giving up.

The waitress came over, and they all ordered a round, plus an appetizer. Jeff waited for drinks to be delivered as well as food before jumping back in. In for a penny, in for a pound, right? For sure.

Jeff leaned toward Tish and was sure to keep his voice low. "You need anything? Another shot of tequila? Any more, and you might need a ride."

Tish kept her gaze straight ahead and took a sip of her beer. "I need a lot of things, but I guarantee not one is a ride from you."

"Hmm, I hear you. I respect you. But I can't help but recall the last time you took a ride from me, you liked it. A lot. A lotlotlot."

Still looking forward, she pursed those puffy lips, and Jeff had to stifle a groan. "Yeah, so? It was good." She shrugged and looked at him. "You give good dick, Jeff. I dug it. That what you want to hear?"

Jeff's stomach did a full somersault, and his cock twitched behind his zipper. "Of course. What red-blooded guy doesn't want to hear that?" He let his gaze travel down to her lips. "But what I really want to hear from that pretty mouth of yours is that you want it again."

She snorted, then pursed her lips. "You like my lips, Jeffrey?"

"Ooh, mami. You know I do."

"Yeah, I bet." She swiped along the bottom lip with the tip of her pink tongue. "What do you like the most about them?"

Damn, she was trying to egg him on, and fuck him, it was working. His dick was thickening in his jeans. Getting hard enough that he needed to adjust it, but there was no way he was going to let her know she was winning this round.

"Arm wrestle me, and if you win, I'll tell you." *Checkmate.* Jeff grinned and planted his elbow on the table, hand in the air, ready for a round.

She smiled before closing her eyes and shaking her head. "No point. You'll let me win, and that's not how I like to win."

"Oh, come on. I won't let you win. I promise." He placed his palm on his chest. "Unless you want me to let you win. But really, how do you like to win?"

She laughed. "Fair and square, like most people."

He shook his head, knowing any minute now this was either going to go his way or blow up in his face. "But it was fair and square, mami. Not like I hid anything from you or tried to pretend. You shouldn't look a gift horse in the mouth."

"Has anyone ever told you that you're a pain in the ass?" Tish stood, her chair screeching behind her.

He should probably brace for the blowup, but maybe not.... With a smirk, Jeff leaned back in his chair, raising the front legs off the ground, balancing on the back ones. "Only you. But, sugarplum, I thought you said you liked it when we did it that way."

"Jeff...wow. Did you really just say that?" The look on Tish's face was a cross between hurt and fury as she picked up her drink and downed the remains.

Okay, so a half explosion then. Damn. Guess he'd blown it again.

After setting down the glass on the table, she turned to him, planted both hands on his chest...and shoved him.

Whoa!

Still grinning like a fool, Jeff tipped backward in his chair, and when his back hit the ground, he was moving so fast, he rolled ass over teakettle.

As he was trying to get back to his feet, Tish stormed out of the bar.

Yep, he'd for sure blown it. *Fuuuuck.*

Jeff righted his chair and looked at his friends. He was not going to hear the end of this one from Derek and Rob.

"I should probably go after her." Rayna got to her feet.

Derek stood and clasped Rayna around the waist. "No, baby. Let her go. I think it's time to go to the Whiskey Barrel."

Rob looked at Heather. "You want to go with them, or do you want to go home?"

Heather slid her glass away and stood. "I think may—"

"Isn't Kim supposed to be over there too?" Derek came around the side of the table.

Heather looked up. "Yep. We should probably get over there."

Jeff moved beside Derek. Best to assess the damage. "So what's the plan, Shirley?"

Derek rolled his eyes. "The plan is, I'm getting you a muzzle and leash, and you're staying with me and Rob while we pay the bill. Also, hand over your cell phone, that way you don't text Tish and make a bigger mess."

He could not be serious. "But—"

Rob raised a hand. "Nope. Shut it." He looked at Heather. "You and Rayna head on over there and find Kim. We'll see you in a few minutes."

"Okay, honey." Heather nodded and turned to Rayna. "Ready?"

"Yes, ma'am." Rayna linked her arm with Heather's. "Why does it feel like we just missed the last five minutes of the final episode in a season of *This Is Us*?" As the ladies walked off, they paused, and Rayna looked back at Jeff. "You should definitely not text Tish tonight, Jeff. I don't know what you did to upset her, but for real, give her a break. Promise me, please?"

Damn Rayna and her sweet, genuine nature. He nodded. "You have my word, Rayna."

After the ladies walked away, Jeff turned to Derek and Rob. "I know, I know...you don't have to say a word. I'll fix it with her. Not tonight, of course, I promised Rayna. But tomorrow. I'll fix it. You have my word on that too." With that, Jeff turned and walked out of the bar.

Yes, he'd been pushing her, but her reaction was more than he'd expected and kind of out of character. Something was up, something she wasn't talking about, and Jeff needed to find out what it was. He was a cop, for fuck's sake. He should be able to figure out what was upsetting his woman.

Yes, his woman.

Chapter 3

Restless, irritable, and discontent feelings from...well, from pretty much everything in life filtered through Tish's veins like poison gunning to shut down all major organs.

With a weary sigh, she unlocked her front door and stepped into her luxury two-bedroom apartment. Luxury was definitely an overstatement, but all things considered, it was still a pretty damn nice place. New construction meant new appliances and fixtures and luxury vinyl—aka indestructible—flooring, plus a gated complex.

After setting her keys, cell, and small clutch down on the narrow entry table, she bent and slipped off her heels. *God, yes.* As she wiggled her toes and rolled each ankle, willing blood flow back into them, she let out a sigh she felt from head to toe. Relieved to be home, she headed to the kitchen in search of a nice cold one.

The night was still young, and a beer paired with some buttery microwave popcorn, with her ass planted on the couch, sounded mighty perfect. As she bent to seek out one of the many craft beer options she had stocked in her fridge, her cell rang.

Probably Rayna calling to check on her. God, Jeff was a raging asshole tonight. He really just would not stop picking at her. It was like the man *wanted* to fight with her.

Swinging the fridge door closed, she stepped out of the kitchen and grabbed the device from the entry table. She focused on the screen and—not Rayna.

The number was one Tish didn't recognize, and she debated letting it go to voicemail...except what if it was Steven?

As Tish started back toward the kitchen, she swiped the screen and put the phone to her ear. "Hello?"

"Hey, Tishy. It's me."

At the sound of the familiar voice on the other end of the line, Tish stopped short just outside the kitchen entrance. She leaned against the wall to steady herself and looked up at the ceiling. *Thank God!*

Blowing out a slow breath, she gave herself a moment so she didn't screech in his ear. "*I have been so fucking worried about you!*" Okay, clearly, a "moment" was not enough time to calm herself. Tish was well aware she sounded *and* felt a tad hysterical, but come on...who could blame her?

She pressed her palm over her forehead and closed her eyes and tried again. "For fuck's sake, where the hell have you been? I thought you were dead, Steven. Seriously! Do you have any idea what that feels like?"

"To be dead? Not personally, no."

"Ugh, Steven!" She sucked in a breath, ready to yell again, but then laughed instead. "Asshole."

He snorted. "Pretty much. Wasn't really sure which question to answer first, so I went with the last one. Figured we could work our way backward from there."

"Fair enough." The wave of relief swamping her system was so overwhelming, she put her back to the wall and slid until her ass met floor. "Where have you been?"

"No place you'd be happy about, so let's not go there."

Of course he wasn't going to tell her. Either way, she wasn't happy about him being MIA for months, so he may as well just tell her. As she rolled her eyes, she gave him a sigh right back. "Okay, fine. Where are you now? Sounds kind of noisy."

"Tempe."

Tish brightened. "Oh! You're so close. You want me to come get you? Give me an address. I can be there in twenty."

He let out a soft chuckle. "Nah. It's all good. I need to stay put for now."

Tish's heart sank. She missed her brother, and what if he didn't call again? God, she just wanted him safe. "Steven, please? I've been sick over this. You don't have to come home with me, but at least let me come see you. Please?"

It seemed like forever, save for the noise of some lunatic yelling in the background and then several other loud voices, before he finally spoke. "Okay, look, don't freak. I got arrested. I'm in Tempe city jail."

Fuck! Goddammit. Sonofabitch! Fuckfuckfuck—*FUUUUCK!* "Fuck, Steven! Again? What are the charges?"

"I said, don't freak. Possession, same as last time, but it was barely a consumable amount."

"Oh, please. You know that doesn't even matter." She frowned. "What drug? Wait...don't answer that. I don't want to know. I just think I do in the moment." Tish got to her feet and headed for her front door, ready to put her shoes back on. "Can you get bonded out?"

"No, I don't think that's going to happen this time."

"Why not?"

"I got a warrant from probation."

"You violated probation?" She pressed the tips of her fingers to the throb that was starting in the center of her forehead. "Jesus, Steven, why would you do that? You may as well just lock yourself up."

"I don't know, Tish. Fuck, will you take it down a notch? I don't really want to be lectured right now." Someone else spoke in the background, but Tish couldn't make out what they said. "Look, I gotta go. They're going to transfer me to County, and then I'll probably be in court Monday."

"Steven, I can't afford another lawyer for you."

"Wasn't asking you for one. They'll assign me a public defender."

Tears pricked her eyes, and she felt them breach her lower lids and run down her cheeks. "It never goes well with public defenders, you know that."

"Yeah, well. It is what it is. Just...I hate to ask, but when I get to County, can you put money on my books so I can buy shit from the canteen?"

"Yes, of course." She sniffled. "Just...I'll be at the courthouse Monday. Do you know if it's going to be Mesa or Phoenix?"

"Nope, I won't know till they transport me."

Tish pulled a tissue from the box on the entry table. "Shit. Okay, I guess I'll call and find out."

"You don't have to come."

She wiped her damp cheeks. "Yes, Steven, I do."

"Don't cry, okay? I'm going to be fine."

She laughed. "Are you kidding? I'm actually going to get a full night's sleep tonight."

"Yeah? Why's that?"

"Because I know where your ass is. Now, be good. Don't cause any trouble."

"Love you, Tish."

"Love you too." Tish pulled the phone away from her ear and stared at the screen.

How the hell was she going to manage this? She needed to find a way to pay for an attorney. Otherwise, he'd likely be going to jail for a long time.

God, why didn't they send repeat drug offenders to rehab? Locking someone up in jail didn't do shit when they were an addict. Half the time, drugs got smuggled into jail too.

Relieved, yet annoyed once again, she went back into the kitchen and resumed her plans. After a few minutes, the popcorn was popped, an icy glass was filled with a superb blonde ale called Strawberry Blonde by THAT Brewery, and Tish moved to her couch.

She could call Rayna and fill her in on the mess Steven had gotten himself into again, cry on her shoulder...but she just didn't have the energy. Planting her ass on the couch, she pulled a blanket over her lap.

Tish let out a slow breath, her head fell back against the cushion, and she closed her eyes. Jeff Pearl's annoying but pretty face flashed in her mind. Tish snapped her eyes open. "Nope. Hell no, not calling him."

With a hard frown, she picked up and engaged the remote. Yes! TLC was playing last week's episodes of *90 Day Fiancé*. Best show to watch when a person felt like shit about their own life.

Tish took a long sip of her beer and then another. Focusing on someone else's train wreck of a life, instead of her own, was preferable any day of the week.

* * * *

Jeff almost dropped the phone when her number came up on his cell screen. He hit the button and pressed the device to his ear. "Hey, you okay?"

"Why were you so mean to me tonight?"

He moved his feet from the coffee table and straightened from his slouched position on his couch. "I wasn't mean, mami. Just pulling your pigtails is all."

"Ugh, you're never going to stop calling me that, are you?"

He smiled. "No. But that's because I know you actually like it."

She laughed and then let out a groan. "God, I kind of hate you, then I really don't. It's so confusing, isn't it?" She blew out a breath. "Okay, fine, if I admit to liking it, do you promise you'll never tell another living soul, ever, evereverforever?"

"Whatever you need, mami." He leaned back and stretched his legs out onto the coffee table again. Her words were a tad slurred, definitely out of the norm for her. Like he'd thought earlier, something was for sure wrong. "You sound like you've been drinking. Where you at, babe? You need me to come get you?"

"Yep and nope."

"Two out of three ain't bad, I guess." Jeff smiled, picturing her defiant little pout. "Will you tell me what's bothering you?"

"What makes you think something's bothering me?"

"Because for one, you're calling me and—" He heard the distinct sound of a can being opened. "Was that a beer or a soda I just heard you open?"

"Beer. Ooh, I bet you'd like this one. You want one?"

Rio let out a low moan and shifted on his dog bed. Jeff glanced at his partner. The dog sighed but stayed sound asleep, all stretched out in front of the gas fireplace.

"Depends on what kind of beer. I am pretty picky, you know. Plus, I don't know where you are. That's still a mystery."

"But you're a good cop. You could probably figure it out." She giggled. "Ever been to THAT Brewery up in Pine?"

Jeff thought for a minute. "Nope, not yet. But I've had their beer before. Which one are you having?"

"Strawberry Blonde." She paused, probably taking a sip of her fresh beer. "Mmm, so good. We'll have to go there sometime."

"Our first official date? I'm game." Yeah, she was definitely buzzing. "How many have you had?"

"How many dates? Hmm, let's see..."

He raised his eyes to the ceiling. He did not want to think about her with anyone else. It was bad enough he had to deal with the fact that she dated constantly, right in front of him. "No, stop. How many beers have you had?"

"In my lifetime? Hmm, let's see..."

Jeff chuckled. "You're kind of cute when you're buzzed."

"I'm always cute, and who says I'm buzzed?"

"Rio said it. Not me." Jeff eyed the dog, whose ears perked up at the mention of his name.

"Awwww! How's Rio doing? I feel like it's been forever since I've seen him."

"Six months, but close enough." Jeff rubbed the back of his neck. "Tell you what, he and I are gonna come by and check on you. Save me one of those Strawberry Blondes, 'kay?"

"Always knew you liked blondes better." She snorted.

"See you in a few, mami."

"Okay, papi." She burst into a fit of giggles.

Jeff disconnected the call before he burst into laughter along with her. He'd rather do that in person, where he could see her eyes dancing with delight and her face alive with happiness.

After getting to his feet and twisting from side to side to crack his lower back, he freshened up in the bathroom. A quick brush of teeth, with a nice mouthful of Listerine. Then a quick finger comb of his hair. Lastly, a refresher of deodorant and then cologne.

If he had more time, he would've showered, but as it was, he figured he had a narrow window to get over there before she passed out. He wasn't wasting it.

On his way toward the kitchen, he called out to Rio. When he got into the small mudroom from the garage into the kitchen, Jeff grabbed Rio's harness and leash. "Come on, partner. Let's go see Tish."

As Jeff slipped the harness onto Rio and clipped on the leash, the dog's tail wagged about a thousand miles a minute, tongue hanging out as he panted. Rio was acting as excited as Jeff felt. Hell, if he had a tail, he'd wag it too. But no matter how excited he was to see her, he had every intention of playing the whole situation cool tonight.

No need to show up like he was starved and desperate for attention. Even if he was. Not the point.

Grabbing his keys, he stepped out into the garage and hit the opener button. "Remember, you gotta play it calm, cool and collected. Hopefully, she'll have a bowl for water for you." He moved to his Tundra. "Yeah, I'm sure she will. She's perfect, so she probably has everything. Maybe even food."

He opened the back door on the driver's side and gave the dog the German command for up. "*Hopp!*" Rio jumped up into the back seat floor and then sprawled across the entire footwell area.

Jeff closed the door, then slid behind the wheel and fired up the engine. "Okay, probably not food. She doesn't have a dog, so that's probably not realistic. But then again, it wouldn't surprise me." He glanced over his shoulder as he backed out of his garage and driveway, and then gave Rio a scratch to an ear before turning around and pulling away from his house.

Fact was, Tish was going to fawn all over the dog and not Jeff, and that was going to suck, but he'd deal.

The drive to her house felt like it took ten years, but according to the clocks in his truck and on his phone, it was barely 11:00 p.m., and she'd sounded completely awake. With any luck, he was in for a long night of one-on-one time with Tish.

* * * *

Tish swung the front door wide and let herself take in all that was Jeffrey Pearl.

Yum.

Six feet of lean muscles, long legs, narrow hips, washboard abs. Tish swallowed, remembering how smooth his skin was, and drew in a slow breath through her nose. All that thick, dark brown, almost black hair on his head was unbelievably soft in her fingers. Those deep brown eyes and sexy-as-sin smile did her in every time she saw him too, though she'd never let it show.

To top all that amazingness off, the man's face was model perfect! High cheekbones, straight nose, chiseled jaw and narrow chin—gorgeous.

She needed to get her libido under control because she'd had a few beers and, as a result, was forgetting all the reasons why it was a bad idea for him to be at her house, and worse, for them to be alone together.

Thank God he wasn't in uniform (which she'd seen before and OMG it was spontaneous orgasm worthy) because if he was, she would for sure be addressing him as Officer Pearl. Maybe ask him for his card with his direct line on it? Maybe ask him to show her his...gun? *Oh my, Officer Pearl...it's sooo big!*

Tish nearly laughed out loud at the thought but bit her tongue to rein it in. Instead, she grinned, stepped aside and propped her hand on her hip. "Wait! How about Rio just comes in, and you stay out?"

"Not a chance, mami." He laughed and looked down at his gorgeous, nearly all-white German shepherd K9 partner. "Dunno, Rio. Maybe we should go back home. She's already being mean to me."

Rio let out a little whine and sat, wagging his tail the whole time.

Tish let out a sharp laugh. "Guess we know who's boss."

Bending forward, he unhooked Rio's leash. "Go on in, young man." Tail still wagging, Rio bolted into her apartment. Jeff stepped over the threshold but stopped when he was face to face with her. "Of course we know who's boss, mami. It's you." He winked and moved past her.

She snorted. *This is suuuuch a bad idea.* Tish closed the door, turned and put her back to it. "You want a beer?"

He was squatted down, removing Rio's harness, and he glanced at her over his shoulder. "You mean you didn't drink all of it?"

"Har, har, har." She moved to the kitchen.

"You have anything dark in there?"

"I thought you wanted me to save you a blonde?" She shifted some other items to find the extra cans she had in the back of her fridge. "I have a brown ale. It's called Coffee Bender, by Surely Brewing Company. Ever had it?"

"Nope, but I'm sure I'll like it." He moved into her kitchen and started opening cabinets. "I'm partial to brunettes—aha, found 'em." He pulled a tall glass down.

"All you had to do was ask, darling." She cracked the top on the can and handed it to him. He started to pour, the dark liquid filling the glass. "Of course, I do have cold ones in the freezer, but suit yourself."

With a shrug, she turned and walked back out to the living room. There was a dog that needed some attention. A smile on her face, Tish moved to Rio and sat beside him on the floor, legs crossed. "You are just what I needed tonight, handsome boy."

Jeff moved past her and found a spot on the couch. He kicked off his sneakers and extended his legs, resting them on her ottoman.

As she continued to stroke Rio's fur and murmur sweet doggie things to him, Jeff watched her. She didn't have to look up to know it. She felt it. His eyes were both a balm to her frustration and a temptation for her libido. She ignored the temptation part but relished in the balm part.

When she'd had her fill of snuggles, she gave Rio a final hug, nuzzling the soft fur on the top of his head. "So sweet. I could cuddle you for hours, Rio." She got to her feet. "Come lay by me, sweet boy."

Tish moved to her spot on the couch, and Rio followed, lying down at her feet. Perfect. She smiled, grabbed her beer, which was still cold, and took a sip.

"You want this?" Jeff held up the blanket she'd been using.

"Nah, I'm warm enough right now." She took another sip.

"Good to know. Is your beer cold enough?"

"Since when don't you like blondes?"

"Never said that."

"Yes you did." She frowned.

"No, I said I was partial to brunettes."

"Okay, but when..." Tish rolled her eyes. "Oh, forget it."

"You want to tell me what's up?"

She ran the tip of her toe on the back of Rio's neck. "His fur is so soft, especially right here."

"It is, yes." He sipped his beer. "So what's wrong?"

"What makes you think something's wrong?"

"Besides all the reasons I already listed on the phone, I'm now sitting in your apartment. Which, considering you won't come near me with a ten-foot pole since that one night, tells me something serious must be up." He shrugged one shoulder. "So tell me what it is. All kidding aside, I care about you, Tish. More kidding aside, I know you know that, but I'm telling you anyway, or reminding you rather. Bottom line, if you're not okay, I want to know why."

"What do you mean you care about me?"

"What do you mean, what do I mean?" Jeff frowned, a line forming between his brows.

Tish wanted to reach out and smooth it but stopped herself. "You care about me how?" She shifted and faced him on the couch. The warmth of the beer buzz pulsed through her veins, making her hyperaware of his presence. "Rayna cares about me. Derek does too. Is that how you mean you care about me?"

She was fishing for something, anything from him really. As long as it was more than the teasing he'd been dishing out since...well, since always. The entire night she'd been an emotional mess, and that call from her brother only made all of it worse instead of better.

Tish felt adrift with no anchor, as if there was nothing and no one in the whole world she could count on, except herself. And truth be told, she'd felt like that her entire life.

It wasn't a bad thing, being self-reliant, but Jesus, sometimes she really wished there was someone to hold her up for once when she felt tired or when she tripped and fell down. She took another mouthful of beer and swallowed the lump in her throat down.

Dammit, all this melancholy was totally the beer talking, and she'd regret it in the morning. That said, for now, she wanted to see what Jeff Pearl intended, where all his teasing and smart-ass comments were supposed to lead.

Besides, even if he did care about her, no matter how, he sure as shit wasn't going to want much to do with her once he found out about her repeat offender, drug addict brother.

Jeff took a long swallow of his beer and then looked at her. "I'm your friend, Tish. No matter what, first and foremost, I'm your friend." He set his glass down on the end table. "But you know damn well I want more. From day one, I have wanted more."

His version of "more" was probably different than others'. Tish looked down into her glass, bit her bottom lip, then looked back at him. "Define more? Another one night? Two nights?"

He frowned, blew out a breath and ran his fingers through his hair. "No, Tish. Not that." He shook his head. "Let me be clearer and spell it out for you: I want every night. I want every day. I want all of you."

He wants all of me.... She drew in a breath and pressed her lips together. If he knew all of it, all of her—there was just no way he'd *really* want her. "You couldn't possibly want all of me, Jeff. There's parts of me no one wants, and no one should ever see."

"You're going to tell me what I could or could not want? Really?" He shifted on the couch and faced her. "Let me tell you something, woman. No bullshit. With me, you get to be the boss, *because I let you.* You get to run the show *because. I. Let. You.* You want it, I give it. From flowers to drinks to control over everything. It's yours, mami. Truly." He shifted and leaned toward her. "But what you do not ever get to do is walk all over me or assume you can tell me *how I feel* or *how to think.*" He licked his lips, and Tish couldn't help but track the movement of his tongue. He wiped the corner of his mouth with his thumb and continued. "Me yielding to you is not because I'm weak. It's because I know it's what you need, and I'm strong enough to give that to you. It's because I know I am the *only* man who can give that to you.

"Make no mistake, Patrice, I will not eat shit for you or from you. That won't ever happen. Sure as fuck, I will never be your whipping boy. Nor will you be able to push me around, ever. That said, hear me now, Tish...I am a man who knows how to take care of his woman and who wants to take care of her, and frankly, there isn't a damn thing about you or your past that would *ever* change that."

Tish felt his words deep in the pit of her stomach, and her throat got tight. Every inch of her skin tingled in anticipation of what his declaration could mean. But beyond that, it was also a complete turn-on for him to both stand up to her and acquiesce to her at the same time.

Fuck it. She leaned forward, coming nose to nose with him. "So...let me get this straight. You saying I'm your woman, Officer Pearl?"

He rolled his eyes. "You know goddamn well you're my woman."

Without moving away, she cast her eyes down and lowered her voice. "Jeff..."

She felt his hand move up her side and give her a soft squeeze. "Yes, Tish?"

She smiled and closed her eyes. "I *need...*"

"I know, mami. I know exactly what you need." In one motion, Jeff stood, pulling her up with him.

He didn't look back at her, didn't say another word, just walked them down the hall to her bedroom.

This was good.

This was what she needed.

There was nothing left to say, nothing that needed to be discussed. She wouldn't have to talk about Steven, or her mounting debt, or the attorney she couldn't afford but needed to get for her brother.

For a couple of hours, she could cast all that aside and instead focus on Jeff, bury herself in him and let him take her away from everything weighing on her shoulders, even if for just the night.

Or maybe even a little longer....

Chapter 4

Jeff stepped into her dim bedroom and headed right for the bed. When he reached it, he turned to face Tish and pulled her close to him.

She needed him, and he sure as fuck needed her right back.

Jeff cupped her face in his palms and stared down at her. The light from the hallway was plenty for him to see her, but still, with her back to the doorway, her features were obscured by the shadows in the room. It didn't matter. He knew how beautiful she was.

Bending forward, he stroked his nose over hers before pressing soft kisses along her cheek to her ear. "Will you let me take care of you tonight?"

She nodded, letting out a soft moan, and he brushed his lips over her ear. "Good. Perfect."

With his nose buried in her hair, he took a moment and drew in a deep breath. Her intoxicating scent filled his lungs—it was the same as the first time he'd been intimate with her. It was a fragrance he'd never, ever forget.

As he trailed his lips and tongue down her neck, the heavenly taste of her skin forced a groan from his throat, and he ran a hand up her back, tangling his fingers in the soft, thick tendrils of her hair.

God, he wanted her. All of her.

Tish arched, her soft breasts pressing against his chest. "Jeff..."

"I got you, mami." Moving from her neck, he went right for her mouth.

She was ready for him, and as their parted lips met, Jeff thrust his tongue inside her mouth, stroking over hers. She moaned, and so did he. Like before, the kiss was wet, hot and no holds barred.

The underlying, low-level current of chemistry that existed between them at all times ignited into an uncontrollable inferno.

Burn, baby, burn...

With both hands tangled in her hair, Jeff deepened the kiss, pulling back only to nip at her lips and then dive back in for more.

Little whimpers and moans came out of her, each sound making Jeff's dick grow harder and harder. She tugged at his shirt, pressing her body against his and pulling him tighter to hers, all cues that she wanted more. Fine with him. He would always want more.

Reluctantly, he released his hold on her hair...but only because there was so much more of her he needed to touch. He slid his palms down her back and found her divine ass. Cupping each cheek in his palms, he hiked her off her feet.

Still kissing, Tish groaned, and as he turned them to move onto her bed, she wrapped her legs around his waist.

Pushing himself up, he broke from her lips but stayed seated between her parted thighs. Staring down at her, he thrust his hips forward.

She moaned and arched, rolling her pelvis, grinding against his dick.

Fucking hell, they were completely in sync.

Jeff drew in a shaky breath. "Do you have any idea how incredible you are?"

She ran her hands under his shirt and up his back. "I could say the same to you."

"Well, don't let me stop you, really. Feel free to share what's on your mind." He grinned and thrust forward again.

She moaned and matched his movement, and fucking hell, the head of his dick was throbbing.

"What's on my mind is, I really want that hard, beautiful cock of yours buried inside my wet cunt." She smirked. "Correction, I *need* your cock inside me. Badly."

"You think my cock is beautiful?" Jeff rose to his knees but remained between her legs. "That might be the nicest thing you've ever said to me."

She giggled and covered her face. "Shut up. I say nice things."

"Not to me, but that's okay. I know you like me." He laughed and pulled her hands away from her face. "Oh, come on now, you don't really want me to shut up, do you?"

"Maybe." She smiled. "It depends on what you're gonna say next."

"I'm probably going to say a lot of things. Naughty, dirty, flirty things." He winked before tugging off his T-shirt and tossing it on the floor.

"Keep it there, and we're all good, cowboy."

Jeff watched her as she watched him. The expression in her eyes was primal and intoxicating. She liked his body, and he liked that she liked it. Being the ham he was, he was not going to miss an opportunity to give her a show. Taking his time, he smoothed his hands down his torso before reaching the waistline of his jeans.

Her eyes were wide, and she licked her lips.

Yeah! Hell fucking yeah! She was right there with him.

"Giddyup." Jeff popped the top button and slid the zipper down. He pushed his pants and boxer briefs down and palmed his hard dick, slowly stroking from root to tip. "Mami, what was it you were saying about my cock?"

"Sweet Jesus." Tish rose up, resting on her elbows. She licked her lips again. "I was saying that your cock is beautiful."

He stroked the length again. "See? That wasn't so hard." He moaned, and a bead of pre-cum formed on the head.

"Looks pretty hard to me." She grinned. "Oooh, I want to taste that."

Jeff caught the drop on his thumb and extended his hand to her. "It's all yours."

Tish licked the end of his thumb and then sucked the whole thing into her mouth.

Arousal and desire raced through his veins, flooding his entire system with nothing but need for her. His cock jerked, bobbing against his belly, the head swollen and throbbing.

God help him, the sight of her plump lips pursed, her cheeks hollowed as she suckled, was enough to nearly have him coming. It was definitely enough to blow his mind. Wanting her desperately, he bent and slid his thumb from her mouth but replaced it with his tongue.

He could fucking kiss her forever.

She moaned and wrapped both hands around his dick and stroked.

Jeff jerked from her lips and arched back, thrusting his pelvis forward. "Fuuuuuck!"

"Oh yeah, let mami take care of that for you." Staring up at him, she raised a brow, and her lips curved into a devious little smile.

Searing heat spread down his spine, settling in his balls, and perspiration broke out all over his body. Jeff smoothed a hand over his face and tried to draw in a full breath.

Holy...yeah. Done. So, fucking done for.

This woman, quite literally, had him in her hands.

To do with what she wanted.

Jeff was totally fucking fine with that and completely unable to take his eyes off her hands as she worked his dick. "Say it again, please?"

* * * *

In complete and utter awe, Tish gazed up at this half-naked god of a man perched between her legs. His abs flexed, in the most delicious way, each time she stroked his steel-hard prick in her fists.

She wanted to swallow the entire length of him to the back of her throat, and she would, it was just...watching him all-consumed by the pleasure *she* was giving him was such a fucking turn-on, she wasn't ready to lose the view.

"Say what again, hmm?" She stroked her thumb over the nonstop ooze of pre-cum gathering at the tip, smearing it over the rim and down the shaft.

Jeff moaned and sucked in a harsh breath.

Fucking magnificent! She knew what he wanted her to say, and teasing him was just too irresistible. Call it payback for all the pigtail pulling... sure, maybe right then was not the time or place, but really, why not?

She had his beautiful dick in her hands. She had all the control. May as well just use it all and get off on it too. Easy peasy, and orgasms all around, right? Damn right.

Licking her lips, she moaned, still tasting him. When he caught her eyes again, she blinked. "Take care of that for you? Is that what you want to hear? But I am."

He shook his head and hissed when she cupped his sac in her other hand, massaging the tender globes. "No, the other—fuck! The other thing. Goddamn, Tish. You're gonna make me come."

"I think that's the idea, honey." She grinned, bent forward and snaked her tongue out, licking the very tip of the head. His sweet and salty flavor was heaven, and she knew she couldn't wait much longer to have him fully in her mouth.

"Oh, God! *Fffuckyeah.*"

"You like that?" As he nodded, his body shook with his arousal, and Tish grinned. "Ask me nice."

He swallowed, his Adam's apple bobbing. "Tish, please suck my cock?"

Tish shook her head. "No, not like that. You know how I want to hear it."

His eyes flashed, and he licked his lips. "Mami, suck my cock, please?"

"Oooh, baby. Mami would *love* to suck your cock for you." Without further preamble, Tish leaned forward, pressed her lips to the tip, and in one steady motion, slid him fully into her mouth.

Oh yes, there he was. Sweet, *sweet* heaven.

Jeff growled, his fingers tangling in her hair and then gripping the strands closest to her scalp.

She moaned at the sexual sting and drew him out, laving the rim with her tongue before sucking him back in. Her pussy was so wet, no doubt she'd soaked her panties. Slurping, sloppy, sucking his cock, Tish moaned and could not get enough.

She wasn't sure whether they had some reverse daddy fetish going with the whole mami thing, but at that moment, she couldn't care less. It was working for her, working in a way she never would've imagined. And apparently, her referring to herself as that turned him on as much as she was turned on by him calling her that.

It was a little twisted, but it was fucking hot.

With a tight grip on her hair, Jeff thrust his hips forward and fucked into her mouth. She moaned again, tasting the salty pre-ejaculate. He was close, and so was she.

"Tish..."

She moaned and sucked the head.

"Tish...fuck. *Tish!*" He jerked back from her, taking his yummy cock with him.

"Wait." She reached for him. "You taste sooo good."

He held his hand out. "No. I don't want to come."

She frowned. "You're not supposed to tell me no."

"Ha. You're right, except I will when it's best for you or both of us." Taking ahold of each of her legs, he gripped behind her knees and yanked her forward, forcing her back to the bed.

Tish let out a half giggle, half squeal, and then groaned. Only this man inspired these kinds of reactions from her. It was so annoying. Too busy complaining in her head, she'd completely missed him getting off the bed. Geez, he'd already shed his pants completely and was holding a condom in his hand. She grinned. "Oooh, is that a present for me?"

His lips arched into a goofy grin. "I love giving presents. What can I say, it's my love language."

Tish blurted a laugh. "You kill me."

"Kill you? No, no. All I want to do is make love to you." After climbing back on the bed and back between her legs, he tore the package with his teeth, opening it. "That's a Heart song, by the way. Great song. So—" He wagged his finger at her. "How about you take off all those things in my way, huh? I'll take care of this part."

"You never stop being a dork, do you?" She rolled her eyes.

He grinned. "You love it."

"I'll never admit that." She pulled her sweater over her head, then did away with her bra.

He positioned the unrolled condom at the tip of his swollen cock head but stopped when her breasts were bare. "You have incredible breasts. I mean seriously, they're fucking perfect."

"Come on, this isn't the first time you've seen them."

"I know, and I should've told you then. I'm sorry."

She tucked a lock of hair behind her ear. He was being sincere, sweet even, no doubt about it. "Thanks."

His tone of voice, the seriousness of his expression, the whole moment between them made her stomach flip-flop. Determined to stay on task and not let any sort of romantic feelings bloom, she undid her jeans and slid them off and then got rid of her very, very damp panties.

Naked, she lay back on the bed and watched. As he maneuvered the latex down his shaft, his arms flexed ever so slightly. *Damn...* Heat spread over her skin. People complained about condoms, but in her opinion, watching a man roll one on a hard cock was sexy as hell.

Once finished, he bent over her. "You ready?"

"Completely." She smoothed her hands up his sides and onto his upper back. "Are you?"

He smirked. "Nope."

She let out a little gasp/laugh. "Why not?"

"Because you're everything, Tish Beck."

She felt that statement...everywhere, and a lump hit her throat. Before she could respond, he kissed her, soft, sweet, stroking his tongue over hers.

Okay, yeah. She'd deal with it later. Kissing Jeff was intoxicating, sexy, and in and of itself, a complete turn-on. She'd never been kissed like he kissed her, ever. The man lit her on fire every time.

But his words, the declarations he was making, were doing things to her body she'd never felt before either. It was as if everything between them went on overdrive and amped up one hundred and fifty percent.

Tish moaned, arching against him. The tip of Jeff's prick nudged at the mouth of her pussy. She moaned again, and Jeff broke the kiss. "Please, Jeff. Please..."

"All of me, for all of you." Jeff pressed forward, his cock entering her tight channel, her body completely ready for him.

"There you are..." She closed her eyes. God, she'd missed him, how good he felt, how perfect and right. She hated admitting that, even if only to herself. Yet... Screw it, she didn't want to hold back, not tonight anyway. "Missed you."

"Ay, mami. Missed you too." He pressed his forehead to hers. "So perfect. You fit me like you were made for me."

Tish moaned, her pussy clenching on his girth filling her. She knew what he was talking about, knew exactly what he meant because she felt it too. But now was not the time for any more talk because she was so primed for him, she was on the verge of coming. "Mmm, yes."

Resting on his forearms, his fingers tangled in her hair, the majority of his body weight was on top of her. It felt good. She loved it that way, loved feeling all of him. With his body pressed fully to hers, Jeff thrust his hips forward and back, grinding against her clit, burying himself completely with each pass.

She raked her nails down his back and gripped his ass. Holding tight, she rocked her pelvis in time with his, her clit getting all the stimulation she needed. Tish's orgasm rose, the tension building in her tummy with every rub of his body against hers, every thrust of his cock inside her cunt. "Jeff...fuck."

With a grunt, he moved faster. Thrusting harder. Gripping her hair in his fists, he tugged her head back and bit the side of her neck. "Ride it, Tish. Let me feel your tight cunt squeeze me."

"Oh, God, yes!" She rolled her pelvis, digging her heels into the bed, taking him as deep as she could. "Harder!"

Jeff growled against her neck and crashed into her, their hips slapping against each other. "Tish..."

"Yes! Now!" Tish's orgasm hit, crashing through her like an ocean wave. "Fuck yes, mami. Give it to me."

Her cunt clenched in little spasms, her clit pulsing as she rode the sensations rolling through her. Her orgasm must've taken him over too. Jeff groaned long and low, thrusting one last time.

Buried deep, his dick pulsed over and over again inside her, spurting his release into the condom. She wished she could feel it, feel his semen spurt from his beautiful cock, filling her. Marking her...

Tish stared up at the ceiling, letting her body come back down to earth. Jeff was still deep inside her, his face buried in her neck. His cock jerked once more, a final spurt of semen, she assumed.

That same longing rose up inside her again. She wanted to be marked by him. She wanted to be his. Tish closed her eyes. Jesus, this wasn't some vampire romance novel. Humans didn't mark each other, not in that way anyway.

Except, Jeff had done just that, hadn't he? He'd marked her—not physically but emotionally for sure.

And that was a realization she wasn't sure she would ever be able to share with him.

Chapter 5

After cleaning up, Jeff returned to Tish's bed. She was resting on her side facing him, one arm tucked under the pillow beneath her head, the other in front of her.

He smiled. "You look comfy. Before I get comfy too, can I get you anything?"

"How long do you think you're going to be comfy for?"

Ooh, she was already trying to get rid of him. Most guys'—hell, every guy's?—dream come true. One-night stand with no attachments, no complications and no cuddling. A different time, different girl, Jeff would've taken that golden ticket and headed out the door, guilt-free.

But this was now, and this was Tish, and he wasn't going any-fucking-where, because in this scenario, *she* was the golden ticket.

"Hmm." Jeff pulled the blanket and sheet back and slid beneath. He turned on his side to face her and mimicked her pose. "I think for however long it takes."

"How long what takes?"

He smoothed his palm across the sheets between them and laced his fingers with hers. She let him, which was surprising, so he took it as a good sign. "For as long as it takes for you to tell me what's up. Actually, correction. For as long as it takes you to tell me what's up and also for you to want me to be comfy."

Her brow furrowed. "You're a strange man, you know that?"

"I prefer to think of myself as unique."

She sighed and rolled onto her back. But instead of pulling free of his fingers, she took him with her, resting the linked hands on her tummy. Jeff took that as another good sign, an even better one.

"There's just a lot going on."

Jeff figured now was the time to shut up, shut up, shut the hell up, and let his woman talk. He'd done enough prompting. The communication ball was in her court.

"I mean, I know everyone has a lot going on. You're a cop, for God's sake. I'm sure you see plenty of people who have a lot going on. So I guess I'm not unique in this." She moved her other hand from under the pillow and began tracing small lines and circles on his forearm. "I don't know what you're going to think of me after I tell you this. Maybe you won't care, maybe you will." She turned her head and looked him dead in the eye. "I'm not supposed to care what you think of me." She lowered her voice to a whisper. "But I do. I really do. And if you tell anyone I admitted that, I swear to God, Jeffrey Pearl, I will never speak to you again."

Fuck, that was a lot, and the last part was not what he was expecting to hear her say. No way he was going to unpack and process all of it as fast as he needed to. She cared about what he thought of her, which was awesome, but she didn't want anyone to know that she cared? Like he was something to be ashamed of? Jeff frowned. What the fuck was he supposed to do with that?

He drew in a breath and decided to put that tangled wreck of emotion aside for a moment and focus on the rest of what she'd said. She had something going on that she was afraid he was going to judge her for. Hell no, he would never... "Tish, there isn't anything you could tell me that would make me think less of you."

"See, I know that about you. You're genuine like that." She focused on the ceiling again. "Except I think this would cross a line for you."

Shit, what did she do? "Did you commit murder?"

She blurted a short laugh. "No, of course not."

"Okay, that's good. Any other major felonies?"

"No." She shook her head. "Not that I am aware of anyway."

"Also good, but I gotta tell you again, even if you were a murderer, I'd never think less of you. I'd even come see you in jail. For realsies."

"Again with the for realsies." She laughed again. "Your crazy ass probably would. Fine. Point made. Guess we'll see."

"Yep, we will." He gave her hand a squeeze and put an imaginary piece of duct tape over his mouth. Wasn't like there was any handy.

"There's so much about me you don't know. No one does, not even Rayna." She pursed her lips, shaking her head. "Not even going to get into all that tonight. I'll just focus on what's now. I guess the first thing is, I hate my job. Well, I don't *hate* being an executive admin, I just hate the guys I work for. They're all pompous assholes in suits who basically do nothing and get paid more money than God to do it. And I can't go someplace else because it's the same BS everywhere, and half the time they all know each other." She shrugged. "It's not like I've got another rung on the ladder to climb, and I'm not really up for a career change. I could deal if I made more money, but who knows. I mean, I don't do too bad for myself, but I have all this debt and then my brother..." She rubbed the center of her forehead. "My brother is in trouble, and I have to help him. I have to."

She has a brother? How the fuck was he just now hearing this? Jeff drew in a slow breath, refocusing. "What kind of trouble?"

She turned her head, looking at him in the pale light from her nightstand lamp. "The kind that ends up getting a person arrested and sent to County."

Jeff cleared his throat and knew he was about to navigate a minefield. "Has he been arrested, or is he on the run?"

"Does it matter?"

He paused, taking a moment to choose his words carefully. She was trying to tell him something, trying to open up to him, and the last thing he wanted to do was taint this moment with him having to put his cop hat on. "I guess it depends."

She turned fully, facing him. "On what?"

"If you're harboring him or you know where he is." Jeff exhaled through his nose.

She stared at him for a long time. So long he wasn't sure if she was going to say anything else, which had a mixture of pissed and fear shooting through his veins. She had to know the legal risk she was taking and the danger she was possibly putting herself in.

For fuck's sake, her silence was killing him. "Tish, are you?"

Her face went stone hard. "No."

Relief sped through him so fast that if he were standing he would've had to sit down. Time for the second part of that question. "Do you know where he is?"

"No. Well... technically yes, but not entirely."

He frowned. "Explain?"

"See? This is why I didn't want to tell you." She sat up, wrapping her arms around her knees. "Just forget it."

"Wait a second. I don't really think you're being fair. Me wanting to make sure that you haven't unwittingly committed a crime is not me judging you, it's me gathering information so I can figure out how to protect you." He sat up too and clasped her upper arm.

Tish jerked from his hold. "I don't need protecting. I can take care of myself, thank you very much."

Where the fuck was all this coming from? He'd never seen her like this... then again, the time they'd spent together over the past year had always been out at a bar, or a party, or...that one night they'd had sex.

"Tish, look, just because you're having some struggles right now doesn't make you less of an independent woman. Or any less strong. But if you don't tell me what's going on, then I can't help you."

She glanced over her shoulder at him, tears glittering in her eyes. "There's nothing you can do to help. Unless you're independently wealthy and want to loan me the money for an attorney."

"For you or for your brother?"

"Are you trying to be a smart-ass?"

"No. For realsi—for real."

She swatted his arm, and he laughed.

"I'm being serious. I swear. I'm not independently wealthy, but I would really like it if you'd lay back down with me and finish telling me what's happening. At the very least, I can help you carry the emotional burden."

Tish's expression softened, and she tipped her head to the side.

My God, that look. He'd give her anything in the world, anything, if she looked at him like that all the time. "What is it, mami?"

"Officer Pearl, you can be the most frustrating person. And then, in a heartbeat, you're the most amazing man on the planet. I don't know what I am going to do with you." She bent toward him and kissed him.

Jeff wrapped an arm around her waist, and as he lay back on the bed, he pulled Tish atop him. Her tongue was smooth, stroking against his, and he loved it, wanted more of it, except this wasn't answering his questions and wasn't solving her problems. It was, however, making his dick hard, which was great, too. But again, not getting him, or them, where he wanted them to be.

Dammit... Reluctantly, Jeff broke the kiss. Cupping the side of her face and head in his palm, he stroked his nose over hers and rolled them to their sides.

There was more she needed to say, and he needed to give her that first.

* * * *

Lying face-to-face with Jeff, Tish gazed at him, his dark eyes soft, sweet, sincere. She needed to try to let him in, at least a little. She just hoped to God he didn't make her regret it. Which, considering this was Jeffrey Pearl she was talking about, meant she had about a fifty-fifty shot.

She closed her eyes and drew in a slow breath. "I'd been trying to reach my brother for weeks. Tonight he called from Tempe city jail, said he'd been arrested for possession and they were taking him to County."

"Okay, we can go bond him out tomorrow."

She shook her head. "No, this isn't his first offense. Plus, he had a warrant for probation violation. There's no guarantee he'll even get bonded out. But even if I could, I don't have the money right now."

"Okay, yeah, sounds like he's gotten himself in deep. But, babe, you know you can't fix that, right?"

Babe...

Warm tingles skittered over her skin. This sweet, serious side of him was such a surprise. The need to kiss him again rose like a wildfire inside her, but she managed to tamp it down. "He might be an adult, a grown man even, but he's still my baby brother. And I can't just let him face this alone. I have to help him, Jeff. Last time, I got him an attorney, and he was able to get him a really fair plea deal. Which is another thing I forgot, he also violated his probation, but anyway, I can't jus—"

"Is that why you have debt, because of the attorney?"

Shame spread through her, weighing her down like a thick, wet blanket. She ducked her face, avoiding his penetrating stare. "Yes." *Plus all the money she was always giving him when he needed it. Plus paying his fines and fees.*

"Hey, hey." He tipped her chin up with his finger. "You don't have to do that. You don't ever have to hide from me, Tish. You did what anyone would do. You were taking care of your brother. Nothing to be ashamed of, babe. Can I ask how old he is? He must be a lot younger for you to feel so responsible for him."

"He's two years younger." Tish shifted her eyes away from his gaze again, and a wave of frantic panic flooded her system.

She needed Jeff to get it. To really understand. These were the things she never shared, and sharing them now was a huge leap of faith for her.

There was a very logical side of her that knew continuing to help her brother was not really helping him, it was only enabling him to continue as he had been. But the other side of her was terrified to let him fall. Tish could not lose him, she just couldn't.

Drawing in another deep breath, she steeled herself and met his gaze once more. "Before you judge me or him, you don't understand what it was like for us as kids."

His expression softened. "I'm not judging. What was it like?"

She squeezed her eyes closed and exhaled. "I can't get into all that tonight. I'm sorry, I can't. It's too much. You're just going to have to take my word for it when I say I've been looking out for my brother since we were little. It's not an exaggeration. But also, I'm not about to stop looking out for him now or ever. I can't. He needs me to stand up for him because no one else ever has."

"Who stands up for you, Tish?"

"No one. I told you, I can take care of myself."

"What if, though, right? What if you had someone..."

He had no idea what he was saying, not really. Pillow talk was nice, and they were friends, but still. No one really stuck it out with anyone or did what they said they were going to do. Especially in relationships, someone always let someone down. That was what her world looked like anyway.

He touched her temple with his fingertip. "I can see those wheels turning."

"Yeah well, my experience has been, people don't follow through."

He trailed his fingertip down her cheek to her chin. "Rayna does."

"She's the exception."

"What about Derek?"

"If Rayna loves him, which she does, then by default he's on the exception list."

"Wait, there are special rules and lists? Are there costumes, too? Is it a game? Wait, wait...do we play this game like D&D or—"

"Oh my God, stop!" She laughed, swatting his arm. Jesus, he was such a dork, but a sweet one. Far sweeter than she ever would've guessed.

"Sorry, got off track, but for realsies, how does someone make it to the special list? Is there an application process? If so, I'd like to apply."

She rolled her eyes. "Yes, there are six forms that have to be filled out in triplicate."

"I'm on it. Wait, do you have those really cool carbon forms? Don't you hate it when people write on one and forget the others are below it and fuck up the whole stack?" He raised one hand in the air, then let it fall onto her lower hip. "God, I hate when that happens, don't you?"

Tish broke into a fit of giggles, and as Jeff laughed along with her, she realized this man was not going to give up until he made her "special" list. Which was fine. He didn't know it yet, but he'd already landed himself there.

The bigger question was, what would happen once he knew that?

A person getting what they wanted sometimes ended up with them no longer wanting it. The literal example of what happened when people made a vow to each other, in front of God and everyone they knew and loved, all because they were riding some "I'm going to love you forever" high, and then ten, five, or even two years later, they sobered up and realized whoops, they didn't mean it anymore.

The man already had what he wanted from Tish. Whether or not he'd keep what he claimed to want so badly, once he knew he had it, remained to be seen.

Jeff slid his arm around her waist and pulled her closer. "Listen, I get that you want to help your brother. I also get that you're super stressed over a lot of things, but it sounds to me like your brother's sitch is probably the biggest stressor of all. That said, I also get that you have a lot of bills and not enough money coming in to handle any more expense." He tipped his head back and pressed a kiss to her forehead. Without pulling away, he continued. "But what I get the most is that you are used to carrying all that stress by yourself. The other thing I get"—he squeezed her waist—"and I hope you get too, is that you can lean on me. I'll be your soft place. I'll be your support. You have my word on that."

Tish pressed her nose to his neck and breathed him in. His warm scent filled her with a sense of home, a sense of security. She closed her eyes. Jeff had made more than a few declarations tonight, all of them filled with sincerity for sure. "Stay with me tonight, please?"

He kissed the top of her head. "Already planned on it."

Tish cuddled closer, as if she could burrow into his warmth. He meant everything he said tonight, she knew that to her core. At least she needed to believe that for the moment, but would he still mean it tomorrow? Or the next day? And for how long?

It was a risk, a huge one. But like everything else so far with him, it was a fifty-fifty game. For tonight, she'd take the odds.

Chapter 6

Jeff woke with the feel of a head resting on his chest along with the warm body attached to it, curled against his right side. Not just any warm body, of course. The most perfect body, which belonged to the most perfectly imperfect woman of his dreams.

It would be beyond unfair if he were dreaming right now. If he was, he did not want to wake up. Except it was Sunday, and dammit, he had to go to work.

Reluctantly, he opened one eye. The crown of her dark brown hair was the only thing he could see. Fine by him, it was a perfect view. Plus, not dreaming, so he was winning all around.

Keeping as still as he could, he drew in a deep breath, reveling in her scent and all the sensations and emotions being with her like this lit off in his mind and body. It was all so overwhelming, but in the best possible way, and he might joke around a lot, but there was no way he'd trade a hot second of any of this goodness with her.

Hmm...based on the light filtering through the curtains on her windows, he could tell dawn hadn't been too long ago, but still, a clock would let him know how much time he actually did have with her.

They'd talked a lot last night, after the amazing sex—PS: he was so going to have more amazing sex with her just as soon as he got off his shift tonight—but anyway, the talking had been enlightening, and Jeff really and truly felt they'd actually bonded.

Okay, maybe not bonded, but they'd for sure crossed some major line with each other, had a sort of breakthrough.

He wanted bonding and breakthroughs, and good and bad, and all the things he'd committed to her last night. He wanted it all so badly he was willing to leash himself and go as slow as she needed them to go.

Really, all he had to do was find out how slow that was exactly.

Speaking of leash, where was Rio? Shit, Jeff raised his head off the pillow and peeked around his side of the bed. His partner probably had to pee so bad his back teeth were floating.

"It's okay. I got up a little while ago and brought him out."

"Wow, you did? Thanks, mami." How had he not heard or felt her get out of bed? He must've been sleeping like the dead. Jeff frowned and stroked her bare back with is fingertips. "How long have you been awake?"

She shrugged. "Dunno, not long. I guess, when you woke up? I'm a light sleeper."

"But I didn't say anything. I've been laying here, still as a statue, totally afraid this was a dream, and I wasn't ready to wake up and have to let you go."

She giggled. "Your breathing changed, and seriously"—Tish raised her head and looked at him—"who are you? When did you get all sweet and gooey romantic?" She flopped her head back down, her thick mane falling over his shoulder. "I'm not sure what to do with this side of you."

Jeff grinned. "Awww, you like me, don't you? It's okay, you can tell me. I won't tell anyone."

"Aaaaannd there he is, the smart-ass I'm more familiar with." She laughed. "Did you happen to have any dog food in the truck for Rio?"

"No, but we can scramble him some eggs." Still refusing to move, because he was not ready, Jeff glanced around the room as best he could. "So do you have a clock in here?"

"Nope, just my phone." She shifted slightly, turned over and grabbed the device off the nightstand on her side of the bed. "It's 6:08, to be exact."

Dammit, he hadn't wanted her to move yet. The loss of her body heat and closeness was profound. Worse, he really didn't want to have to leave her yet either. He lifted up on an elbow and ran a fingertip down her upper arm. "Doesn't really give us much time."

Looking all sleep tousled and sexy, a crooked little grin formed on her lips, and she raised a single brow. "You should know, I'm not a fan of morning sex. The morning breath is just way too much to handle."

Well now, he couldn't argue with that. He raised both brows and chuckled. "Noted. But I meant not enough time for me to make you coffee and breakfast."

"Oh." She tipped her head to the side. "I don't think I knew you worked Sundays. Does that suck?"

He dropped back down onto his pillow. "Only if I didn't get enough sleep Saturday night."

A hint of pink hit her cheeks. "Ooh, ouch. Sorry about that."

"I'm not."

She looked over at him, an expression he couldn't quite read in her eyes. "You sure about that?"

Okay, so that was what doubt looked like on her. Jeff allowed all his feelings to show in his expression because it was looking like she needed to see it. But also... "I've never been so sure of anything in my life, mami."

She turned, facing him. "Okay, soooo then...what do we do next?"

"First thing is, we both brush our teeth so I can give you a good-morning kiss."

She bent forward and pressed a closed-lip kiss to his mouth, her grin spreading from ear to ear. "Good morning."

He chuckled. "Who's the goofy smart-ass now? How about a better good-morning kiss? Assuming you have an extra toothbrush, right? If not, I will use my finger."

"I do."

"Because you're awesome—"

"Not really, Jeff. Lots of people have extra toothbrushes. It's not a life-defining quality."

"Au contraire. You have no idea how people live. Cop, remember? I see a lot of different kinds of people, and let's just say not all are living their 'best life.' And won't be anytime soon." He smoothed his palm up and down her arm. "After we brush our teeth, and after I kiss you so good you'll be thinking about it all day, I'll leave to head home and get ready for work. I get off at six p.m., provided there's nothing crazy going on. How about you meet me at my place at seven?"

She smiled. "What happens at your place at seven?"

"Sunday dinner of course."

"You mean no Netflix and chill? Jeff, I'm shocked."

"Naughty girl. All you need to do is ask for what you need." He winked. "We can do that after Sunday dinner if you want."

"I didn't—I don't—" She shook her head and rolled her eyes. "You kill me."

"I thought I made this clear last night. The Heart song, remember?"

She rolled her eyes again. "Now I'm going to have to look the damn song up."

"My work is done here." He laughed and rolled away from her. Finding his boxer briefs on the floor at his feet, he donned them and stood. "Come on, mami. Let's brush our teeth."

* * * *

Standing in her small en suite bathroom, clad in only panties and a T-shirt, Tish brushed her teeth and did it watching Jeff brush his. It was all very comical and cute and entertaining, and the worst part was, she was enjoying every foamy minute of it.

Such an odd and yet intimate thing to do with him. If someone had told her yesterday that today she would be doing something so personal with him, she would've told them they were out of their fucking gourd.

Plus, she'd never had this level of openness with any other man before, had never allowed anything like this. She sure as hell would never have imagined being this intimate with Jeff, yet here she was, and here he was, and now it was time to spit.

She bent to the sink, spit, and brushed her tongue (managed not to gag), then rinsed, then spit then...Holy shit, was this what things had come to? Had she gotten herself so far off the emotional balance beam that brushing her teeth (and now spitting and rinsing) beside Jeff Pearl in her bathroom was comforting and about to become some new brand of normal that she somehow enjoyed?

She didn't even want to answer that question. And just her luck, she wasn't going to ask it out loud to anyone, so she'd never get an answer anyway. Perfect.

As he did the swish and rinse as well, she had a moment of sheer terror blaze through her. She straightened and took a step back, figuratively and literally.

What the hell was she doing? She didn't want to want this. Or God forbid, need it. She needed to stop this right—

Jeff turned and moved right to her. Wrapping an arm around her waist and cupping her cheek in his palm, he tilted his head and kissed her. As she was learning was his way, there was no playing around, no working his way in.

He went straight for the kill, open mouth, lots of tongue. The kind of kiss that branded a woman, made her forget everything except who she belonged to.

Tish didn't belong to anyone, she never would, but she liked the way he kissed her and the way those kisses made every inch of her skin tingle, made her belly get tight and made her crave more.

Tish gripped the wrist on the hand cradling her cheek and wrapped her free arm around his shoulders. Holding on, she moaned and gave herself over to the kiss and to Jeff, letting him take her where he wanted her to go.

Good God, he was an outstanding kisser.

Jeff broke the kiss, giving her bottom lip a little nip. "Good morning, beautiful."

Tish swallowed and blew out a slow breath. "Good morning to you too."

He rubbed his nose over hers and gave her a soft peck. "Are you going to go back to sleep for a little while?"

"I don't know. Maybe? It is rather early."

"I think you should." He took her hand and walked them out of the bathroom back to her bed.

She sat on the edge and watched him as he got his clothes back on. Gorgeous body, truly. "Let me at least walk you out."

"It's fine, honey. Really."

"Yes, of course, but I need to lock the door after you go."

"Christ, I'm failing cop duty for sure. That's twice now. Thank God Rio's here."

She frowned. "Why do you say that?"

Fully dressed, he took her hand and walked her out to her living room. "First, you got out of bed at zero-dark-thirty and went and walked my dog, alone, and I didn't know it. Didn't feel you get up or hear you leave. That's not normal. Second is me not thinking about the fact that I can't lock your deadbolt for you." He shook his head. "No key."

Jeff bent and put Rio's harness on, then his lead.

Tish blinked, staring down at him though not really seeing him. Was he? No...no way he really thought she'd give him a key to her place, did he? He had to be kidding. Tish cleared her throat, hoping to sidestep that little hint drop. "I was being really quiet, and I think you're a little sleep deprived, so..." She shrugged a shoulder. "I wouldn't be so hard on yourself."

"Sleep deprived and on duty don't mix well, mami. I'm fine. But truth is, you wore me out, stole all my mojo. It's the only explanation."

She crossed her arms, tipped her chin down and raised both brows. "So now it's my fault? I don't recall tying you down to my bed."

"Meeeoww! That might be fun. Can we do that later?" Circling her waist, he pulled her close and nuzzled her neck, growling a little.

God, he moved so fast. She giggled, unable to stop herself. "From meowing to growling? Suits you, because you are a tomcat!"

"A tomcat who knows a good thing when he gets it." He grinned, still holding her close.

Caught in his gaze, her giggles faded, and once more she fell into the warm pool of his soft, brown eyes. "What am I going to do with you?"

"Pfft, that's easy. You're going to meet me at my place at seven, remember?" He brushed a soft kiss over her lips and let her go. "Gotta run or I'll never make it. See you tonight, mami. Don't be late." Turning from her, he opened the front door. "Let's go, Rio."

Tish watched until he got to the end of the walkway, and then he was gone from her view. She yawned and closed the door, locked it, and headed back to her bedroom.

Tired was an understatement. With all that had happened between them, and then the emotional conversation after, she'd had a hard time sleeping—hence why she'd gotten up and taken Rio out for a quick walk.

She climbed into bed and pulled her soft sheets and comforter around her. There was even more on her mind now than before Jeff had come over. Which of course was one thousand percent her fault, not like she could blame the beer. Though maybe she could?

Except she really didn't have any regrets about the sex or the talking or the cuddling or...any of it.

Fear, sure, she had that in buckets.

Did she trust him? Nope, not one bit.

Was she willing to play around with him a little longer, have a little fun? Yes.

Tish closed her eyes and rolled over, curling around a pillow. Maybe when all was said and done, they'd end up friends, not lovers.

She was okay with that.

Chapter 7

Tish knocked on Jeff's front door, and as she waited for him to open up, she swiped a stray hair away from her eyes and smoothed down the front of her shirt. A nervous thrill, in the form of a thousand butterflies, had taken up residence in her tummy.

What would it be like once he opened the door? Would he kiss her right away? God, she was actually feeling a little giddy.

Figuring they'd be hanging out on the couch, she'd dressed semi-casual, jeans but a soft comfy top and a pair of black high-heeled ankle boots—the boots adding a little bit of spice to an otherwise boring outfit.

They had ground rules to discuss, and maybe after they'd gotten their arrangement all settled, then they could get naked and see if they could top the night before's beneath-the-sheets play.

She shifted the bag she held to the other hand and knocked again, this time a little harder. Did she have the time wrong? She glanced at her watch. Nope, seven o'clock on the dime. Plus, he'd texted her his address, just to be sure she had it (she already did but whatever) and reiterated the time.

The door swung open. "Hey! Hi, hi. Come in." He held his arm out, motioning her inside.

"Hey. I got a little worried that maybe you weren't home." Tish moved past him.

He closed the door. "Nope, I'm right here."

She smiled and held the bag out to him. "This is for you."

"Awww, you brought presents? I love presents. Let me see." He took the bag from her, but instead of looking inside, he set it on the ground, pulled her to his chest and laid one of his inferno-inducing kisses on her.

When he broke from her lips, she was breathing heavy and, to her surprise, realized she had gripped his T-shirt in her fists, but worse, she hadn't let go yet. "Whoops, sorry."

Giggling, she let go of the fabric and smoothed the wrinkled cotton. How had she done that and not even realized? Proof right there that the man's mouth was made of magic. Made her wonder what else he could do with that tongue...

"You okay?"

She dragged her gaze from his mouth to his eyes and grinned. "Uh, yeah. Why?"

He smirked, and then he pursed his lips. "You're looking at my mouth with a naughty little gleam in your eye. What's on your mind, hmm?"

Tish felt her cheeks get hot. Damn, she needed to stick to her agenda. "Not even going to try and hide it. I've got lots of ideas, but how about I share them with you *after* we eat and talk?"

"Whatever you want, dear." He grinned and stepped back. "Can I open my present?"

"Dear?" She chuckled and rolled her eyes. "Yes, please do."

He picked up the bag and looked inside. "Ooh, one white and one red! Perfect." He leaned in and gave her cheek a peck. "Very thoughtful, thank you."

She followed him to the kitchen. "You're welcome. I wasn't sure what you liked or what we were having, so I figured get both and poof, we're covered."

"Sounds like a good enough justification in my book." He glanced back at her as he pulled two glasses down from the cabinet. "Which one do you want?"

She looked around, taking a moment to appreciate his home. She'd been only one other time, that one night to be specific, but hadn't really looked around. She definitely hadn't been in this back part of the house that had clearly been remodeled into a huge great room.

"Did you remodel this house yourself?"

"Yeah."

Wow... "You mean, you can do all this?" She motioned to the cabinets, the large island.

"Yeah. Well, I don't do granite counters. I had to pay someone to do those. But—" He glanced around the large space. "Yeah, I can do all this, why?"

"No. Nothing, I'm just...surprised, is all. Not something you've ever talked about."

"Stick around, Patrice Beck, I'm full of surprises." He winked and then leaned his ass against the counter and motioned to the two bottles of wine. "Now, which one do you want?"

Tish couldn't stop the grin that formed on her lips. "I don't know. What are we having for dinner?"

He placed his palm on his forehead. "Oh em gee. You want dinner too? Pfft, mami, you so high maintenance."

Tish burst into laughter. How the hell was she going to have a serious, ground-rules discussion with him? He made everything silly, or somehow less serious. Either way, she was outnumbered by the many sides of Jeffrey Pearl.

"I'm kidding. Of course I made dinner. I made ravioli with no-meat sauce. So I'm going to have red, but there are no rules, really. It's all about what makes you happy." He uncorked the red and set it back down on the counter.

Only then did Tish notice the pot of sauce boiling on the stove. And right then the delicious aroma hit her nose. How the fuck had she missed that? Jesus, she was beyond preoccupied, and he probably thought she was fucking crazy. "I think I'm losing my mind."

He moved to her and placed his palms on her hips. "Why do you think that?"

She frowned, blinking. "I've been here at least ten minutes and I didn't even notice the pot on the stove, and I didn't smell it cooking either."

"Hmm, well, you've kind of got a lot on your mind right now."

She exhaled. "I always do."

He shrugged. "I'd like to hear about it. But for the record, the wheels turning on overdrive constantly can have some serious side effects."

She smoothed her hands down his shoulders, feeling the strong muscles. "Like not noticing things, right?" She rolled her eyes. "I guess it's as good an excuse as any."

He touched the tip of her nose with his fingertip. "Not an excuse. A fact. Now—" He took her by the hand and led her over to the large island. "How about you have a seat and drink some wine, have some olives. Do you like olives?"

"I do, yes."

"You want white or red?"

"Red." She sat where he indicated.

"Perfect." He moved around the island and poured them each a glass, then set hers in front of her. "You sit, eat olives, drink wine, and I'll finish dinner."

"Deal." She clinked her glass to his and took a sip. "Mmm. I love red blends."

"Me too!" He grinned and moved to the fridge and pulled out a small tray with an array of olives on it, as well as a few cheeses. He slid the tray onto the counter, then grabbed her a small plate and set it in front of her, along with a napkin. "Here you go."

Tish's eyes went wide. How the hell did he do all of this? "Did you get off work early?"

"No, why?"

"Because when did you find the time to get this spread together?"

His brows pinched together, and he shrugged. "I had all of this in my fridge already. Didn't take me more than five minutes to put it together. Sauce only takes an hour, hence the no meat." He picked up his glass. "But if you want to think it makes me awesome, I will not stop you." With a wink he took a sip.

"I see you, Jeffrey Pearl. I see you crystal clear." She smirked and ate one of the Castelvetrano olives.

"Good to know. I like you seeing me." He nodded and got a pot of water on the stove to boil.

Tish sipped her wine and snacked on olives and cheese while Jeff finished meal prep.

* * * *

Within thirty minutes, he had gotten them arranged at his kitchen table, raviolis with extra sauce plated up, and a couple slices of perfectly toasted garlic bread.

He raised his glass. "Here's to beginnings."

Tish smiled and raised her glass to his. "Beginnings with guidelines."

He raised both brows. "Guidelines?"

She sipped the burgundy-colored fluid, savoring the taste for a moment before swallowing. "Yes, because, well, if this is happening—"

"It's happening, Tish."

She swirled the wine in her glass. "Well, then for sure we need guidelines."

"I don't need any, but I'm sensing you do."

"I do." She nodded.

"Okay, like I said, whatever you need, you get." He cut into a ravioli, and halfway to his mouth he stopped. "Wait, do I need to get a pen and paper, or should I get my laptop? If there's going to be a test later, I want to make sure I'm prepared."

"Are you making fun of me?"

"Never, mami." He set his fork down and leaned toward her. "I'm just pulling pigtails."

She rolled her eyes. "Same thing. In that case, yes, after dinner, get a pen and paper. You can write it all down, and we can both sign it like a contract."

"How Fifty Shades of you!" He laughed. "Now I'm really intrigued."

Tish let out a loud sigh and cut into a ravioli. "Fantastic. Let's eat, and then we can have more wine while we negotiate."

When they'd finished eating and she'd helped him clean up the kitchen, Jeff pulled out another bottle of wine. The same one she'd brought in fact.

He opened it and then pressed a kiss to her forehead. "Let the negotiations begin. You pour, I'll get a yellow legal pad out of my office."

He seriously had yellow legal pads? Tish grabbed the bottle and filled both their glasses. This wasn't supposed to be a negotiation, but he was definitely going to turn it into that. She may as well just prep herself for it. He'd get things out of her she would not want to give, but based on how things were going so far, she'd give in, but she'd drive a hard bargain before she did.

At the end of all this, really she just needed things to go slow, and stay casual, if that made any sense. Jeff would likely be good with that too. But more importantly, she also needed things to stay strictly between just them.

And she had a feeling that one wasn't going to go over so well.

* * * *

"Grab our wine, my darling, and meet me on the couch." Yellow legal pad and pen in hand, Jeff moved past her to the living room area.

"Okay then."

Jeff got settled on the edge of his large sofa and gave a low whistle for Rio. The dog trotted over from his dog bed and sat. "How's my young man doing tonight?" He scratched around Rio's ears. "You tired from our first day back to work?"

Tish came around the front of the couch and held his wine out for him. "Here you go."

"Thanks."

Before she moved to sit, she gave Rio some attention, stroking the top of his head. "Sweet boy. I bet you are tired. Up half the night at my place, then working hard all day. You catch any bad guys today?"

Jeff watched, loving how she was loving on Rio. "No bad guys today, and we were both okay with that."

"Sounds fair to me." Stepping away, she sat on the other end of the sofa. Not ten seconds later, Rio moved to her, lying down at her feet. With a smile, she leaned down and smoothed his ears. "Aw, that's sweet."

"Uh-oh, clearly he's already attached to you." Satisfaction filled Jeff's heart and soul. Rio liked his woman. His woman liked Rio. Life was good.

She glanced at him. "Is that a bad thing?"

"Not. At. All." Jeff smiled. "You ready to get into this? There are other things I want to 'discuss' after we get this part done."

Tish laughed and made air quotes. "I bet."

No matter how goofy he looked, Jeff could *not* stop smiling. He had no idea what she was going to put on this list of guidelines of hers, but it didn't matter. He'd roll with them, whatever they were.

At the top of the paper he wrote: Tish & Jeff Guidelines, Agreements and Rules. Dropping down a line, he put a 1. He held the notebook up so she could see it. "How's this? A good start?"

Her brow furrowed as she read the top line, and then she smiled. "You're so funny. Yes, that's fine."

"All right, mami. What's number one?"

"Okay, if we're going to do this, it's really important that we keep things casual. What I mean by—"

"Hold up. Should I be writing all this down, or are you going to summarize when you get to the end of your explanation?"

She tipped her head slightly forward, one brow raised, and gave him a look of annoyance coupled with humor. He hoped humor anyway.

"What? I'm being serious." He chuckled.

She drew in an exaggerated breath and then exhaled, also exaggerated. "I will summarize for you."

"K-k." He set the notebook down. "Continue, dear."

She shook her head, chuckling. "As I was saying, I need things to be casual. Now, I realize that leaves things open to interpretation, so I want to be really clear. You can date other women if you want. You are a free man to do what you want, but I would ask that you don't have sex with them. Truth be told, I date a lot. I don't want to stop doing that. But I don't have a lot of sex, so I guess what I'm trying to say is, the only commitment I can make to you is that I'll be monogamous with you but still be free to date other men."

Jesus Christ, he did not expect this. Jeff took a deep breath. Then another. A beat of panic sped through him. How the fuck was he going to handle her dating other guys? Needing to get a grip on his emotions, he forced himself to try to talk through this with her. He cleared his throat. "So let me see if I have this straight. You want to date other people but only have sex with me?"

"Yes."

He blinked. "And you want me to date other people but only have sex with you?"

"Yes." She sipped her wine.

Deep breath—in and out, in and out. "I guess that's..." He looked down at the notepad. "I guess we call number one: Monogamous, non-exclusive dating."

"But are you okay with that?"

He glanced at her. *Not a chance in hell.* "Yeah, that works."

"Okay, good." She smiled.

He took a sip of his wine. A feeling of dis-ease filled his stomach, keeping company with the wine. With every fiber of his being, Jeff wanted to tell her how he really felt about her casual dating idea, but he knew he couldn't.

The truth was, he had no interest in dating *any* other woman, because she was it for him. But worse, the idea of her going out on a date with some dude she met on Tinder and said dude touching her, kissing h— Jeff closed his eyes and managed to swallow the growl that nearly erupted from his chest.

Nope, not going there. Bottom line, he was going to have to find a way to give her the space she needed, without actually giving her enough free time to go any dates. And if she did go on any, they would all pale in comparison to him.

That wasn't arrogance he was projecting either, it was just fact. He and Tish were a true match, soul mates even. He'd known it when he first met her. Eventually, she'd figure it out too. It was only a matter of time.

"Jeff, are you sure?"

Nope. "One hundred percent." He nodded and added the next number. "Okay, what's number two?"

She blew a breath out and then licked her full lips. "I want this to stay between us."

Wha... He could not have heard her right. "Come again?"

Her stare did not waver. "I don't want our friends to know. I want it to stay between us only."

"Tish, that's..." He ran his fingers through his hair. *What the fuck, really?*

"I know it's a lot to ask. But Jeff, hear me out. Seriously, we don't even know what this is between us. The last thing I want is for things to go south, and if that—"

"That's not going to happen, Tish."

"Come on, it could happen. It happens all the time to people."

He shook his head. "Yeah, sure, it happens all the time, but it's not going to happen to us."

She crossed her arms. "Fine, maybe you're right, maybe it won't, but either way, right now, I don't want them to know. It's too soon and too much of a risk."

Fucking hell, this was harder than the first request. Was she ashamed of him, of them together as a couple? Was she scared? Was she just *that* screwed up with *so* much baggage that she had to hide something this awesome from their friends? "This is a lot to ask, Tish. We love our friends, they love us. They already think we're together. What you're suggesting is that we lie to them. Every single day."

She held her hand up. "I am not saying lie, just not tell them."

"Withholding is tantamount to lying."

"Tantamount?" She chuckled. "That's a ten-dollar word."

He picked up his wineglass. "You're okay lying to Rayna then?"

"No, not at all. But I won't be lying to her. Besides, she would never ask me about you. Especially if I am going on regular dates with other guys, she wouldn't even think to ask." She shrugged and drank more of her wine.

Jeff ran his palm over his face and leaned back. Tish had a lot of issues, of that he was certain, some he was pretty clear on, but others he had yet to discover and figure out. He'd assured her that he'd give her what she needed, no questions asked. That he was strong enough to give what she needed.

He just hadn't expected this would be what she needed. Guess it was time to put up or shut up. "Okay, mami, I'll do this for you, but...I will not do it forever. If we make it to the six-month mark, then we tell our friends. Deal?"

She licked her bottom lip, then rubbed both together. "I guess that's fine. If we make it six months, we can talk about it then."

Clever girl. He smirked. "You just loopholed me, didn't you?"

"I don't know what you mean." She swirled her wine in the glass and took a long sip.

"Fine. I can loophole you back." He focused on the notepad and wrote down their agreement, and then read it to her. "For the next six months, no friends or personal acquaintances can know we are dating and sleeping together."

She laughed. "Sure, that works."

Jeff set the notepad down on the end table. "Come here."

"No. *You* come here." She grinned and set her glass down.

"Rawr." Jeff crawled over the two cushions separating them. When he got to her, he slid his arms under her legs and ass and scooped her up. "The temptation to toss you over my shoulder and carry you—"

"Don't you—"

"—to my bed is almost—"

"I'm warning you."

"—too great to ignore. Which of course, now I will not ignore it." Shifting, he tossed her up and over his shoulder, and then swatted her ass for good measure.

Tish let out a squeal and then a giggle. "Jeff!"

"You got no one but yourself to blame." He started toward the hallway.

She laughed. "Ugh, put me down, pretty please?"

"Now Miss Manners shows up? Since you asked nicely, will do. Just as soon as I get to the bedroom. PS: we're coming back to the guidelines list later. I have a few items I want to add to it, too."

"Whatever. Don't be such a girl."

"A girl? Really?" He stepped into his bedroom, flipped on the light but hit the dimmer. With the lighting where he wanted it, he moved to the bed and bent forward, flopping Tish down onto the mattress.

She giggled, smiling up at him, her dark hair spread out all over his pale gray comforter.

Once more, he lost his breath at the sight of her.

Chapter 8

Damn, it was about time! Tish was starting to think they weren't going to be having sex tonight. And that would've sucked because, although she'd been thinking about a lot of things all day, she'd also been thinking about how fucking good the fucking was.

Jeff bent over her, pressing his fists into the bed on each side of her. "My, my, my, you look fine in my bed."

"You look fine. Full stop." She traced his lips with her fingertip.

"Ay, mami. You so sweet. I need a taste." With a grin, Jeff dipped close and took her mouth in a kiss.

Oh yes, there he was. Apparently she'd needed a taste too, more so than she'd thought. Heat pooled in her tummy, then spread to her limbs.

Giving herself over to the lust spiking in her system, she moaned and raised her knees up to his hips. Jeff groaned and lowered himself between her parted thighs. Tish welcomed the weight of him, the heat of his body and his decadent scent.

With their tongues tangling, Jeff shifted his weight onto one forearm and tugged her shirt free from her jeans. Sliding his hand up her torso, he found her breast and cupped the full mound in his palm, squeezing just enough to draw another moan from her before dragging his thumb over the tight peak of her nipple through the fabric of her bra.

She whimpered, arching beneath him.

Jeff moved from her mouth, trailing kisses down her chin to her throat and then the side of her neck. "So, so sweet."

Tish clawed at his shirt, tugging a handful of fabric up his back. "Want you naked."

"Ditto." Jeff pulled away long enough to yank his shirt over his head.

She did the same, sitting up just enough to get her shirt off, but before she could lose the bra, Jeff pushed her back down on the bed. "Hey, I was—"

As his mouth closed over her hard nipple through her bra, Tish forgot what the hell she was saying. Again, she arched. The feel of his hot wet mouth through the fabric was intense. Then he let go and blew over the wet tip. The wet instantly turned to cool, and her nipple got tighter.

"Oh yeah, look at that tight little berry." He pinched it between finger and thumb, and Tish bit her bottom lip, groaning. "Gonna nibble your nips all fucking night."

Her clit throbbed and her pussy clenched, her panties soaking with arousal at every little thing he did to her. "Promise?"

His gaze shifted from her breasts to her eyes. "Always."

Tish pulled him to her lips for another mind-numbing kiss.

As he gave her what she wanted, he tugged her bra cup aside and played with her nipple. Little bolts of pleasure arrowed from the hard tip, straight to her clit, taking her higher.

Tish planted a heel in the bed and rolled them.

"Well now, that was unexpected."

Tish pushed her hair out of her face, settling herself astride his hips. "I'm full of surprises, too."

Jeff framed her waist in his palms. "I bet you are."

Tish reached behind her back, unhooked her bra and tossed it on the floor. Cupping both breasts in her palms, she stared down at him.

"Show me. Let me see."

Exactly what she was hoping he would say. Tish closed her eyes and tugged her nipples, moaning at the sweet sting.

"Fuck, that's gorgeous."

She rocked her hips, rubbing against the hard length behind his zipper. "Want you inside me."

"Yeah, mami. It's yours. Take it."

Tish bent and kissed him before sliding off the bed and removing her jeans.

Jeff stayed where he was and did the same, and as he was fishing in his nightstand, Tish assumed for a condom, she bent over and licked up the length of his beautiful cock.

"Fuuuuuck!"

"Well, what can I say, you're sweet too." Tish climbed on the bed and settled between his thighs. "Go head, get the condom ready. I'll be down here getting reacquainted with little Jeffrey."

Both his brows raised so high they nearly hit his hairline. "Little?"

Tish giggled and glanced up at him as she made a show of licking over the rim.

His eyes rolled back in his head, so she did it again.

No, his dick was not little, not in the slightest. It was an average-sized cock, but prettier. A little thicker than average maybe, which was perfect for her. Not that it mattered, anyway. With their chemistry, no matter what his size was, it would've been perfect for her.

With the shaft gripped in her fist, she slipped the head past her lips and suckled him.

Jeff let out a groan, and his hand landed on the back of her head.

God, she loved this, loved having this control. Tish sucked him to the back of her throat.

Another groan, and he tangled his fingers in the length of her hair. "Tish..."

"Mmm." She curled her tongue as she fucked him with her mouth. "Tish!"

He was going to stop her, and as much as she didn't want that because she really did enjoy sucking his dick, she was so amped up, she was ready for him to be inside her cunt instead.

She let him go and stroked the length in her fist. "Yes, honey?"

He swallowed and held his hand out to her. "Here."

"Ooh! For me?" She took the wrapped condom from him and tore it with her teeth. "Yay, I love doing this almost as much as I love watching you do it."

"Whew. Yeah." He nodded, licking his lips. "Mmhmm."

Tish grinned and rolled the condom down his shaft. Once done, she pressed a kiss to his abs, then straddled his hips. "I'm soaking wet for you."

Jeff stroked two fingers between her folds, dragging her wetness to her clit. "Wow." He glanced to her eyes and then back between her legs where he touched her. "Fuck yeah, you are."

She was so worked up, the light touch of his fingers had everything clenching. "Mmm, you eat pussy, Jeff?"

With a devilish glint in his eyes, he pulled his hand away and sucked his two fingers, coated with her honey, between his lips. He moaned, parted his fingers into a V and then licked down the center. "Mami, I will eat your very bare, very smooth pussy on command. You say when, and I'll get on my knees."

Heat spread over her skin, and her clit pulsed. Of all the things that turned her on, she never would've anticipated something like that would do it for her. The idea that she could command him to get on his knees and give her head was nearly enough to cause a mini orgasm. "That is so going to happen soon—" Tish grabbed his cock, positioned him at the mouth of her pussy and slid down. "Fuck. God, that's soooo good."

Jeff gripped her hips and thrust up. "Mmgggood is an understatement."

"Mmhmm." Tish nodded, no longer able to focus on words. Leaning forward over him, she tipped her pelvis back, dragging his length in and out of her wet core.

He grabbed her breasts, squeezing them before sucking her nipples one at a time between his lips, biting each just enough to bring that slight sting.

"Yes, baby. Harder." Tish reached between their bodies and rubbed her clit.

Jeff held her tits together, rubbing them over his face before he pinched both nipples, tugging them away from her breasts. "Look at that! So fucking hot."

"Yes, fuck, yes." Tish rocked faster and kept at her clit. She was going to come. "Close."

"Get what you need, mami."

Jeff took one hard peak between his teeth, biting hard enough that she cried out. Tish gripped a handful of his hair in her other hand, holding him to her as her climax raced to the surface. His hands landed on her ass, and he grabbed hold of her skin, rocking her back and forward.

Tish's orgasm hit like an earthquake, and she froze, his cock deep inside her. Hot ripples plowed through her over and over, and she closed her eyes, giving herself over to the sheer mind-numbing pleasure filling her entire being.

He pressed a soft kiss to her chest. "The feel of you when you come for me? It's like being buried inside heaven."

Tish's tummy jumped at the rawness of his words....

But before she had a chance to respond, to show him how special he'd made her feel, he rolled them over. With an arm around her back and waist, he held her above the bed, bringing her to his lips, and then stole her mind with another kiss.

God, this man. He was too good. In damn near every way.

Moments like this, the things he said, how he made her feel, was exactly why she needed to be careful. If she didn't keep some sort of guard up, she was going to get addicted to him.

And Tish didn't get addicted to anything...or anyone.

* * * *

Jeff pulled back from the heated kiss. Tish's lips were so perfect, all moist and puckered, her cheeks flushed...the body doing its thing it knew to do when sex hormones were on overload.

When he closed his eyes and relived how she looked with her mouth wrapped around his dick, he risked blowing his load right then and there. Whew...

Laying her back down on the mattress, he stayed kneeling between her thighs. "Spread your legs nice and wide for me." She did, and he positioned the head of his cock at her glistening cunt. So fucking erotic. He let his gaze travel up her gorgeous body to her gorgeous face. "Want to watch you take my cock from this angle. Nice and slow, and deep."

He pushed forward, taking his time.

Tish's eyes went wide, and she bit her bottom lip.

Yeah, those lips. "You know how fucking sexy you look sucking my cock?" He pulled back and slid in again. "Do you have any idea?"

Tish shook her head, moaning.

Jeff curled his fingers around the bend of her knee and parted her thighs farther. Shifting his pelvis forward, he watched as her dark pink labia stretched around his shaft, her pussy swallowing his cock deep.

Tish gripped his wrists, whimpering. "Babe..."

"So fucking beautiful." He gritted his teeth, moving in and out of her, his pace quickening.

"I want it."

"What do you want, mami?" He drove into her harder, faster, his orgasm tingling at the base of his spine. "Tell me."

She let go of his wrists and moved both hands to her clit, her fingers rubbing the engorged little nub. "Mmmgggod yes. Oh, fuck, yes. I want it."

Jeff couldn't take his eyes off her finger, her cunt, and his dick—the whole scene registering as off-the-charts erotic. "Tell me."

"Come for me. On *meeeefffuck*! Come on me." Another orgasm hit Tish, and she arched her back off the bed, letting out a loud moan.

"Fuuuuuuck!" Each wave of her orgasm had her tight cunt clenching down around his dick. The way she looked in the throes of ecstasy combined with how she felt, Jeff nearly went over. Pulling from the sweet heaven of her heat, Jeff rolled off the condom, palmed his rock-hard dick. Stroking from root to tip. "This what you want?"

She nodded, pressing her lips together. "Mmmhmm."

Yeah, he was so good with that too. Jeff stroked his cock, building his orgasm again. It hadn't gone far, that was for sure, especially because she was now lazily rubbing her wet pussy while watching him jack himself off for her. "Where do you want it?" He jacked himself a little faster, on the verge of climax. "Hurry."

"My belly." She moved one hand to her breast and pinched her nipple. Her plump lips arched into a devilish grin. "Or my tits."

"Naughty, mami." Jeff bent forward and kissed her, sucking her tongue and then nipping her bottom lip before pulling away.

With no reason to hold back any longer, Jeff increased his strokes. Panting, his body tensed, and his climax boiled up and out of him. With a deep moan, his semen shot from his shaft, landing in ropey spurts all over her stomach.

"Yes!" Moaning, Tish spread the creamy fluid over her skin.

"Goddamn." That light-headed euphoria from his orgasm hit him, and he bent over her, resting his weight on one hand as he continued to pump his cock, spurting one last time onto her tits.

She raised up and took his lips, her tongue penetrating his mouth, and she wrapped her wet hand around his fist, and finished stroking with him, until sensitivity won, forcing him to let go, taking her hand with him.

Jeff linked his fingers with hers, palm to palm, and pressed their hands to the bed. Out of steam, he lowered himself to her body, shifting slightly to one side to spare her his full weight. With his face buried in the side of her neck, he lay there, trying to catch his breath, but also trying to figure out how he would ever live without her again.

"You marked me." She stroked his back with the tips of her fingers. "Thank you."

Thank you? He raised his head and squinted through one eye. "Um, you're welcome?"

She laughed. "Um, yes? Hasn't anyone ever thanked you before?"

"Phhsaw, of course. Two, three times a week. I go around coming on people, and they always thank me for it. I mean it's that way for everyone, isn't it?"

She laughed, her head tipping back on the pillow as she did. God, she was beautiful. He couldn't help but laugh with her. She was kinky, too. But only a little. That was perfect, since he was only a little kinky too. But who wasn't nowadays.

When they'd both stopped laughing and an easy quiet settled between them, she smiled an almost demure smile at him. "What can I say, I liked it. A lot. Figured I should let you know how much I appreciated it."

Jeff drew in a slow breath and let the way she was looking at him in that moment flow through his body. "There you go saying nice things again. Giving me that sweet side of you. Thank you for letting me see it."

"Well, don't tell anyone, mister!" Her eyes went wide, and she giggled.

"That's not part of the guidelines list, and it's not your turn anymore. Nah, nah, nanah nah. I can tell anyone I want." Jeff stuck out his tongue.

She pouted, and he immediately felt it in his balls. Jesus, she had him by the short hairs for sure.

When he didn't do anything but grin at her, she rolled her eyes. "Fine. So...I seem to be a little messy. You think I can get a towel?"

"A towel? Already trying to get rid of me?" Jeff frowned, sticking out his bottom lip in a pout. "But mami, you said you liked it."

She cupped his cheek, chuckling. "Aw, baby, don't pout. I do like it, but you know, once it gets cold and sticky, it's time to clean up."

Jeff gave her an exaggerated groan. "Fine, if you insist."

"I do, I do. For sure." She giggled.

Jeff gave her a quick peck and rolled off her and out of the bed. In his bathroom, he wet a washcloth with warm water and brought it out to her.

He climbed onto the bed and knelt beside her. "Arms up."

"Ooh, okay." She grinned.

Jeff started at her chest and gently wiped off each breast. After he'd cleaned the area, he bent and pressed a soft kiss to her sternum. Coming back up, he wiped off her stomach, and then all the way down to her hairless mons. He moved the washcloth down over her clit, then between her legs, cleaning her labia. "Why is this so smooth? Do you get it waxed?"

She lowered her arms. "I got it lasered off. A few years ago."

"Wow! Didn't that hurt?"

"Hell yeah, it did. But it was worth it. This way, except for a few hairs, it's never growing back."

"That's awesome." Jeff smiled and looked down at her bare skin. "I love how smooth it is."

"What was that you said earlier?" She took the washcloth from him. "Something about on command? Hmm— Oh, that's right, I remember." She dropped the washcloth on the floor and spread her legs farther apart. "Jeffrey, eat my pussy and tell me again how smooth it is."

Jeff felt a primal growl roll up his chest, and somehow he managed to swallow it back down. Yes, he was ready to pounce on her, his cock instantly hard, and do some more marking. But having her on his tongue was just as good, if not better. This woman, goddamn! Would she ever stop blowing his mind? He stroked her swollen clit with his fingertip. "Yes, mami."

She sucked in a hard breath, and he shifted, kneeling between her parted legs.

Jeff spread her labia, parting her folds to see the glistening mouth of her pussy. She was beautiful, perfect, and laid out for him like a fucking buffet.

Tish moaned, and he moved to his stomach, stretching his legs out behind him. With her sweet cunt right in front of him, he was right where he needed to be. Once again, he parted her labia but then moved his thumbs up and rubbed her clit. With her right there for the taking, Jeff licked at the mouth of her pussy, moaning as he swallowed her honey down.

Tish's head fell back, and she circled his shoulders with a leg.

He pressed one hand to her lower abdomen, and as he rubbed her clit with his thumb, he buried his tongue in her core.

Heaven, he was back in heaven.

Chapter 9

Tish walked out of the courthouse, her purse straps hanging from one hand, a tissue gripped tight in the fist of the other. She had managed not to let any real tears go while she was in the courtroom, but once she got in her car, all bets were gonna be off. She sniffed and wiped her nose with the tissue.

Watching her brother get sentenced to six months in jail was not the way she'd wanted to start the day off. Wait, five months technically, since he'd already been in County for a month, but still.

The damn judge probably didn't even read the letter she'd written for Steven, practically begging for them to put him in rehab instead of jail. But no, of course not. Why should they try to help him? As far as they were concerned, he was just another number on the docket. And that public defender assigned to his case had sucked too.

With her heels clicking on the pavement, she moved through the parking lot and crossed the street to the visitors' lot as fast as she could. When Tish reached the car, her phone vibrated in her purse. She ignored it, hit the unlock button on her key fob, and slipped behind the wheel.

Closing herself in, she set her purse on the seat next to her and dug out her phone. It'd stopped ringing, the notification saying the caller had been Rayna, likely calling to see how things had gone.

Tish wasn't sure she could talk to anyone yet, not without bursting into a dribbling mess of tears. Dropping her phone in her lap, she gripped her steering wheel and leaned forward, pressing her forehead to the cool leather.

Why was this happening?

Why was everything so goddamn hard all the time?

Why couldn't Steven just stop what he was doing and accept the help he so badly needed?

Why did it end up here? After everything she'd done to try to help him, this was still where they landed. She couldn't make any fucking sense of it.

Tish tightened her grip. The tears broke free, and she raised her head and banged it (a little more than gently) against the wheel. Why was he letting their shitty childhood beat him, beat them?

Why couldn't he see, listen, just...be different?

She sniffled, tears racing down her cheeks. Fuck, she was so tired. Why was she so tired? All the goddamn time? When was it going to feel better?

Would it ever feel better?

The vibration of her phone in her lap forced her to wipe her cheeks and eyes. Tish turned the phone over and focused on the screen.

Goofball: *Checking in on you, mami. How's it going?*

Tish grabbed another tissue and blew her nose. A couple of times. She was surprised he was texting and not calling. But then again, he was giving her space...which was what she wanted. What she had asked for, too.

But sometimes Tish didn't want space at all. Sometimes she wished someone else would take over for a little while.

Pulling down the visor, she opened the flap on the vanity mirror and attempted to clean up her smeared mascara and eyeliner. Hello, raccoon eyes. Shit, a makeup wipe would go a long way right now.

She glanced at the time: 2:20 p.m. Tish closed her eyes and let her head fall back against the headrest. God, she was tired. Curling up in bed for the rest of the day and night sounded like a fine idea, except...she should probably go to work.

Letting out a resigned sigh, she reached in her purse and pulled out her small makeup bag. After finding her eyeliner, she focused on the mirror again and tried a small repair job.

When she was done, she went back to her phone and stared at his text.

Jeff was sweet and attentive, and yes, a total goofball. Somehow, the man managed to make her feel better. For short periods of time anyway. Mostly during sex...which, hello? Was awesome with him.

Feeling better, with all those nice orgasm hormones kicking in her system, combined with having intense attention from a hot man, was to be expected, sure.

But...truth was, Jeff made her feel better even when they weren't naked—though she would never admit that to him. No way she could. His ego would get even bigger than it already was. He'd think he conquered her, and then boredom would set in and...poof, he'd leave.

After all, she wasn't that fascinating.

Tish Beck: *I'm okay. Thanks for checking in on me, honey. Think I'm going to head to work.*

Goofball: *Work? No, nope. Nah. Listen, no one likes a party pooper, Tish. How about you come play hooky and meet me for a coffee?*

She laughed. God, this man. He said the stupidest shit, and it always had her cracking up in laughter.

Tish Beck: *Aren't you on duty right now?*

Goofball: *Yes, but it's a slow day, and I do get breaks, you know.*

Tish Beck: *Please don't tell me you want to meet at DD.*

Goofball: *Dungeons & Dragons? There's a place called that in the valley?*

Tish burst into laughter and then typed a long string of LOLOLOLOLOLOLs to him.

Goofball: *I say something funny? Wow, I wasn't even trying. Hey, here's something funny. Pick up.*

A second or so later, her phone rang, vibrating in her hand. She swiped the screen and hit the speaker button. "Hey."

"And there's that voice I dream of. How's it going?"

She started her car. "Dunkin' Donuts, *not* Dungeons & Dragons."

"Oh."

"Wait." She chuckled. "You were serious?"

"Uh, which answer will get you to come meet me?"

"Sadly, neither." She brushed some lint off her pant leg. "I should get a few hours in."

"Tish, my gorgeous angel...I know you're going to do what you want, I get that. I respect it. But...your brother got sentenced to jail today, my guess is for at least a few months, and that's gotta be hard on a person. So hear me out. This is what I'm thinking. You listening?"

She smiled. "Yes."

"Mmkay, good. *I'm* thinking you should give yourself the day, you know? Just chill and feel and process and stuff. Come see me, or go see Rayna. Or hell, go home and take a nap. Just, don't fucking go to work."

"But it'll take my mind off everything, and I need the distraction."

He tsked her. "Well, humor me then, okay? Rio misses you. He hasn't shut up about it all morning. Right, Rio?"

Tish heard the dog let out a short yelp, which sounded too adorable, and she couldn't wipe the smile off her face. Dammit, she hated when Jeff brought Rio into things. It was a guaranteed loss for her. Total sucker for that dog. "You know I can hear him, and that is a big fat no fair."

"Hey, I never promised to be fair. It wasn't on the list."

"And I am totally renegotiating our agreement at the six-month mark."
Shit...why did she just say that? Ugh, she really needed to stop doing that.
"Stop distracting me. Where are we meeting?"
  "I knew you liked me."
  She shook her head, grinning. "You're incorrigible. *Where are we meeting?*"
  "I love encouragement. Oh, uhhhh...BoSa Donuts, if you please."
Yum. "Which one?"
  "I'll text it to you."
  "Fine. You win. See you in a few." She ended the call before he tossed in another smart-ass comment.
  Tish plugged her phone in to charge, and then the text with the address she needed came in as expected. Knowing she'd totally just given in, Tish backed her car out of the space and headed for Jeff. And donuts.
  She was only going for the donuts.
  And also because he'd made her smile when all she had wanted to do was cry. The donuts were a close second, though. Icing on the cake.

* * * *

  Jeff looked over his shoulder when he heard the bell ding on the entry door into BoSa's.
  There she was, his woman.
  Unable to stop his smile, he moved to her and pulled her into his arms. Even wearing all his body armor and gear, she managed to get her arms almost halfway around his waist.
  She needed him.
  He knew it.
  She knew it too...but she would rather do *anything* in the world besides admit it to him and probably not to herself either. It was all good. He didn't need her to admit anything.
  It'd been a month since they'd become a real (albeit non-public) couple, and over that time, she'd told him all he needed to know in quiet moments just like this one, and a thousand others. Although today was different. Today was more.
  Jeff smoothed his palm up and down her back and kissed the top of her head. After another moment, Tish tipped her head back, her ice-blue gaze searching his face. No mistaking it, there was a lot of pain lingering in the depths of her amazing eyes. She was hurting.

He bent and brushed his lips over hers. "Glad you came."

"I want sprinkles." She smiled, baring her straight teeth.

He chuckled. "You can have anything you want."

She squinted at him. "So you keep saying."

"Well, you have a built-in forgetter, so I'm just making sure the statement stays put." Stepping back, he took her by the hand and moved to the counter.

She giggled. "I have a broken what?"

Jeff cleared his throat and focused his attention on the donut guy working the counter, ready to take his order. "Yeah, can we get one of each of the sprinkles and—" He glanced at the case filled with donuts. "Two chocolate glazed and two coffees."

"Ooh, yum. Donut holes too?"

God, he was crazy about her. Freaking donut holes.

"A bag of donut holes to go, please. That should do it."

Once they'd fixed their coffees with the essentials of cream and sweetener, they took a seat in one of the booths.

"Hmm. Cops and donuts." She winked. "You're kind of a walking cliché, you know that, right?" With a crooked grin, she bit into the chocolate frosted with colored sprinkles.

Half of a pink sprinkle got stuck to her upper lip. Jeff got it with his fingertip, popped it into his mouth, and winked back. "Why you gotta hate?"

"Don't hate the player, hate the game." She raised both hands and shrugged as she leaned back in her seat.

"Damn, that's my line." He sighed and then sipped his coffee. He really wanted to jump right in, ask her about Steven and court. How was she doing with it? However, being with Tish Beck had taught him patience in ways he'd never have thought possible. "So which one is your favorite?"

Jeff took another sip of his coffee. Maybe it was his training as a cop. Maybe it was a combination of many things. Or maybe it was just her, he honestly didn't know. But somehow he managed to shut his pie hole and not say every damn thought that galloped through his brain, and because he'd learned how to shut up, she was doing a fair amount of talking.

So far, Tish had told him things about herself he'd have paid his life savings to learn. She also told him things that meant nothing but meant everything at the same time. Little by little, she was sharing herself with him, and Jeff was falling deeper and deeper for her. She wasn't an open book yet, but they'd get there. Just needed more time.

"I think the chocolate sprinkles is my favorite, but at the end of the day, regular glazed is always the best."

"That's how I feel about chocolate glazed." He took a bite of his donut.

"I don't think I've ever had the chocolate glazed here. But I do love the chocolate glazed Munchkins at DD."

"Gasp!" Jeff pressed his hand to his chest and leaned forward to lay it on as thick as possible in order to get the reaction he was seeking. He lowered his voice almost to a whisper. "Are you trying to get us kicked out of here?" He pressed his palm to his forehead. "You can't just go throwing around the Dungeons & Dragons name, you know? That's like real life, for realsies blasphemy and stuff."

Tish gazed at him over the rim of her coffee cup. "Were you dropped as a child?"

He let his donut fall to the table. "Dammit. Why does everyone ask me that?" She was mid-sip and pulled the cup away, then covered her mouth with her palm. When she'd finally swallowed, she pointed her finger at him. "Are you trying to kill me?"

He hooked his pointer finger with the one she was pointing at him. "Why do you always ask me that?" He pulled her to lean across the booth table. "Remember...all I want to do is make love to you? Sheesh, mami."

"Noooo! Ugh." She laughed. "I still haven't looked it up."

"Do it. You'll thank me later." He tapped the edge of her coffee cup with his. "Speaking of later, what's your plan tonight?"

She swallowed the mouthful of donut she'd been chewing, then took a sip of coffee. "I don't have one. You can come over if you feel like it."

"Since you mentioned it, I always feel like it."

"Good." She smiled and ate another bite of donut and then focused out the window beside their table. "Is your police truck running?"

"Always. He's fine, probably napping. I can take him out before we go."

"I didn't even say anything about Rio, but yeah, cool. I'd like that." She glanced at him and gave him one of her famous eyerolls but then returned to looking out the window. After another thirty seconds or so, she spoke. "So, Steven will be in for five months. Technically six, but they took a month off for time served."

There it was, exactly what he'd been standing ready for her to share. Jeff reached for her hand. "I'm sorry. I know you were hoping for a different outcome."

She let him hold it but kept her gaze trained out the window, even as she wiped beneath one eye. "I just wish they'd listen, you know? He needs rehab, not jail."

Rio's specialty was drugs, and sadly, Jeff had seen his fair share of guys like her brother. Bottom line, repeat offenders were usually long out of second chances. There was no way a judge was going to give someone who'd already proven he was an active user, and wasn't afraid to steal from someone or hock their mother's fine jewelry to buy a fix, a second or third chance.

He stroked his thumb over the back of her hand. "Do you think when he gets out he'd be willing to go into rehab?"

She drew in a breath, her chest rising with the action. She shrugged and focused on him once more. "I don't know. I hope so. It's what I want and definitely what he needs."

"I agree, but with things like that, people have to *want* it. Do you think he does?"

She frowned, her brow furrowing. "You know, I don't really care what he wants. He needs to get his shit together. Christ, he's a thirty-two-year-old man-child, acting like a completely reckless idiot."

"From what you've told me, I don't disagree. I just don't want to see you making yourself crazy trying to fix him, babe. It's not good for you."

Her frown deepened. "I get it, but he's my brother, Jeff. I won't turn my back on him. Please don't expect that from me."

Damn, he just went a little too far. *Reel it in, Jeff.* "Not at all what I am saying, hon. I'm just thinking of you, that's all."

"Yeah well, don't worry about me. I told you before, I can take care of myself." She pulled her hand away from his and crossed her arms.

God, he wished that were as true as she believed it was. Tish didn't do shit to take care of herself. Not the real kind of care anyway. Frustration filled his gut, and all the words he wanted to say burned in the back of his throat.

With her agitated, there was nothing else to say, no way she'd be able to *hear* him. He needed to let things settle down a bit and then come back to it later. "Not trying to piss you off, mami. Please don't take it that way. I know you can take care of yourself; you do it every day without fail. But I will remind you, I am right beside you, whatever you need is yours."

She blinked at him, her lips pursed in annoyance.

Jeff continued, raising a hand, palm up. "Not that you'll need anything because, hello, you got this. Truly, you do. But just in case—" He leaned forward over the table, getting closer to her so he could lower his voice. "If you need a little tension relief or any other relief, I got you."

Her expression softened.

He kept going, relief moving through him. "Remember? You like me. A lot. I'm your guy. You're my mami."

She sighed. "It always amazes me how you can be so charming while you're talking about yourself."

"You got this." Jeff smiled.

She nodded. "Yeah, yeah."

"We got this. Together."

"Okay, enough." She laughed.

He chuckled. "Too far?"

"For you? Never!" Still laughing, she slid out of the booth. "Come on, let's go. Don't you have some protecting and serving to do?"

"You mean other than for you?" He handed her the bag of donut holes and got to his feet.

"Thank you. Yes. You know, the kind that pays your bills?"

"Oh, right! But..." He wagged his brows and bent to her, his lips hovering right above hers. "When it's for you, it's so much more fun."

She smirked. "Incorrigible."

"You love it." Jeff gave her a soft kiss. "Come on, let's go see Rio, and then really, I know you need me right now, but I *must* get back to work."

Laughing, she swatted his arm but let him take her hand and followed as he led them out the door.

Not an easy convo, but not too bad either. Tish had opened up just enough to let him see she was hurting and share a few inner thoughts. If he'd been able to keep his comments under wraps, she'd have gone further.

It was all right. He'd get another chance to shut his trap and let her do the talking tonight at her place. To him, she was worth every bite of his tongue and every minute of his time.

Chapter 10

After Jeff parked in the dirt lot behind the Whiskey Barrel, he headed inside to meet everyone. Heather and Rob, and Kim were there already, all crowded around one of the center tables near the dance floor. Derek and Rayna were on their way.

Tish was taking a Lyft to meet them all there, which was what she always did—which he thought was insane because they could just drive together, but that was beside the point. Seriously, no one was going to notice them getting out of the same vehicle. For real. They could even enter the bar separately, but Tish was against it. End of discussion.

They'd been together about three months, and it looked like there would be no budging on operation "don't tell anyone we're together" guideline. Yes, he was grateful to have her, to just be with her, but man, *as a* man, sometimes it was really fucking hard to not shout to the world what she meant to him.

When a man loves a woman, everyone should know about it.

"Rhonda! Have you lost weight?" Jeff clasped fists with Rob and pulled him in for a hug and back slap. "You look fab."

Rob pulled back, grinning. "Aw, Nelly, you say the sweetest things."

"I know, but you make it so easy." Jeff winked and turned his attention to Heather and Kim. "I swear the two of you are the most beautiful women in here."

Heather rolled her eyes, laughing. "Such a charmer."

Kim laughed and gave Jeff a hug. "You mean until Tish gets here, right?"

"Miss Kim, I have no idea what you mean by that." Jeff stuck his tongue out at her.

"And he dodges again." Rob laughed.

"No idea what you're talking about either." Jeff wiggled his way between Rob and Heather. "'Scuse me while I hug your woman. Come here, gorgeous." Jeff wrapped his arms around Heather's waist and, pulling her off her feet, gave her a brotherly bear hug.

"Best hugs ever." Heather giggled.

"I know, right?" Jeff set her down and straightened the cowgirl hat on her head. "This is adorbs, by the way."

Heather smiled and tipped the brim. "Thank you."

Jeff moved around to the other side of the table. "Now that I'm here, we can get the party started. What's everyone having tonight?"

Kim raised her tall glass filled with a fruit-punch-colored liquid. "I got my usual to drink and mixed one of my sugar-free powder flavor packs in." She smiled and took a sip through the straw. "I'm on a budget, but I did order the mac and cheese."

Jeff smiled. "Aw, I got you, girl. Get what you want."

"Hey, y'all." Tish stepped up beside him. She set her small bag on the table before shifting her hip to the side and bumping his. "What is Kim getting that you're giving her?"

"Speak of the devil, and the devil will call." Kim laughed. "All good, mamacita, already covered myself. It's ladies night, hence drink specials." Kim came around and gave Tish a quick hug and then returned to her side of the table.

When she turned back, Jeff nudged her hip with his own. "I didn't even see you come in."

"Falling down on the job?" She gave him a smug grin.

He shrugged, tipping his head to the side. "What can I say, I was distracted by shiny things."

"Figures." Tish stepped away and went and hugged Heather and Rob.

Jeff watched her, wishing he'd already gotten a drink. She was going to pull the jealous girlfriend game, something she always did (and denied doing), and he'd let her.

A small part of him loved when she couldn't help but let her green slip. Beyond that, it served a purpose for them, or for her rather. It made everyone think they were sleeping together and hiding it from them.

Which technically, yes, they were sleeping together and hiding it, but totally not the point. The point and purpose was everyone thought they were sleeping together from the very beginning, and they weren't or... hadn't been, and the plan was to let them keep on thinking it.

If all of the sudden Jeff and Tish stopped their back and forth banter, then everyone might get suspicious. Plus, Rayna and Derek both assumed they'd know firsthand if something was really going on between their BFFs.

Which, when Jeff gave that fact any bit of thought, it made him feel like a fraud because essentially it meant lying to his best friend. He was not that man. He did not lie to his friends.

Basically, if he focused too much on any of the situation Tish required they be in because of her "guidelines," he felt like shit about it. They'd had a couple tense moments because of the matter, each time Jeff finding a way to suck it up and let it go.

"Hey, guys! Good to see you." Bethany, their favorite waitress, delivered Kim's mac and cheese and then came around the side of the table and gave Jeff a hug. "I didn't see you and Tish come in."

Jeff grinned. "My dearest, Little Bit, that is always the plan. Tish would rather *die* than let anyone see us come in together."

"Aww, you two aren't fooling anybody." Bethany laughed and waved her hand, dismissing his comment.

Bet a gazillion dollars we are. Jeff grinned. "That's the rumor. But we keep trying!"

Tish came over. "I think he needs a Piehole Porter."

God, she had amazing timing. Like their act was practiced or something. Jeff leaned his chin on his fist and plastered on an obnoxious grin. "She knows me so well. That's exactly what I wanted. And I know she for sure wants a Three Skulls Block Orange."

Bethany laughed, shaking her head.

"Perfect. Oh, and a shot of tequila please, Little Bit?" Tish smiled.

"Of course. You want any food?" Bethany motioned to the menu.

"Yes, but I'm gonna wait for Rayna and Derek to get here." Tish looked to him. "You?"

He batted his eyes. "Nope. I'll wait for you and share."

Tish rolled her eyes and looked back at Bethany.

"Okay then, back with your drinks in just a few." Grinning, Bethany turned and stepped away.

The band queued up their version of Jennifer Nettles's "Playing with Fire," and Jeff glanced at Tish.

"I love this song!" Heather bounced.

"Come on, bombshell, let's go dance." Rob smiled, took Heather by the hand, and off they went.

Jeff wanted to dance with Tish. They never really had before. Maybe it'd be playing with fire, like the song? God knows that was what they were already doing. "Maybe I should go request some Bonnie Raitt."

"Oh yeah, which song?"

"Here you go." Bethany set their beers and Tish's shot down.

"Thanks, Little Bit." Tish smiled, picked up her shot glass and faced Jeff. "Here's to 'nothing to talk about,' right?" With a wink, she put the glass to her lips and tipped it back.

"Yes, mami." Jeff picked up his beer and took a long drink. As he set his glass back down on the table, Derek and Rayna came through the entrance. Time to really ham it up. "Here they are."

"Oh, good. Was wondering where they were."

As the two approached, Derek was smiling, and Rayna was waving to Tish. Jeff leaned forward on his forearms. "Probably fucking in the 4Runner."

Tish burst into a fit of laughter, falling against his side.

"Well, well, now. Aren't you two cozy." Derek clasped palms with Jeff.

Jeff grinned. "How goes it, Shirley."

"Oh yes, they do look cozy." With her lips split in a grin, Rayna came around the other side of the table to where Tish was sitting. "And what's got you laughing so hard, Tish? Jeff say something funny?"

Tish managed to rein it in and gave Rayna a hug. "Doesn't he always? And nice to see you too."

"He's consistent, that's for sure." Derek clapped his hands together. "I need a beer. Doc, you want beer or wine or booze?"

"I just had a shot." Tish sipped her beer.

"Ooh, after the day I had, I want a shot too. Or I could just get a margarita and call it a day."

"You getting salt on the rim?" Derek grinned. "Pretty please get salt?"

Rayna laughed. "Of course, honey."

Tish slapped her hand down on the table. "Oh my God! You two? Jesus, will you ever get sick of each other? You only want her to get salt so you can watch her lick it off the rim before each sip. By the way, you do realize how that looks, right?"

"How what looks?" Rayna's eyes were all wide, an innocent expression in them.

Derek blurted a laugh.

Jeff let his head fall into his palm. "Sweet baby J, save us from this extraordinary and amazing innocence."

"You know she's for real, right? How do you not know that yet?" Tish laughed.

"Oh, I know. Believe me, mami."

Rayna gasped and rolled her eyes. "You're just jealous."

Jeff nodded and gave her a cheesy grin. "Pegged me."

Tish blurted a laugh.

Jeff looked at her, and for a minute he wasn't sure wha—

Oh, hell. Did she just take that where he thought she did?

* * * *

Tish could barely get her giggles under control. Had he really said pegged? Considering how often he told her "she was in charge," maybe she should suggest some literal pegging to him?

That could be interesting.

Warmth hit Tish's tummy and spread to her limbs. Honestly, she wasn't sure if the idea was titillating or not. But it could be....

"You gonna share?" Rayna was smiling ear to ear.

"Maybe if I have another shot or two?" She grinned and eyed Jeff.

"Maybe it's time to cut you off?" With a blank expression on his face, Jeff lifted his beer and took a swig.

Which meant he'd picked up on what she was laughing at. The man was no dummy. What she couldn't tell was if he was mad or not. If he was mad, it'd be a first. The man had the patience of a saint with everyone. Especially her. Especially in regard to the front she needed him to keep up in front of their friends, too.

He didn't like it, but he did it anyway.

For her.

And sure, on occasion he'd slip something in. Example, the Bonnie Raitt comment, but that was it. Plus, those comments worked to their advantage anyway.

Besides, she'd be making it up to him later. Maybe with some pegging. Tish slapped her hand over her mouth to keep in the laugh that wanted to burst out into the world.

The band started, the lead singer and backups belting out Tim McGraw's "It's Your World."

And Jeff looked at her, an expression in his eyes she was afraid to read, but really, did she have to? The damn words to the song said it all. She rolled her eyes.

Heather and Rob came back to the table.

"Hey, kids! Glad you made it." Rob clasped hands with Derek.

Heather gave Rayna a hug.

Tish drew in a slow breath, eyes still locked with Jeff's, each word of the song a hard slap to her face. Dammit, this was not where she wanted things to go between them. Bitterness and resentment taking the place of happiness and acceptance.

And she was happy. To the point she almost forgot that what they had could be lost, that he could up and change his mind at any minute. Nothing like a song to remind her of exactly why their friends didn't need to know what was going on between her and Jeff.

So fine, it *was* her world. It had to be. So be it.

As the song came to an end, Jeff raised his glass and took a drink of his beer. Thank God that was over. The next song started, one Tish didn't recognize.

"May I have this dance?" Jeff held his hand out.

"Wow, I don't think you two have ever danced together. You should." Rayna smiled, resting her chin on both fists. "Go for it."

Tish shrugged. "I don't really like to dance."

"What do you mean?" Rayna frowned. "You used to."

"How about you fake it?" Jeff took her hand and pulled her behind him.

Oh, God! What the hell was he thinking? How was this supposed to work? They'd never even danced together before. Hell, she couldn't recall ever seeing him on the dance floor with anyone. Shit, did he even know how?

Worse, Tish had no idea how she was going to maintain appropriate distance while he whisked her around the dance floor to—"What the hell song is this?"

Jeff walked them to the center of the floor and pivoted to face her. "It's called 'You and Tequila' by Kenny Chesney."

"Oh." Yes, she knew that one. Between the last song, and now this one? The music gods were most definitely conspiring against her. And the words to this song, well, it was as if Jeff was trying to tell her something.

"Let's do this." Jeff wrapped an arm around her waist, pressed his hand to her back and scooted her close to his body.

Instinctively, she placed her hand in his, and not a moment later they started moving in a slow, country swing. Well then, guess he knew how to dance after all.

This close to him, Tish breathed in his scent, loving his cologne and how it mixed so perfectly with his body chemistry. She wanted to bury her nose in his neck, but no way she could do that, too many eyes on them.

The song was slower than she typically would've preferred to dance to, but as Jeff moved them, their steps fell right in line with the beat, and to her surprise, with each other. Then again, they'd been in sync from the minute, three months ago, she'd stopped fighting him.

He gave her hand a slight squeeze, and Tish crossed in front of him. He spun her back and then out again. Tish pressed her lips together and followed him. His hand on her mid-back made her feel supported, and the loose clasp he had on her hand also made her feel like she could hold on or let go. Her choice.

He turned them, and she crossed in front of him once more before spinning back then tucking under his arm to scoot behind him as he ducked under hers.

Geez, she'd missed this and couldn't stop the smile that formed.

Another turn and then he dipped her, singing the chorus to her.

She could not take her eyes off him. Between his dark brown eyes, his sweet lips and the sound of his voice singing these words to her? Tish was caught in his web of charm and good looks and something deeper in his expression.

It almost felt like his heart was breaking...but hers might be, too.

Jeff pulled her up slowly and then started them moving again. When the song finally ended, Tish wasn't sure what to do. She wasn't out of breath, but her heart was beating as if she'd been running a race.

As the bar applauded the band, Jeff took a step back from her and clapped too. "That was fun. We should do it more."

Tish swallowed. "I didn't know you could dance like that."

The next song started, and Jeff took her hand and off they went again. The cover band rocking "You Look Good" by Lady Antebellum.

Jeff grinned. "Still full of surprises, mami."

He moved, pivoting them in a series of turns, navigating the perimeter of the dance floor area. Her pelvis was tight to his as he rotated his hips, sexy as sin, taking her along with him.

Coming back to the two-step, Jeff pushed her out to a double spin before looping her back in to him.

"*You are* killing me." She laughed. "Oh my God, do not even say it!"

Jeff shook his head as he sang along with the song, moving them around the floor, smooth as hell, showing off—showing her all his skills.

Yeah, she was impressed.

And completely and totally turned on. Maybe he was trying to tell her that, too.

* * * *

Jeff could see that look in her eye, the one that said she wanted him. Damn if he didn't live for that look from her. The dancing had shocked her *and* turned her on, a twofer for sure.

Although he'd give her what she wanted, no doubt, there was no ignoring he was also filled with a mixture of emotions from how the night had gone, and also from the dance.

Tipping his glass, he took a swig of his beer and watched her from the corner of his eye as she talked with Heather and Rayna. Did the woman have any idea the power he'd given her? What a big deal that gift was?

How many guys were willing to go to the lengths he was going to win a heart? Not many. Shit, more than half the cops he worked with (male and female) walked around filled to the brim, polluted with their toxic-masculinity-type thinking.

In his opinion, suffering really, but don't bother trying to explain any of that to them. Again, too caught up in "feelings are for pussies" or "I'm a guy's guy" or...whatever stupid shit they pulled out of their asses.

That was not him, never had been. Yeah sure, he played a good front, goofed off a lot, and although he'd never thought like a caveman, he never knew he had it in him to give so much of himself, knowing in the end he could lose anyway.

That said, Jeff was one hundred percent sure about Tish. Had been from the first time he laid his eyes on her in the same bar they were standing in right now. Even if she left his ass, he wasn't going to lose her, lose her. Not forever.

Whatever kind of sense that made, it didn't even matter. If his ego had to make way for her to run the show and find her feet, he'd do it because it was worth it.

She was worth it.

They both were.

"You guys want to do some training this weekend?" Derek leaned over the table.

Rob set his beer down. "I'm game. When are you thinking?"

"I gotta check my calendar and get back to you. Was thinking about some OT this weekend." The excuse was real, sort of. Yes, there was OT available this weekend, which he would not be doing because he and Tish had made plans, though sort of tentative, aka not entirely firm yet because she hadn't fully decided. But then again, he also needed some downtime with his buddies. Plus, the training would be good for Rio.

With a half grin, half frown, Derek jerked his head back. "Huh? Check now, Nelly. You got your calendar on your phone."

"Bossy bossy, Shirley. It's not a good look on you." Jeff chuckled and slipped his phone from his front pocket and started scrolling through his calendar.

"Whatcha doin?" Tish leaned into him, pressing her shoulder and the side of her boob against his arm.

"Nelly's checking his calendar to see if he's got time for training this weekend." Rob rested his elbows on the table.

"Training?" Tish raised both brows. "Like, do you guys go and play cops and robbers or something? Is that legal?"

Jeff looked at her. "Did you have another shot of t'killya with Rayna?"

She raised both brows. "Maybe? What's it to you?" She grinned at him. "Are you the tequila-shot police now, because if so, let me just say, feel free to arrest me, ociffer."

Oh yeah, she was buzzing. And still had that look in her eye. *Rawr...*

"That's right, you tell him, girl." Kim laughed.

"Right?" Tish tapped Kim's glass with hers. "Just sayin'."

Derek laughed. "Oh, damn."

"'Oh, damn' is right." Rob nudged Heather. "We need popcorn."

This was about to get interesting. Jeff wasn't sure how to proceed, so he took a moment to think back to the days before they were together, how he would have reacted back then, because throwing her over his shoulder and carrying her out of the bar might feel right but was definitely a hell-no option.

Deciding to roll with the game and see where it went (hopefully not right into a brick wall), Jeff set his phone down, turned to her and rested his hand on her waist, giving her a gentle squeeze. "Oooh, mami, look at you all warm and fuzzy and, dare I say, flirty?"

She grinned and took a sip of her beer. "Flirty? Will you be adding that to the charges?" She giggled and pressed her fingertip to the center of his chest. "I mean really, Jeffrey, don't you think it's enough? All this pussyfooting around?"

Jeff took a second to glance around at the five pairs of eyes watching them like they were some hit movie on the big screen. He blew out a long, slow breath. It was time to give her some sort of typical smart-ass but flirty comment to call her bluff, and then she'd back down, get pissy with him, and poof, show over.

Jeff tipped his head to the side, curled his lips into a devious grin and gave her side another gentle squeeze. "Now that you mention it. Can I just take a pause and say, *meee-yowww,* mami! I mean, your kitty is *exactly* where I've been trying to be for over a year now." He winked and then glanced at all their friends. "But as always, and you all know this, no such luck for me. I'm blocked from the goods." He pulled his hand away and shrugged, making sure everyone saw it. "I kinda stopped trying. The amusement park is always closed. No fun in that."

Rob laughed. "Boo, hiss. The poor man!"

Jeff took a swallow of his beer, his work done. Operation "distract the group from the flirty, warm and fuzzy his woman was throwing his way" was well under way.

Tish frowned and narrowed her eyes at Rob. "What. Ever. Poor man, my ass." She flipped her hand in the air at Rob and then focused on Jeff. "Begging for a slap to the back of the head again, aren't you? At this rate, Rob might need one too." Grinning, she glanced at Heather, and luckily, the woman was laughing and nodding. Tish refocused on Jeff and brushed her hair off her shoulders. "I've had two shots and one and a half beers. So yes, I have a nice, manageable buzz going, and whoops, my bad for tossing you a bone." She put her hands on her hips. "One and only shot, dude. Won't happen again. All good with me."

"Noted." Jeff raised his beer to toast her. "Here's to back-of-the-head slaps, shots and thrown bones."

Tish blurted a laugh and raised her glass to his. "And to lost chances."

"Whatever that means." He grinned and then took a swig.

She drank from her beer and shook her head while swallowing. "Whatever is right."

"You two really need to get a room." Derek slipped his arm around Rayna's shoulders.

"And there's another country heard from." Tish nodded before finishing off her beer and turning the empty glass upside down on the table. "Two beers."

Giggling, Rayna gave Tish a high five. "Yeehaw! Get it, girl."

At that point, everyone burst into laughter, and Jeff just shook his head at the lunacy of it all.

"Well, kids, this has been tons of fun, but I think it's time to go." Kim stood, stuffed her cigarettes back in her small purse and started making the rounds giving hugs. "Let me know if anyone is out and about this weekend."

"Of course." Heather smiled and hugged Kim.

When Kim came Jeff's way and hugged him, he could feel the daggers from Tish's eyes. He really hoped Kim hadn't picked up on it too. "Night, my friends." Kim leaned and hugged Tish. "You good getting home, or do you need a ride?"

"Nope, all good." Tish held up her cell. "Calling my Lyft in just a minute."

No, she would not be calling a Lyft, but whatever.

Jeff stepped away and headed to the far end of the bar to close his and Tish's tab without prying eyes. He glanced over and waved bye to Derek and then motioned with his hand that he'd call him later.

Derek nodded, and then he, Kim and Rayna walked out.

Tish gave Rob and Heather a hug and then walked away heading toward the back of the bar, likely for the ladies' room.

After another wave goodbye, Heather and Rob left too.

And...scene!

Another successful friend night in the bag.

God help him.

Chapter 11

Buzzed, restless, irritable, and above all of that...horny. With her hands tucked in the back pockets of her jeans, she made her way to Jeff's truck in the parking lot behind the Whiskey. He was walking beside her, in silence. Thank God, because considering how she was feeling, talking was probably not the safest idea at the moment.

To his credit, he seemed to be picking up on that. Bright one, that Jeff Pearl was. She honestly wasn't sure if she wanted to pick a fight with him or fuck him. Both seemed like a great idea.

And why the hell did she keep getting all stupid jealous over Kim? Tish knew, deep down, there was nothing there to worry about. Yes, sure, Kim was hot. But if she and Jeff were going to get together, it would've happened a long time ago.

Tish drew in a slow breath...maybe that was what had her all on edge? Had they ever been a thing? She didn't really know. As they got to the truck, she turned to him. "Have you fucked her?"

He stopped, rested his hands on his hips, and stared down at the gravel in the parking lot. Without looking up at her, he said, "Why would you ask me that? I've fucked a lot of people in my past, Tish. So have you."

"Ugh, I know. I know. And our past is our past. It doesn't matter." She covered her face with her hands and then pulled them away in a huff. "Except in this case...it matters." Tish shifted and leaned back against the side panel of the truck.

Jeff moved closer and raised his arms, one on each side of her, resting his hands on the side of the truck bed, caging her in. "It should not matter. Especially because we're all friends."

He was so close, close enough to kiss her. She took in his features, the muscle that ticked in the side of his jaw, his eyes filled with desire *and* frustration.

Well, good, she was frustrated too—with herself and with him. "The fact that you haven't said no confirms it."

"It confirms nothing. So don't put words in my mouth." He shook his head. "You know, I don't get it. You were the one that wanted things open between us, yet here you are, worried about another woman? What kind of shit is that?"

"You agreed no sex." Smoldering unease spiked in her gut. Was he? Had he? *Oh, God.* "There's not supposed to be sex with other partners, Jeff. You agreed."

"Yeah, and how's that working out for you? Any good dates lately?" The expression in his eyes got dark, angry.

Again his jaw flexed, and between that and the look in his eyes, Tish wasn't sure if she was scared or turned on or pissed that he was acting pissed. Maybe she was feeling all of them combined?

Yeah, awesome. And what the hell did he have to be pissed about anyway? In order to keep from doing anything stupid, she fisted her hands at her sides. "That's completely un-fucking-fair."

"It's one hundred and fifty percent fucking fair." He smirked. "Give me a break, woman. All is fair in love and war, *and* casual relationships, right? They're your rules, mami, and *now* you don't want to play by them?"

Anger beat through Tish in time with her heart, and she stomped her foot. "No fucking way are you going to throw that in my face. You agreed!"

"Yes, I did. But let me fill you in on a little fun fact, and make sure you listen because this is the last time I'm saying it—" He drew in a deep breath, his chest heaving with it, and then he exhaled through his nose before he leaned in closer, their bodies touching, no more than three inches separating their mouths. *"No one* else gets my *dick* but you."

"How am I supposed to know that!" Raw panic and insecurity sped through her veins. Her entire body shook with it. The idea of him with another...she couldn't handle it.

His eyes went wide and then he narrowed them, glaring at her. "Because I'm telling you the fucking truth and you have no reason to doubt me. And for the fucking record, so it's clear, I have never fucked Kim Duke!"

A wave of relief crashed through her, and she exhaled a breath she hadn't realized she was holding. But it was also clear, unlike her, Jeff was not relieved. He was still pissed. Apparently, she'd pushed him too far. "Okay."

"Okay?" He scowled. "That's it, that's all you have to say, just okay?"

She scowled back. "What do you want me to say?"

"I don't fucking know, Tish! This is your goddamn game, and you started this argument."

Okay, fair point. She had started the argument. But it wasn't a game and...maybe it was time they (God help her) removed one of the guidelines. Drawing in a slow breath, she placed her palms on his chest and rolled her lips together. "Listen, first, this isn't a game to me. It's never been a game, Jeff. Second, I haven't been out with anyone since we started...whatever this is between us. And I don't want to be. Is that a better answer?"

His chin jerked back into his neck, and he pushed back from her body and turned his gaze away from hers. Although he'd put a small distance between them, he was still right in front of her, his arms still caging her in against the side of the truck. She'd had to let her hands drop back down to her sides though.

"Jeff?" She wanted to touch his cheek or something but then lost her nerve. "Say something, please?"

He refocused on her, his eyes dark and serious. "You really mean that?"

Staring into his eyes, she knew that even if she was terrified to trust him, even if she thought what was between them wouldn't last, plus all the rest of what she was so sure of regarding relationships, she was also sure she didn't want to see anyone else. And she didn't want him to see anyone else either. "Completely."

Once again, he moved close, pressing his body to hers. "Last chance to back out." He licked his lips. "You sure you're sure?"

In order to keep eye contact with him, she tipped her head back. He was breathing heavy, his lips so close to hers there was barely a breath separating them, and he still looked a little pissed.

With their gazes locked, Tish placed her hands on his sides and slid them around his back and held him to her. His big body against hers was solid and strong, something she could hold on to—something she *wanted* to hold on to. "I'm sure, Jeff."

With what sounded like a strangled groan, Jeff closed the remaining distance between their lips and took her mouth in a hot and hard kiss.

Tish's world spun as she was swept up in the tornado known as Jeff Pearl. He always kissed her like this, possessed her with his lips, his hands, his body...like she was his. As if she always had been and always would be.

In these moments, she gave herself over to that feeling, even if she knew it wouldn't last forever. Some was better than none.

And she'd never had anything like this man before. She wanted to savor him for as long as he'd let her.

* * * *

Jeff had been pulled down deep, drowning in the undertow of Patrice Beck. Letting go of the side of the truck, he buried his hands in her luscious hair and held her to him, stroking her tongue, taking everything she was willing to give him, though he'd always want more.

How dare she lay that shit on him about Kim and then blindside him with the rest? She no longer wanted to see anyone else but him? Fucking hell!

Great.

Awesome.

Perfect.

It was *exactly* what he wanted, what he'd been praying for, but *did not* see coming. Fuck's sake, she was always saying he was trying to kill her, but really it was the other way around.

Her wandering hands found his dick through his jeans, and she moaned. So did he. The damn thing was rod hard and throbbing for attention. She tugged the top button open, slid the zipper down and slipped her hand inside—

Jeff yanked from her lips. "Fuuuuuck!"

"Good idea." She grinned and squeezed the head. "Let's do it."

"In the truck now."

"Oooh, so bossy. I kind of like it." Her eyes flashed, and it only made his dick harder.

After pulling her hand out of his pants, he held onto it, took two long strides and opened the back door of his truck. "You like it, huh? Then try doing what you're told for once. Get in and get your pants off."

She giggled. "Yes, papi." She trailed her fingers over his abs before hopping into the back seat.

Yep, she was definitely the one doing the killing.

He closed the door and walked around to the other side. Good thing he'd parked in the back of the lot, most of the cars were gone, and if anyone came out, they wouldn't be able to see them though his tint. He opened the door and got in beside her.

He had no idea how she'd done it so fast, but she'd stripped out of all her clothes. Perched, all sweet and innocent, her legs tucked under her, beautifully naked holding an unopened condom between her fingertips.

Jeff shook his head and wanted to scream.

She was so fucking sexy, so fucking beautiful. More than he'd ever dreamed he could have.

He cocked a brow. "Whatcha got there?"

She grinned. "A present."

"I like when you give me presents." Lifting his hips, Jeff slid his jeans down, freeing himself.

She eyed his cock as it lay rock hard against his lower abdomen. "I like when you give me presents, too."

Tish leaned to him. Jeff curled his hand around the back of her neck and pulled her to his lips. God, her taste, there was nothing like it. Even with the booze and beer, she was heaven on his tongue. She gave as good as he did too, thrusting her tongue into his mouth.

As they kissed, he reached around her and played with her very wet slit, while she moaned and wiggled, unbuttoning his shirt.

Tish broke the kiss and parted his shirt. "Want to feel your skin against my nipples."

"I want to feel your wet cunt on my hard dick."

She blurted a laugh. "Good thing neither of us minces words, huh?"

"Mami, shut up and get that condom on my dick so you can fuck me."

"Yes, sir!" She laughed, tore open the package and rolled it on. Wasting no time, she straddled him, and staying up on her knees, she positioned the head at her entrance.

"You're so fucking beautiful." Jeff stared at her in the dim light inside his truck, caught in her web, and not fighting it one bit.

Her expression went soft, and she slid down his cock. "So are you."

Her words flowed out on a breathless moan, and Jeff gritted his teeth, pressing the back of his head against the headrest. Heaven...

Tish wrapped her arms around his neck and took his lips in a kiss, thrusting her tongue in and out of his mouth as she rocked her pelvis back and forth, fucking him with a kind of intense intimacy they'd not shared before.

This was different.

Jeff grabbed her ass, helping her move on him, but then he let go with one hand and slipped it between them to rub her tight clit with his thumb. Breaking from her lips, he moved to her neck. "Ohh, fuck yeah, mami. Take it."

"Baby..." She moved faster, her fingers tangling in his hair. "You're going to make me come so fast."

"I'll go when you go." He nipped her collarbone.

She arched back, holding on to his shoulders, whimpering, rolling her pelvis and doing it with her eyes locked with his.

So fucking sexy, so gorgeous.

Jeff gripped her waist tighter on one side and kept at her clit. Her cunt clenched around his shaft, and he almost blew his load. "Tish..."

"Yeah, baby?" She moved a hand down to his and pressed her fingers to his thumb, rubbing her clit harder than he'd been doing.

"Show me how you like it."

A small smile arched her full lips, and as much as he wanted to kiss her again, he needed to see her take what she needed from him.

Her muscles clenched around him again, and Jeff gritted his teeth. If she didn't come soon, he might grind his molars to dust. "Tish..."

"Oh, God! Yes, yes!" Tish threw her head back, her orgasm hitting. She froze, his dick buried to the hilt inside her. The only thing moving on her were the walls of her sweet cunt, steady pulsing, squeezing his dick with each wave of her orgasm.

Jeff blinked, feeling more than he should in the deepest parts of his heart, caught up in the beauty of her body coming for him. Jesus, it was a moment he'd never forget, watching her in the throes of climax, that pleasure being something he gave her—something they were giving each other.

When she'd come down enough, she started moving again. The head of his cock was throbbing with the need to come, his balls full and pulled up tight. "Want to feel you without a condom on." She wrapped her arms around his neck again, bringing her chest-to-chest with him. Tish pressed her forehead to his, rising and falling on his cock. "Want to feel you come inside me. Tell me you want that too."

Fuck yeah, he did. That didn't mean it was going to happen though. Jeff wrapped his arms around her waist and held her tight. She tipped her hips back, raising herself off him just enough so he could drill up into her. The sound of the flesh slapping together filled the cab and all he could do was grunt...because this close to coming so hard he might go blind, words were not a priority.

She smiled, as if she knew she had him in the palm of her hand. "Harder, baby. Let me feel it."

"Tish!" Jeff buried his face in her neck, squeezed his eyes closed and came. Hard. Harder than he'd even expected. Cum spurted into the condom, his dick kicking over and over and over. The kind of orgasm where a person saw stars.

Spent, he collapsed against the truck seat, and Tish collapsed against him. Her nails traced little circles in the back of his neck at his hairline.

"You good?" Jeff released his hold a little, only to smooth a hand up and down her back, soothing her, but also getting the pleasure of feeling her soft skin.

"More than good. You?" She pressed a soft kiss to his shoulder.

I love you... The words were right there, caught in Jeff's throat, hanging in the silence. Three little words that he knew had no place between them at that stage, so he kept them to himself.

He gave her a gentle squeeze. "Mami, with you, I'm perfect."

She giggled and sat up to look at him. "That's some high praise, my friend. I'll take it, even if you're just being a smart-ass."

My friend...

He traced her bottom lip. "Smart-ass? Nope. I speak only non-smart-ass with you."

She raised both brows. "Is that so?"

"It's very so. Fucking you? Dream come true for me. There's not a damn thing about that where smart-ass applies."

Her eyes got soft, and he felt it in his throat. Jeff closed the distance between their lips and kissed her. This time it was slow, sweet, intimate.

When she broke the kiss, she moved her lips to his neck, then his ear. "I was serious. I don't want to use condoms anymore."

Jeff blinked, needing a moment to process that ask. For sure, with her announcement regarding monogamous dating, aka a real relationship, that could mean they could go ungloved, and he wanted that.

Things had changed, they'd changed.

He just hadn't thought about no condom as an option, but going that route was definitely a bennie he didn't know he wanted. He guessed that answered it right there. He wanted it. What guy wouldn't?

He smoothed his fingertips up and down her spine, loving the feel of her in his arms, against his chest and still holding him inside her. "I'm all for that. But I haven't been tested in a while, so even though I'm pretty sure I'm clean, I want to do that first."

She sat up, tucking a piece of hair behind her ear. "Good idea. I'll get tested too."

"What about birth control?'

She grinned. "I have an IUD. I barely even get periods anymore. It's fucking awesome."

"Good to know." He smiled. "You ready to go?"

"I am, yes." She rubbed her nose over his.

Sweet. So sweet. "Your place or mine?"

"Yours. I want to see Rio."

He nodded. "Good. Betting he wants to see you too. So...you know we can't drive home like this, right?"

She looked down at their bodies. "You mean naked?"

He laughed. "No, I mean with my dick still inside you, and us in the back seat."

"Ohh, right, yes." Her eyes went wide, and she shrugged. "Tell me, why is it you don't have a chauffeur, again?" Giggling, she slid to one side.

He helped her shift over to the seat beside him. As much as he hated losing her, he needed to take care of the condom.

She slipped on her panties. "You got napkins in the center console?"

That would be better than leaving it in the parking lot, which even though he was a guy, was fucking gross. "Yes, would you mind?"

"Not at all." Tish bent forward and opened the console, somehow managing to get inside around the opened lid. "Aha! Got 'em." She raised a pile of napkins in the air.

"Thank you." Jeff cleaned up, wrapped the spent condom in the napkin and pulled up his pants.

Tish finished getting dressed and climbed over to settle in the front passenger seat.

Jeff got out of the back seat and then slid back in, but this time behind the wheel. He glanced at Tish and started the truck. "Are you—"

"I'm hungry."

He laughed. "Yep, it's what I figured."

"Are you?"

He put the truck in drive and pulled out of the parking spot, then the parking lot. "I could eat, yeah."

"You have anything at your place, or should we hit a drive-through? Oooh, maybe donuts?" A smile so bright hit her face it practically lit the inside of the truck up.

Jeff flipped a bitch and headed in the opposite direction. "BoSa's donuts it is. Cop, remember?" He glanced at her and winked. "Don't have to ask me twice about donuts."

She laughed. "We all have our things...."

"Yes. We certainly do." Jeff glanced at her once more and then focused back on the road.

She had no idea really. Of course, everyone had their things, but for him, it wasn't donuts. It was Tish.

Tish was his thing. Tish was his dream. She was his everything.

Jeff focused on the road. "By the way, I got you a toothbrush to keep at my place."

Chapter 12

Jeff stepped out his back door onto his patio, a beer in each hand. "Have no fear, the barley and hops is here."

Derek took one of the bottles. "You're so good to me."

"You know it." Jeff resumed his seat and tipped his bottle back. He eyed the small blaze in the fire pit. "You add more wood?"

"Yeah, figured we'd be hanging a little longer." Derek threw the glow-in-the-dark rubber ball into the darkness of the backyard, giving the dogs the German command for fetch. "*Bring!*"

Axle and Rio both darted out after it.

Derek sighed. "I think I could sit and play fetch all night long."

"Me too. It's the repetition. Totally relaxing."

"True words, my friend. True words." Derek raised his beer and took a sip.

Rio came back, ball in his mouth, and dropped it in Jeff's lap. He palmed the damp ball. "I could do without the spit though." He laughed and looked at the dogs, both panting and ready for him to throw the ball. "*Sitz!*"

Without hesitation, both animals sat, almost in unison. Jeff grinned and threw the ball. Rio and Axle took off for it again. Rinse, lather and repeat.

He and Derek sat in silence, drinking their beers, chilling in front of the fire, playing with the dogs...relaxing. As cops, downtime was always welcome, and good for the soul.

"Feels like forever since we've done this. Speaking of, where's Rob tonight?"

So much for the silence part. Jeff grinned. "Dinner with Heather at her parents'."

Derek visibly cringed. "Ooh, tough break. I do not envy that at all."

"Me either." Jeff tipped his beer back.

"So what's new? You seeing anyone?"

Apparently the silence was *really* a no-go tonight. Damn. But worse, his best friend just asked a question that in order to answer meant Jeff had to lie. He hated lying to Derek. Hell, he hated lying to anyone.

"Nah, not really interested in anything like that right now." Jeff took another swig of his beer and picked at the label.

"You and Tish still dancing around?"

Jeff chuckled. "We don't dance."

"I dunno." Derek shrugged. "Some might say, a couple of months ago, you two seemed to dance pretty good together."

"Bah, it was all fun and games. Doesn't mean anything." Jeff tipped his beer, taking a large gulp, and focused on the wild flicker of the fire.

He loved his friends, needed the downtime with them and their canines. But spending time with them, especially Derek, was getting harder and harder. This was the perfect example of what kept happening.

Bottom line, it sucked balls not being able to share about his life.

A couple of weeks ago, he almost gave in to the need to share and said he was seeing someone, telling the guys it wasn't serious enough to bring her around the crew yet. No way that'd work though. After all, Derek and Rob, aka Shirley and Rhonda, were two guys in committed relationships, but more, were completely head-over-heels *in love* with their women.

Point was, they were a couple of hopeless romantics who wanted Jeff to have what they were having. Therefore, both would want to know her name, who she was, where she lived, how long they'd been dating...etcetera.

Jeff wouldn't be able to share any of those details or that info with them. That included no disclosure to Heather and Rayna as well. Plus... for the record, and his own sanity, then he really would officially be lying.

So, no.

No story.

No bullshit.

He'd keep it to himself. He'd hate it, but he'd do it.

* * * *

"I think I want a new pair of cowgirl boots." Tish shifted a shirt over on the rack and examined the next. "A set of red ones maybe."

"You should. We can head to Boot Barn after this if you want," Heather said from beside Tish. "Rob would *love* it if I got a pair."

On the other side of the rack, Rayna's eyes got big as saucers. "Oh my goodness, you don't have cowgirl boots yet? How is that possible?"

Heather laughed. "Just haven't bought any?" She shrugged. "I don't know. Been a little busy."

"You been busy all right. Busy riding that cowboy of yours. Forward, backward and upside down, no doubt." Tish grinned. "All without cowgirl boots apparently."

"Well yes, it cannot be denied." Heather winked, tucking a lock of hair behind her ear.

Rayna put a hand on her hip. "Sweet Lord, please don't go all rated R on me in public again."

Tish and Heather burst into laughter.

"I'm serious, you guys." Rayna rolled her eyes, shaking her head before focusing on the clothes on the rack again.

Tish got her giggles under control. "What if we just go PG-13? Would that be okay?"

"You are too much, I tell you what." Rayna rolled her eyes again.

Heather moved around the rack to where Rayna was standing. "Okay, okay. I promise, no rated R." Heather crossed her heart. "Though, I gotta admit, I *am* curious where Miss Tish has been spending all her time lately. Always busy. No time for us. Makes me wonder if she's got a hot piece on the side she's keeping a secret."

Tish glanced up from a shirt she was examining. Heather had no idea how right she was, not that Tish was going to cop to anything. No pun intended. "Well, Miss Heather, you should know by now that I *always* have a hot piece on the side. But I assure you, they aren't what's taking my time away."

Heather's brows popped. "Uhh...back up. They?"

"No, not they as in *they*. Sheesh." Rayna laughed. "My Tish might date a lot, but she doesn't do multiples. Yes, *could* be a new guy maybe, one I haven't heard about yet, but—" She held a sweater up to her body. "I'm betting it's the job."

"Hard no to that sweater. It's too matronly." Tish scrunched her face, shaking her head. "And yes, the job is a pain for sure."

"Brat. I like matronly." Rayna pouted and hung the sweater back up. "Soooo, *is* there a new guy?"

Tish held a sheer, white tunic up to her chest. "No one worth mentioning... but if there were, do you think he'd like this?"

Heather nodded, grinning. "*That* is sexy."

"Right? Especially with a white lace bra underneath it." Tish draped it over her arm. "Sold."

"Or a black lace one." Heather winked.

"Ooh! Naughty. I love it!" Tish grinned.

Rayna crossed her arms. "So, wait, which is it...are you seeing someone new?"

Tish glanced up. "Don't worry your pretty little ginger head. You know I'd tell you if there was someone new."

"Case closed, I guess." Heather wrapped an arm around Rayna's shoulders. "Let's go get some boots."

"Okay, I'll go get in line to pay." Tish held the sheer shirt up again, looking at it. As she made her way to the registers, Heather and Rayna went out to wait in the car.

Jeff would say she'd just lied to her friends, but Tish didn't really see it that way.

It was easier this way. Them not knowing. Even though things were going seemingly good for her and Jeff, eventually things would shift. There was no point in risking friendships over a fling.

Plus, she didn't want their friends picking sides or feeling like they needed to pick sides anyway. They were a great group, had become a family to her, and frankly, she needed them to stay that way.

Steven would be getting out soon, and Tish was going to need their support more than ever, even though Rayna and Jeff were the only ones who knew about her brother—well, Derek probably knew too, but that was to be expected. Heather and Rob didn't need to know in order for Tish to feel their support. Maybe that didn't make sense to others, but it made sense to her.

She handed the shirt to the clerk and took her wallet out. Hopefully, things would keep going a little longer with her and Jeff, and then she'd have him, too. She wasn't under any illusion that once things ended between them, they'd be able to easily go back to how things were before, but she hoped they could at least coexist among *their* friends and keep it cordial.

She just hoped that her hope didn't bite her in the ass when all was said and done...the best laid plans and all that mess.

Chapter 13

"Baby..." Tish drew in a slow breath, letting the feel of him overtake her as it always did...but refused to close her eyes. Watching how Jeff's expression changed to one of ecstasy the minute he entered her was nothing less than...perfection.

"I know."

Naked in his bed, him on top of her, nestled between her thighs. They'd stopped using condoms over two months ago, thank God, and she still wasn't used to how unbelievably good his cock felt as it slid deep.

Especially when he did it all slow and intense, like he was doing right then.

Based on what she was seeing in his face, he wasn't used to it yet either. And Tish was good with that.

She ran her hands down his back and continued to his perfect ass. Gripping the hard muscles, a thrill ran through her, feeling those muscles bunch and flex with each thrust of his hips.

After a little over five months together, she'd learned missionary with Jeff was not just typical vanilla missionary in any way, it was so much more.

Resting on his forearms, which he'd looped under her arms, cradling her, Jeff tangled his fingers in her hair. Gripping the strands tight, Tish gasped and he took her lips, sliding his tongue into her mouth, stroking over hers.

She moaned, and her tummy got tight. She liked the feel of him, loved it really...the way the weight of his body felt pressed to hers, from chest to pelvis. His skin against hers. His strong legs and back, and ass—

He withdrew fully, just so she could feel the ridge of the head catch on the mouth of her cunt when he slid back in, doing it in a way that his pelvis ground against her clit. Tish whimpered into his mouth, dug her heels into the bed and rolled her body, moving in harmony with him, meeting the slow and steady thrust of his hips.

Lust spread through her like hot molasses, her orgasm hovering just out of reach. He was building it inside her. Slow. Steady. And so fucking intentional, that when she came, she knew she'd see stars.

Tish spread her legs wider, which changed the angle of her pelvis, and dug her nails into his ass cheeks. Pulling from her lips, he groaned without breaking stride and thrust in again. Not faster, but a little harder, a little deeper, a little more intense.

Fucking hell, this was sexy. He was beyond sexy, and the tension in her grew tighter, her orgasm inching closer with every penetration. Tish moaned, getting completely lost in him.

"I know, mami." He slid his hands to the side of her head and stroked his thumbs along her jawline. "So fucking perfect."

"Baby—"

The sound of Rio barking filled the room, his nails clacking on the flooring as he ran toward whatever his reason for barking was.

Tish and Jeff both froze.

Tish felt her eyes go wide. "You think someone's here?"

He looked to his bedroom doorway. That was when the doorbell rang, the sound sending Rio into another round of barking, a few whines and yelps mixed in. Jeff looked back to her. "Sounds like it."

"Shit!" She pushed at his chest, frantic to move. "Go, babe. Get up."

"Go easy." Jeff shook his head and, before he pulled away, pressed a soft kiss to her forehead. "Good thing your car is in the garage."

BARKBARKBARK-dingdong-BARKBARKBARK

"Right?" Her eyes went wide. "Ohhmygod."

Once he'd sat up and shifted to the edge of the bed, Tish did the same, scanning the floor for her shirt, something. Anything. Where the hell were her clothes?

Jeff stood and pulled up his boxer briefs, then his jeans. "Clothes are in the kitchen, mami. Remember?"

Tish looked up and felt her brows hit her hairline. "Shit! Okay, um..." She eyed his tall dresser, ran to it, opened a drawer and nabbed one of his T-shirts. She pulled it over her head and caught sight of Jeff, still sitting on the side of the bed.

BANGBANGBANG—BARKBARKBARK-BARK

What was he doing? Was he... Tish put her hands on her hips. "You're enjoying this, aren't you?"

He stood and ran his fingers through his hair. "For the record, I was balls deep in your sweet cunt, so no, I am not enjoying this, I was enjoying that."

Tish felt that between her legs, and she clenched in response.

Jeff moved to her. "But let's just say, if that's Derek or Rob at the door and they find you, I won't be upset about it."

Of course he wouldn't. He wanted them to know. Damn him. She pursed her lips. "And exactly how would they find me, unless you tell them I'm here?"

He eyed her, his gaze roaming over her face. "It's fine. Stay here."

She sighed. "Whoever it is, they're awfully persistent and aren't afraid of the dog, that's for damn sure."

"That's a good sign." He walked out of his bedroom, disappearing from her sight.

Tish moved to the door, closed it, but not completely. She wasn't sure who it was but was hoping she might be able to tell once Jeff let them in.

It was only when Rio stopped barking that she could hear anyone. And yep, it was Derek. She eyed the clock on Jeff's nightstand: 10:30 p.m. Apparently Derek was stopping by on his way home. Fabulous.

Padding across the carpet back to Jeff's bed, Tish lay on her side and pulled a pillow to her chest. Hopefully, he'd get Derek out of there and come back to bed, because yeah, she'd been enjoying him too.

* * * *

Jeff stepped back from the door so Derek could get into the house. "Hey what's up? Everything okay?"

"Yeah, are you okay?" Derek looked Jeff up and down before letting Axle off his lead.

The dogs did their ass sniffing, nosing each other routine before taking off into the kitchen.

"Right as rain." Jeff stretched an arm in the air at an angle and yawned, making like he was tired. Which he wasn't, but technically he would be had he finished intensely fucking his girl, milking at least two orgasms from her, then spurting his seed deep, like she liked him to do. "Was catching up on my beauty sleep."

Derek crossed his arms. "Dude, what the fuck? Why are you in bed already? It's only ten thirty. Are you sick?"

"Shirley, I realize ever since Rayna hitched her star to your wagon, keeping track of my needs is no longer your priority. I get it. I forgive. I know my place. And I don't complain either, even though I was your one and only before her." Jeff pressed his palm to his bare chest, covering his heart.

Derek rolled his eyes.

"Where was I?" Jeff tipped his head to the side and looked up at an angle. "Oh right, me. Anyway..." He looked back at Derek. "You get my point. So no, I'm not sick. But I do have to get up early tomorrow for my shift...at seven a.m. Any of that ringing a bell?" Jeff winked. "Hence, I was sleeping, right where I should be, getting my beauty sleep."

Derek stared at him for what felt like ten minutes but was probably only ten seconds before he frowned and responded. "When did you start going to bed so early?"

"Seriously, darling, I love you too. I really do, but did you come here so you could flip me shit in the middle of our workweek because I'm catching some Zs?"

Derek frowned. "Yeah, no. Of course not." His friend shrugged. "I just thought maybe we'd have a beer or something. I texted, but I'm guessing you didn't see it."

Jeff glanced around, wondering where he'd left his phone. He hadn't seen it since he'd stripped Tish naked in the kitchen. Which reminded him, her clothes were in there.

As much as the idea of making her wait in his bed for him while he drank a beer with his bestie appealed to him, it would likely piss her off, which would ensure he didn't get to go back to being buried deep inside her tight cunt, at least not tonight anyway. Fuck him! "Nope, can't say that I did. Sorry, man. How about a rain check?"

"Yeah, that's cool. Rayna and Heather were talking about a real all girls' night Thursday, so maybe we can go out too and then meet up with the girls later on?"

"Sounds like a date." Jeff grinned before letting out a quick, sharp whistle for Rio.

Sure enough, Rio and Axle emerged, trotting one after the other, from the hallway (likely from the bedroom) into the living room. Jeff eyed Rio, and the dog came up and sat beside him.

"Cool." Derek nodded. "All right, man, I'll let you get back to it." Derek bent and linked Axle's lead back onto his harness.

A sudden feeling of dread filled Jeff's veins. "Hey, everything okay with you and the doc?"

Derek shook his head. "Yeah, yeah. No, we're good. Got some stuff I can share, but no worries, it'll sit until Thursday night."

Okay, not dread, just guilt. Guilt sucked but not as bad as dread.

Jeff drew in a deep breath, feeling only a sliver better than he had. "Look forward to hearing all the juicy gossip. First round's on me." He clapped Derek's shoulder and shifted toward the door.

Derek laughed and stepped outside. "Isn't it always?"

"What can I say? I'm generous like that." Jeff grinned and blew Derek a kiss. "Get home safe, Shirley. I'll text you in the morning, when I get on shift."

"Touché." Derek laughed. "And I will not answer because *I'll* still be sleeping." He turned and walked across the front lawn to his patrol truck.

"Oh, you mean like I was?" Jeff laughed and watched as Derek rounded the truck, got Axle in his seat in the back, and then slid behind the wheel. When the engine started up, Jeff gave one last wave before his best friend pulled away from his house.

He closed the front door, and instead of going back to the bedroom, he stood there, his back against the closed door, wondering if his best friend would ever forgive him for keeping his relationship from him, or if he and Tish would ever move past this charade she insisted on keeping up.

Speak of the devil....

Tish appeared at the end of the hall, looking a little nervous. "All clear?"

"I hope so, because if not, it's a little late now."

"Very funny." She moved to him, and when she got there she placed her palms on his bare stomach. "The dogs came to visit me."

He kept his hands at his sides. "I figured as much."

"You okay?" She tipped her head, a small frown pinching her brows together.

He blew out a breath. *Nope, not at all.* "I'm fine."

"You don't look fine." She rose on tiptoe and linked her arms around his neck. "What's up, baby?"

Unable to resist the need to touch her, he rested his hands on her sides. He wasn't sure if he should even bring the matter up with her again. They'd had a talk about it a couple of weeks ago, and although it wasn't an argument, she'd made her point clear she still wasn't open to sharing what they had.

Jeff sighed and deflected. "Dunno, just a little worried about Derek. He seemed like he needed to talk, so I feel a little shitty shooing him off." That was not a lie. Derek did say he had stuff to share. He gave her sides a gentle squeeze. "Has Rayna said anything?"

"Shit, you think something might be wrong between them?"

He shrugged. "Could be?"

"God, I hope not." Tish settled back onto her feet but kept her arms around his neck. "She hasn't said anything, but Rayna is *not* a talker.

Believe me when I say, I'd have to ask her directly, and specifically in the right way, if everything was okay with her and Derek. Only then would she tell me, but only because she would rather cut off her own arm than lie."

He sighed and pressed a kiss to her cheek. "It's probably fine. He mentioned something about a girls' night on Thursday. Guess the guys will head out too and then meet up with you all later in the night."

"I haven't heard about that either. But I'm guessing I will soon enough." She pressed her lips to his sternum. "You ready to get back in bed?"

Jeff yawned. "Yeah, but I'm sorry, mami, Derek kind of killed my mojo, and honestly? I actually am tired."

She stepped back. "Oh. Uh, okay. Yeah, I'll grab my things."

"You don't want to sleep over?"

"I'd love to, but I didn't bring anything with me, and I have an early day tomorrow too, so..." She shrugged. "May as well head out, and we can both get some sleep."

Jeff gave himself a mental kick in the ass. He did not want her to go. That was not in his plan. Damn, he should've just taken her back to bed and picked up where they'd left off, but he really *had* lost his mojo. "Okay, mami. Whatever you need."

She gave him a small smile before pressing a soft kiss to his lips. "Gonna grab my clothes."

"Good idea." Before she stepped away, he gave her bare ass cheek a little pat.

"Don't go teasing me, now." She rolled her eyes, turned away and headed for the kitchen.

Jeff drew in a slow breath and crossed his arms. How was it that the greatest time in his life was also the hardest? How was that even fair? He moved to the couch and plopped down.

If he gave the whole situation too much thought, it started to feel like he didn't exist. Maybe he didn't? After all, "they" as a couple didn't exist, at least not to the outside world.

If things ended for them right now, he'd have to move forward as if nothing happened, as if he'd never had her in his arms.

As if he didn't love her.

Pretending like that? Sweeping what was between them under the rug so no one saw it?

That might be the one thing he'd struggle to be able to give her.

Chapter 14

"Oh my God, of course you can stay here when you get out!" Surprise bubbled over inside Tish. Grinning from ear to ear, she pulled the phone away from her ear and put it on speaker.

Her brother cleared his throat. "Sweet. Thanks. I gotta give an address for probation, so they know where I'll be."

"Of course. No worries." Tish set the phone down on the bathroom counter so she could put on a little makeup. "I'm excited. How much longer before they let you out?"

"Not sure. In the next week or so, I'm guessing."

She leaned toward the mirror to put on a layer of mascara. "Should I try and call myself and ask?"

"Nah, it's all good. I'll call you as soon as I know. You think you'll be able to come pick me up though?"

Tish pulled the mascara wand away and straightened, thinking for a moment if she could pull that off. She shrugged and bent to the mirror again. Her bosses would be dicks, but oh well, she'd figure it out and they'd have to get over it. Her brother was coming home. That was what was important. "Absolutely! If it conflicts with work, I'll figure it out."

"Okay, gotta go."

"Yay! Love you! It's gonna be great, Steven. I just know it." The sheer anticipation of her brother getting out of jail and coming home again raced through her, and she smiled in excitement, how could she not?

The call disconnected and Tish hurried, finishing her makeup. She was meeting Rayna for happy hour, and for the first time in forever, she had something awesome to share.

* * * *

Tish entered Postino's and waved to Rayna when she spotted her. Her best friend had gotten them an awesome table along the side. The outside, on the back patio, was completely full. Not a surprise considering it was springtime in AZ.

"Hey, honey!" Tish gave Rayna a peck on the cheek and took her seat.

"Look at you all smiles. You look beautiful." Rayna's mouth was arched in a cute smile.

"Aw, thank you. But...does that mean without a smile, I'm not beautiful?" Tish chuckled, unrolled her napkin and placed it on her lap. "I'm kidding. Don't answer that."

"Good, because you know that's not true." Rayna rolled her eyes. "Let's get some wine and you can fill me in on what, or rather who, has put that smile on your face."

"Deal." Tish eyed the menu. "Did you want to get a bottle?"

Rayna shrugged, sipping her water. "I think that's the special, isn't it? The boards and wines?"

"Oh yeah. True. Okay, red or white?"

"White. It's so nice outside, I want something light and springy."

Tish eyed the list. "Yep, yep. I agree. I think we need a nice white blend. You decide the boards we're eating."

Rayna held her menu up. "On it."

Tish waited until they'd placed their order and the wine had been delivered before she shared.

"Let's toast." Tish raised her glass in the air.

"My beating heart, I can barely wait any longer for whatever this news is." Rayna held her glass up, a curious gleam in her eyes. "Lay it on me?"

Tish laughed, her smile bigger now than before, she was sure. Her poor best friend probably thought Tish was going to tell her she'd met Prince Charming or was maybe getting a raise or promotion (although, just to say a raise would not be unappreciated), but to Tish, the news she had was better than anything like that. "Let's raise our glasses and drink to fresh starts and new beginnings!" Tish clinked her glass to Rayna's.

"Time out." Rayna frowned and pulled her glass away. "Beautiful toast, honey, really, but you are speakin' in code right now, and before I come clean outta my skin from the undiluted anticipation, will you *pah-leeeze* tell me *what in the world* is goin' on?"

Tish laughed again. She loved when her bestie's southern accent made its presence known.

Rayna glared. "Pahhtrice Marie Beck—"

Tish held her hand out. "Okay, okay. I'm sorry, you know I love your accent. It makes me smile every time I hear it and—"

Rayna cleared her throat and crossed her arms over her chest.

Tish snorted and then covered her mouth. After taking a breath, she started again. "Steven is getting out of County and coming home!"

Rayna blew out a breath, dropping her arms. A soft smile formed on her lips, and she extended her hand across the table. "Honey, that's so, so good. I'm so relieved for you."

A wave of melancholy poured into Tish, and she took Rayna's extended hand. "Thank you. I'm relieved too."

"This is definitely worth celebrating." Rayna smiled, and after she let go of Tish's hand, she raised her glass again. "Here's to fresh starts and new beginnings."

After a successful clinking, Tish had her first sip of the wine. "Mmm delicious."

Rayna pulled her glass away from her lips, swallowing. "Mmm is right. Yum-*meeey.*"

"I'm so glad he's made it. Six months isn't long, but to me it felt like a lifetime." Tish swirled the wine in the glass. "Then again, sometimes it feels like it just flew by."

Her friend nodded. "I feel that way all the time now. One minute time is crawling, and the next an entire month has passed and I feel like I hadn't done more than blink."

"I think it's because we get so deep in our routines, you know? Wash, rinse, eat dinner, then do it all over again...repeat." Tish took another sip, then set her glass down. "Though, my routine is for sure going to get turned on its side now. At least for a while, anyway."

"Why do you say that?"

"Here you go, ladies," the waiter said, setting down their two boards chock-full of various bruschetta and artisan cheeses.

As the kid answered a question Rayna had, Tish sat back, thinking about how life would work once Steven moved in. She hadn't even thought twice when he'd asked if he could come live with her. She'd never turn him away, so it didn't really matter.

But for sure, her brother being there would impact her relationship with Jeff. Right off the bat, Tish was not going to have the time she had before. Likely, she'd be busy getting Steven settled, as well as on the right road to recovery.

Jeff was used to having her...well, all to himself. And that was no longer going to be the case. To be honest, she'd gotten used to having him too, but she couldn't worry about that now. What she wanted and what Steven needed didn't compare.

Without question, Tish would do whatever her brother needed, to make sure he succeeded. If that meant she and Jeff needed to pump the brakes, so be it.

"Sorry, what were we saying?"

The sound of Rayna's voice pulled Tish from her deep thoughts. She focused on her friend. "Um, routines I think...."

"Right, right." Rayna nodded, spreading some cheese on a small piece of toast. "Why is your routine going to get turned upside down?"

"Because Steven, he's going to be moving in with me, you know, until he gets on his feet."

"Ooh, honey. Is that a good idea?" Rayna took a bite of the cracker.

Tish frowned. "Of course it's a good idea. Why wouldn't it be?"

Rayna chewed and then took a sip of her wine. "Well, I just..." Rayna pressed her lips together. "Honey, I mean no disrespect, and I don't want to cross a line. I just...I get it, he's your brother, but considering his pattern, maybe it's not—"

"Rayna, I know you worry about me, know you love me. You're my friend, and I love you too, I cherish you. But...*he* is my brother. Hard stop. There is no 'but.'" Tish leaned forward, flattening her palm to her chest. "Please understand, I will never give up on my brother. That simple."

Her best friend drew in a slow breath and nodded. "Okay, Tish. I hear you."

"Thank you." Tish extended her hand. They clasped fingers for a moment and then let go. "Now, can we devour some of this food and celebrate?"

"Absolutely."

"The brie with apple and fig is my fave." Tish grabbed the piece off the board and bit into it.

"Oh yes. Mine too." Rayna grinned and selected a nice slice with warm artichoke spread on it.

Tish smiled, chewing her mouthful. Life was good and was only going to get better. Her brother was coming home, and she just knew this time he was going to make it. He was going to turn over a new leaf and get his life together.

Finally, Tish was going to be okay...because Steven would *finally* be okay too.

Chapter 15

Tish used the garage door opener Jeff had given her to open the door and pull her car inside. Shutting the car off, she grabbed her purse and decided to leave her overnight bag where it was.

Tish was too excited to share the good news to bother with it now. She could always get it later. She opened the door into the laundry room and was met with Rio's dark snout, perky white ears and wagging tail.

She dropped her purse on top of the washer and bent to the dog. "Hi there, my handsome boy!" She pressed a kiss to the top of his head and scratched all around his ears. Rio's tail went into double time. "Ooh, that feels good, doesn't it?" Rio nosed her chin. Tish giggled. "Yes, yes. I missed you too, I know."

"Why, hello there, gorgeous. Good thing Rio's paying attention. I didn't even hear the car."

Tish looked up to see Jeff leaning against the doorjamb. She straightened, taking him in. Arms crossed over his broad chest, the short sleeves of his T-shirt stretched tight over his biceps. Dark hair a little damp from the shower he'd likely taken. Faded Levis, just tight enough to show his muscular thighs. Feet, bare.

Desire pulsed in her veins, and she licked her lips. Good God, the man was looking especially sexy tonight.

"You're looking at me like you're hungry."

"Mmm." She moved closer to him. "That's because I am."

The tried and true chemistry they shared arced between them, and Tish felt the heat hit her tummy.

"Rawrrrr." Jeff hooked a finger in her belt loop and tugged her against his lean body.

Tish giggled as he nuzzled her neck, nipping at the skin behind her ear and purring. Holding on to his shoulders, Tish let her head fall back. He knew exactly how to touch her, and her body automatically responded to him.

It didn't seem like she'd ever get enough of him. Eventually, sure, but not yet. She was going to have to find a way to continue their arrangement after Steven came home.

Somehow, they'd work it out.

Jeff kissed up her throat to her jawline. "Miss me?"

"Maybe." As she smoothed her hands along his upper back and then circled his neck, she gave him a wink. "How about I show you if I missed you or not? Actions do speak louder than words."

Jeff frowned, his brow furrowing. "You do know I love it when you're naughty, right?"

Tish raised her brows. "And this is a problem, why?"

"Because dinner is ready, and now, instead of eating food, I want to set you on the washing machine and devour *you* for dinner."

Her clit pulsed. "Mmhmm. I see how that could be a problem." She glanced past his shoulder to the kitchen. "Can we just...keep it warm?"

Jeff blew out a breath and rolled his eyes to the ceiling. "I slave over a hot stove for the woman, and all she wants is my dick?" He shrugged. "If you insist."

Tish blurted a laugh and swatted his arm. "Some men would find it a compliment, you know."

"Oh, believe me, I do." Jeff picked her up, and she parted her legs, wrapping them around his waist. He set her down on top of the washer. "Good thing I didn't buy the stands that go with this set. They're at the perfect height as is."

"I guess that's one way of looking at it." Tish glanced down at the side-by-side pair, but then her attention was back on Jeff. "Hey, I thought it was me showing you, not the other way around."

Tugging her top button open and handling the zipper, he grinned up at her. "Eh, semantics."

"I am not touching that with a ten-foot pole." Chuckling, Tish bent forward and took his mouth in a tender kiss.

His familiar scent hit her nose, clean soap and light cologne, and Tish moaned, tangling her tongue with his. Yeah, she'd missed him. *Dammit.* It hadn't even been twenty-four hours since she'd seen him last, but to her dismay, she missed him anyway.

She couldn't let him know that, though. No way. The man might actually think he had some power over her. And Tish couldn't have that. She'd learned early on, as a child, that she couldn't trust her vulnerabilities to anyone.

In fact, the only person she'd ever really trusted was Steven.

Jeff broke from her lips and urged her to lean back.

As she raised her hips for him, he stripped her jeans and panties off and dove between her legs. He latched onto her clit, and Tish let out a harsh gasp and landed her hands on his head. He groaned and dragged his tongue through her folds before sucking her clit again.

Tish arched, flexing her fingers in his hair. "Jeff!"

Continuing his assault on her clit, he slid two fingers inside her and curled them, hitting her G-spot.

Tish's orgasm flew to the surface, and she bit her bottom lip, staring down at him...his eyes locked on her as he fucked her with his fingers and mouth.

Holy. Fucking. Shit.

"Oh, God!" Tish reared up, coming hard. As wave after wave rolled through her, her body shook from head to toe, her pussy clenching around his fingers, her clit pulsing in time with her heartbeat.

When she came back to herself, she focused on Jeff, who was intently focused on her. The expression in his eyes told her more than she should ever try to decipher. He pressed a gentle kiss to her mons. "Most beautiful thing I've ever seen, mami."

Tish felt the truth of that in her gut. He wasn't just giving her lines. Or pillow talk. Or any other kind of bullshit she wanted to try to pretend he was sending her way. He meant what he said, and as much as she wanted to, she couldn't let herself fully believe in him.

Afraid of saying something she'd regret, Tish bent to him, took his face in her hands, and kissed him instead.

* * * *

Jeff broke from her kiss. "You totally missed me."

She rolled her eyes. "Mmhmm. Whatever."

"Sooo, you think that orgasm was enough to tide you over until after dinner? I know how insatiable you are." He grinned and stroked her inner thighs with his thumbs. She was going to slap him, and he was okay with that. Nothing had changed for him. He'd still take anything she wanted to give him.

"Don't make me beat you." She laughed and pushed against his chest. "Move so I can get my pants back on."

"Ay, mami." He hissed, sucking air through his teeth and stepping back. "You gonna spank me?"

"Maybe I should." She grinned, hopping down from the washer. "I can use one of your wooden spoons."

"Tease." Jeff gave her forehead a kiss. "Get dressed. I'll get dinner on the table."

Stepping away from her, Jeff went to the sink and washed his hands. From the corner of his eye, he caught a glimpse of her as she disappeared down the hall, probably needing the bathroom.

What an absolutely perfect way to start their night. One orgasm down (more would come later), then next, dinner and wine, and once that was done, he'd take her to his bed and make love to her.

Six months they'd been together, and he was beyond ready to take things to the next level—or at least one small step forward—with her. He'd already planned on broaching the subject while they ate.

Hopefully, the orgasm he just gave her would work in his favor, and she'd be willing to revisit the "no reveal of their relationship" guideline. If they didn't get past that, how on earth could they move forward?

In a short amount of time, Jeff got everything out on the table, and Tish had poured them both wine. Nothing fancy, just a couple grilled chicken breasts over a bed of quinoa with a nice side of fresh asparagus.

"This looks delish, baby." Tish unrolled her napkin. "And I still love the fact that you use cloth napkins."

"What can I say, I had a fancy grandmother. She liked place settings." He draped his napkin over his lap.

"Don't get me wrong, I am *not* complaining. I'm not even teasing. I really do love it." She raised her glass, smiling. "Anyway, I have some exciting news."

"More exciting than that orgasm I just gave you?" He winked, raising his glass. "Tell me?"

"Cloth napkins, yet absolutely no verbal filter." She rolled her eyes, but her smile stayed. "Okay... Sooooo... Steven is getting out sometime this week!"

"Sweetheart, that's awesome!" Jeff clinked his glass to hers and took a sip.

She was glowing with her excitement, so much he could see it in her eyes, her face, everything. Jeff smiled, absolutely in love with seeing her filled with joy. This brother of hers must be pretty amazing. His rap sheet was definitely amazing, impressive even.

Not the sort of thing a guy wanted on his resume for sure, yet there it was. Jeff knew that sometimes good people stumbled and hit a rough patch, but Steven's rough patch seemed to keep going and going and...giving the Energizer Bunny a run for its money.

"It is, I know. I'm so excited, and God, let me just say, I'm beyond relieved he's going to be staying with me until he gets back on his feet."

Jeff nearly choked on his wine. He set his glass down, coughing a little. Had he heard her right?

She touched his arm. "Babe, you okay?"

He nodded, wiping his mouth. "I'm sorry." He cleared his throat again. "What now?"

"Oh. Uh." The expression in her eyes changed, and she pulled her hand away. "My brother, he's going to be staying with me."

Okay, what the flying fuck was she thinking? "Tish, I don't think that's a good idea."

"And why's that?" She frowned, her brows pinching together.

"I'd think it would be obvious." He sipped his wine. "There's a ton of reasons. You really need me to list them out for you?"

She sighed through her nose, pursing her lips. "If you're worried about having time for us, you don't have to, I'll figure out how to make it work. Obviously, at first, I'll be a little wrapped up in getting him settled, but once that's done, we'll be able to see each other often enough."

Utter shock spilled through him, and he jerked his head back. "Is that what you think I'm worried about?"

"Yeah, what else would you be worried about?"

"You!" He shook his head, trying to digest the fact that they were so out of sync. "Holy shit, I'm worried about you, Tish. Your safety. The fact that your brother is a criminal. That he's a drug addict. Plus, he's on probation and a repeat offender. Does any of this ring a bell?"

"My brother would never hurt me."

"You don't know that."

"Yeah, actually, I do." She stood. "I'm suddenly not hungry anymore." She grabbed her plate and took it to the sink.

Jeff got to his feet and followed. "Listen to me, he should go to a halfway house or something, but he should not come to live with you. All that's going to do is enable him. I know you don't want that."

She scraped her plate into the trash can and set it in the sink, and not gently. She turned, glaring at him, the fire in her expression evident. "You have *no* idea what I want or don't want. You don't know my brother at all, and fuck you for thinking you have some sort of say in this."

Well, shit, this escalated quickly. How did they get here so fast? Jeff shoved his hands in his pockets. "Listen, I don't want to fight about this. Please understand, I'm coming from a place of love. I'm worried about you, babe, and you're right, I may not know your brother, but I know his type. This kind of thing, it never goes well. I can't let you do this."

She crossed her arms. "Let me? Interesting, considering the last time I checked, I was a free woman, able to do what I want, when I want, with no one just 'letting me' do anything. Speaking of, what happened to me getting 'anything I want or need from you,' hmm?"

Jeff jerked back. "That's not fair. Nor does it apply to this situation."

"Yeah, well the way I see it, you don't apply to this situation."

"Not for anything, but you don't apply to this situation." Tish shook her head and raised her finger, pointing it at him. "Frankly, this is none of your goddamn business, Jeff, and PS: I don't recall even asking your opinion."

"Are you serious with this right now? This is how you talk to someone you're supposed to care about?" He raised his arms out to his sides. "Tish, you shared this news with me, remember? What did you think would happen? That I wouldn't say anything or have an opinion about it? Just smile and nod? Sorry, mami, but that's not me, won't ever be me. Apparently, you forgot that, so here's a reminder for you: I'm not your fucking bobblehead puppet, Tish. I don't just smile and nod my head in agreement, and then poof, everything you wanted just falls into your lap. You want that? Then go find yourself a spineless 'yes man' because that'll never be me."

Tish glared at him, her arms crossed, her eyes on fire, and not in a good way.

Jeff drew in a breath, and with that, a weird calm moved through him. Things were spiraling, and that was the last thing he wanted. He needed to get them back to a place where they could talk without the anger. "Tish, look—"

She shook her head and raised both hands, palms facing him as if she was pushing back. "Nope. No more. I'm done...this is done."

Done?

"What the fuck are you saying?"

She stalked past him and grabbed her purse off the counter. "I don't care what you say, Jeff. You don't understand, and seriously, you just showed me you never will, so I guess, thanks for that? You did me a favor. Now I know. Therefore, I'm not doing this with you anymore."

Jeff wanted to take her by the shoulders, shake some sense—or maybe kiss some sense—into her. Anything really, but he could tell by the tone of her voice, and also just looking at her, she'd made up her mind and nothing he said or did, at least at that moment, would change her mind.

Fuck him, she was ending things, really?

God, he was honestly unsure of what to do next. *Deep breath, Jeff.* She was just upset. Maybe she would cool off, and they'd talk later or tomorrow, and everything would be okay. He needed to get things calmed down right now if there was any hope of salvaging this.

Jeff leveled his gaze on her. "Tish, please don't do this. I get it, you're upset, but just...what we have? It's a good thing. Don't end it over one fight."

She raised both brows. "One fight? Really?" Tish put her hands on her hips and stared down at the ground for what felt like forever before she looked up at him. "I gotta say, you *really* do not fucking get me. This wasn't a fight, Jeff. This was the front row reveal of a huge chasm between us, one I didn't know was there until now." With a stone-cold glare in her eyes, she moved to him and pointed her finger at him. "Hear me when I say this...I will *never* not help my brother. *Ever.* We spent our lives being abused, abandoned and cast aside, and I would rather *die* than ever do that to him. Not for anything or anyone. And certainly not for some guy, who in a few months or maybe a year, won't be around anymore anyway. Honestly, better to end it now before things got further entangled and complicated."

Those last words hit him square in the chest like an anvil, the pain radiating outward, making his limbs tingle. "Tish..."

She shook her head and walked away from him. Just before she stepped into the laundry room, she paused, looking down at Rio, who was sitting, waiting for her. The dog knew something was wrong. Then again, Rio didn't have to be a police dog to know that.

His partner gave Tish a little whine.

She bent, pressed a kiss to the top of his head, and then walked out of his house.

Jeff scrubbed his hands down his face and looked up at the ceiling. What the fuck just happened?

Chapter 16

"Hey, you awake?" Tish poked her head in the door to the guest room, which as of two weeks ago had become her brother's bedroom.

Steven moaned from beneath the pile of blankets.

"Come on, sleeping beauty." She plucked the bottom of his foot sticking out from the comforter. "Come have coffee with me, please?"

He tucked his foot back in. "Dammit, Tish, knock it off."

She giggled. "I'm making you a coffee." She walked out of the bedroom but then turned and stuck her head back in. "And waffles."

He flipped the cover off his head and stared at her out of one partially open eye. "What kind of waffles?"

"The Eggo kind. That you love so much." She grinned, triumph filling her gut. "Meet me in the kitchen, sleeping beauty."

Tish went to the kitchen and got to work. She popped two frozen Eggo waffle disks into her toaster and was sure to turn the temp down a bit. Those suckers had a habit of burning, or maybe it was her that did the burning...ouch.

Steven made it out of his bedroom. Dark brown hair, too long and a disheveled mess. Beard, full and longer than she'd ever seen it. He needed a damn head-to-toe makeover. Plus, he needed to gain about forty pounds. Her baby brother was practically skin and bones.

"Here you go, sir." With a smile, Tish handed him his coffee.

"Thanks. Mmm. Smells good."

"The coffee or the waffles?" She grabbed a small plate from the cabinet and got the syrup out of the small pantry.

"Both." He tilted the cup to his lips. "What time is it?"

Tish made a show of looking at the clock on the stove, then the one on the microwave, and then the small decorative one she had hanging on the wall. "Hmm... Survey says: 10:41."

"A.m. or p.m.?" He leaned to the side, trying to get a look out her sliding glass balcony door.

"Honey, the sun is up, so I'm thinking a.m. is the only option."

He laughed. "Sounds good to me."

The toaster popped, and Tish yelped, nearly jumping out of her skin. She pressed her hand to her pounding heart. "Shit, that scared me."

Steven glanced at the silver two-slice toaster and then back to her, a crooked grin on his face. "You good?"

She looked to the ceiling, shaking her head. "Yep. Perfect. Totally fine. Go have a seat at the table, and I'll bring this over."

"You don't have to wait on me, Tishy."

"I know I don't, Steven. Just to say, don't get used to it though." She grinned and pointed toward the small dining table just outside the kitchen area. "Now, go, please? Take a seat."

Shaking his head, with his coffee cup in hand, Steven walked out of her kitchen.

She plated the waffles and grabbed some fresh fruit and a can of whipped cream from the fridge. Grabbing the extra toppings first, she brought them out to the table. Next came the waffles, butter and syrup.

When she'd gotten that all settled, she returned with her coffee and took a seat to his left. "Eat up."

He looked up from squirting a healthy amount of whipped cream onto one of the waffles. "Aren't you eating too?"

She sipped her coffee. "Already ate."

He nodded and added syrup to the other waffle. On both, he sprinkled some of the fresh berries and melon.

"Looks pretty damn good." She grinned and took another drink.

"Would've given my left nut for real Eggos in County." He cut into a waffle, severed a big chunk and shoved it in his mouth. He closed his eyes, chewing. "Mmm. Heaven."

Tish smiled, this time on the inside *and* the outside. She loved seeing Steven happy. Loved being able to give that to him. Having him with her again had been wonderful.

Last night, for the first time since he'd gotten out of jail, he'd gone to see a friend. It worried her, but she tried not to let it. She figured he'd be home around midnight or so, but by twelve thirty, he hadn't gotten home yet, and she was already half asleep.

Later, she could've sworn she heard him coming in and a quick glance at the clock had told her it was past four a.m.—not that she was keeping track or anything. Maybe he'd met a girl? God, she hoped not.

He needed to focus on his recovery, not nailing some chick he didn't know. Tish cringed at the thought. At least she wouldn't have to worry about running into anyone in her house in the middle of the night. Steven knew he couldn't bring women there.

"Do you want to check out that AA meeting tonight with me? The one I found when you first moved in?"

Steven stared at his phone screen (the one she'd paid to turn on for him, and if he didn't get a job soon, unfortunately she'd be paying the monthly bill when it came in, too) and said nothing.

"Steven? Yoo-hoo?" She waved her hand in front of him.

He moved his eyes to hers. "What's up?"

Annoyance crept up the back of her neck, and she frowned. "Did you hear me?"

"Sorry, was reading something." He shoveled in another bite and then talked around his food. "What'd you say?"

Trying for calm, she sighed and leveled her tone. "AA meeting? With me? Tonight?"

"Ah, right." He stretched. "I dunno. Can I think about it?"

"You have to get court papers signed at the meeting, as proof you attended, don't you?"

"Yeah, but—" He shrugged. "There's no rush. I don't go see my PO until the end of the month, so I got time."

"Steven—"

"Plus, I'm not an alcoholic, Tishy." He shrugged again. "No point sitting there listening to drunks."

"Okay, well, what about NA, you know, Narcotics Anonymous? I could look up to see where those meetings are if you want. I'm happy to do that."

"I guess, if you want." Steven ran his fingers through his hair and then took another swig of coffee.

"Perfect." Tish nodded, relief filling her veins. "Oh, did you call that guy about the entry level construction job I found online?"

"Not yet, no." He took another bite.

Frustration hit with a vengeance, chasing away the relief she felt moments ago. "Steven, we talked about this. You *have* to get a job. And not just because I want you to and it's the right thing to do, but as a condition of your release. I saw all the paperwork, remember?"

He shoved his plate away. "Was this your plan? Ply me with food and then nag me about meetings and jobs? You know how hard it is to get hired when you have a fucking criminal record—"

"First off, there is need to—"

"No, you don't." He stood, the chair screeching on the laminated wood floor. "You got no cl—"

"Steven, I'm just trying to hel—"

"Stop. Just stop trying to help me."

Tish got to her feet, anger making her hands shake. "What the hell are you saying? You're the one who asked me to help you in the first place!"

"Yeah, for a place to stay. That's it. The kind of help I don't need, or want, is to be nagged twenty-four fucking seven." Steven frowned, a snarl forming on his lips. "Jesus Christ, you're not my mother, Tish. How about you get the hell off my ass." He took a step away, but paused, looking back over his shoulder, a snide smirk on his face. "In case you didn't get it, that was not a question, it was a statement." Looking away, he walked off to his bedroom.

Tish blinked, frustration, anger and hurt swirling together in her stomach. She wasn't sure if she wanted to scream, cry or throw up. Maybe all three.

It'd only been two weeks since Steven's release from jail. And already this was where they were, with him barely doing what he was supposed to do based on his terms of probation or what he had committed to do with her.

Tish sat and rested her forearms on the table, holding her coffee cup between both hands. This just plain sucked and was beyond hard, the stress of it already starting to take its toll. Plus, she missed...*him*.

Him being the one and only, drop-dead gorgeous, goofy asshole she'd ever fallen for. She sipped her coffee, swallowing down the lump in her throat. God, no doubt Jeff would be really pissed that she was upset. The red flags, small as they might seem to others, were already present, telling her Steven was already on his way to fucking up.

Knowing Jeff, he'd let her vent about everything she was frustrated about, and he'd do it standing by her side—while also reminding her, in some goofy-ass way, that he'd told her so.

The lump in her throat returned, and a wave of deep sadness swamped her chest. Tish dropped her head to the table, feeling the cool wood on her forehead. She wasn't supposed to miss him this much, but dammit, what choice had she had?

None.

For fuck's sake, he'd pushed her, given her an ultimatum—well, sort of—but still, he was heading there for sure, and no way Tish would ever tolerate that kind of shit. So yes, she'd cut it off. Not that anyone could blame her. Blood was thicker than water, as the saying went. Bottom line, nothing would ever come between her and her brother.

Certainly not a man.

Whether she had strong feelings for that man or not.

Didn't matter.

It didn't....

She raised her head from the table and frowned. Okay, sure. If it didn't matter, then why did it hurt so much?

Chapter 17

"Sorry, the mailbox is full—" Tish groaned and disconnected the call. Steven was not answering his phone.

She'd been trying him all day, ever since she found cash missing from her purse this morning while at work. Not that forty bucks was much, but still. It was enough to buy drugs, she was sure.

Tish let out an exasperated sigh and eyed the clock: 9:48 p.m. Was he even going to come home tonight? For Christ's sake, it had only been a month, and all signs were pointing in the wrong direction.

He hadn't attended any meetings, not any that she was aware of anyway. And he was supposed to meet up with his probation officer in a few days. Obviously he was going to fail the drug test if they gave him one.

She didn't have to see him actually using the drugs to know he was for sure using. Maybe she should call his PO? Shit, he'd never forgive her if she did that.

A deep sense of failure and sadness filled Tish's heart and gut. Why couldn't she help him? What was she doing wrong? She'd done everything she could think of, and nothing worked.

Heading into the kitchen, she pulled out the bottle of white wine she had in the fridge and poured herself a glass. Tish moved to her living room and plopped down on the couch.

Fuck, and now he'd stolen from her too? He'd never done that before. It was like a hard slap in the face. Tish let her head fall back on the couch. Did she spend the money and forget that she had? She thought back over the last week, trying to find a moment where she had her wallet out, what things she bought. Maybe she could've dropped the money?

It was possible.

Maybe.

Ugh, who was she kidding. Tish sipped her wine. The way the billfold inside her wallet was shaped, it would make it pretty hard to lose money, especially if she was just pulling out her credit card to pay at the grocery store, which she'd done just two days ago.

God, how could her sweet baby brother steal from her? Was he really this far gone that even his only family was fair game?

This was exactly what everyone was worried about. Rayna hadn't said it, but Tish could tell she was. No way she could talk to her best friend about this now. Jeff wasn't an option either.

Of course, he had said plenty about her moving her brother in, hadn't he? This was the exact thing he was worried about too. Dammit, she hated that he was right. Hated that she was wrong. And hated that with everything she'd done trying to fix things for her brother, to make things better, easier and to save him, her brother was spiraling anyway.

Tish picked up her cell and dialed Steven's number again. It rang and rang and then voicemail picked up. "The mailbox is full—"

Fucking hell, if she could only leave him a voicemail, it would make her feel better. Tish hit end call, pulled up messages and sent him another text.

Tish Beck: *Steven, please just let me know you're okay. I'm really worried.*

Wasn't this a quaint déjà vu. A little over seven months ago, she was sending texts just like that one. Steven was missing, and she was obsessed with finding him. The stress of it all had sent her into her own tailspin.

Looking back on it now, when he'd ended up in jail, relief had blanketed Tish, giving her the emotional reprieve she'd so desperately needed, so much so that she was able to turn her attentions on to Jeff.

But that was over now. And she was alone.

Except she had her brother, thank God, and as long as she had him, she'd never truly be alone.

But God help her if she ever lost Steven. Then she'd truly be alone.

* * * *

As the door opened, Jeff cleared his throat and made sure to plant a smile on his face. When he saw who it was, the smile turned genuine. "Why hello there, beautiful."

"Hi, Uncle Jeff!" Megan, Derek's daughter, smiled, a blush forming on her cheeks. "Aw, hi, Rio." She held her hand out to Rio.

Rio responded immediately, eating up the attention. Such a ladies' man. With a giggle from getting a dog tongue to the cheek, Megan backed up to let Jeff in, and then knelt down to pet Rio again.

Jeff closed the door behind him. "Girl, how old are you now? Didn't I just see you last week? You weren't this tall. Are you driving yet?"

"I'm eleven and a half. I was this tall, and nope, I'm not driving yet." She laughed again, scratching Rio's ears. "You're so funny, Uncle Jeff."

Jeff grinned and gave her a wink, then glanced around. "New place is looking good. Your new room all set up?"

"Yes, it's so pretty! I love it." She jumped up. "Hey, can I take Rio outside to play with Axle?"

Just then, Derek came from somewhere, walking toward him down the long center hallway of the house. Axle was beside him for about two steps before he saw Rio and bounded for him, tails wagging on both dogs.

Jeff grinned and glanced at his watch, waiting for Derek to reach him.

Derek chuckled, holding out his hand. "Hey, man. Glad you made it."

They clasped fists. "Shirley, always a pleasure."

Derek laughed and held an arm out to the side. "So what do you think?"

Jeff nodded, looking around again. The two rooms on either side of the main hall were meant to be formal spaces. He could see Rayna would put her touch on them, but it'd be interesting to see what Derek would choose, too. Pool table maybe? "You sure it's big enough?"

"Right?" Derek chuckled. "Come on, it's not *that* big."

"Two of your old house, or two of my house put together?" Jeff nodded, widening his eyes. "Maybe you're compensating for something, huh? I get it, not all of us are blessed."

Derek busted up. "Yeah, that's totally it."

"Shame, really. Poor Rayna." Jeff smirked, trying like hell to hold back his laughter. "I guess a house will have to fill the void."

Derek rolled his eyes, then clapped Jeff on the back. "Come on, Nelly, let's go to the kitchen."

"Should I grab a snack?" Jeff motioned over his shoulder with his thumb. "I can get one out of the truck. Is it a long walk? Wait, do we need a golf cart?"

When they got to the kitchen, Rayna turned from the sink, wiping her wet hands on a dishtowel. "Hi, Jeff. So glad you're here. We've missed you."

Jeff went to her and gave her cheek a soft peck and smiled. "Aw, missed you too. Thanks for having me, kids."

"Beer?" Derek opened the fridge door.

"Yeah, that'd be great." Jeff took a seat at one of the stools in front of the island. "Anyone else coming?"

Derek set a can down in front of Jeff. "You want a glass? I have some chilling in the freezer."

"Sure." Jeff looked down at the can, and a knife sank into his heart. Strawberry Blonde by THAT Brewery. The same beer Tish was drinking that night, seven months ago, when she'd called him because she was upset about her brother. He rubbed the center of his chest and tried to remember how to breathe.

"I had asked Tish to come, but she says she's tied up with her brother. Honestly, I'm starting to get concerned. I haven't seen her in a month at least. She's too wrapped up in him." Rayna looked up from slicing a tomato.

His best friend set the frosted glass down in front of him and put his hand on his shoulder. "Hey, you okay?"

Jeff glanced over from Rayna to Derek. "Listen, all kidding aside, I'm really happy for both of you. I mean it. What you found with each other? It doesn't come along every day, so hold on to it. Cherish it. Never take it for granted."

Rayna had stopped what she was doing and just stared at him. "I think that's the sweetest thing you've ever said to me."

"Me too." Derek crossed his arms. "Which really makes me wonder, are you okay?"

Jeff cracked the can open and poured the light amber beer into his glass. "Yep, right as the rain."

"Mm. Okay, cool. I'm going to get the burgers started. You want cheese, Jeff?" Derek grabbed a platter out of the fridge.

"You know it! I'm all cheese." Jeff grinned and tipped his beer to his lips. Fuck, the brew was good. Damn, Tish knew her craft beers. Cue another round of chest pains. Man, having a broken heart sucked big-time.

Jeff had basically spent the last month isolating—aka licking his wounds. In an effort to avoid running into her, he hadn't seen any of his friends, especially Derek and Rayna. It was just too painful.

Tonight was an exception, though. They had invited him to come over and share dinner in the house they'd just bought together. He had to come, had to be a good friend.

Part of him prayed to God that Tish wouldn't be there. It would just be too hard to put up the front, pretend like nothing had happened or gone down between them. But the other part of him had hoped against hope that she would be there.

Just to see her...to hear her. To be near her. It would be torture, for sure, yet he'd take it. But to what end? Jeff shook his head and took another mouthful of his beer.

He could not let her go. He wasn't sure if he would ever be able to.

Chapter 18

A noise startled Tish awake, and she bolted upright, caught in that half awake and physically shaky state, trying to determine if the noise was the neighbors upstairs or...

Another bang—her heart jumped into her throat.

Oh my God, someone was in her apartment!

Throwing the blankets off, she ran into her closet, punched in the code for her small safe and took out her .22 pistol.

After making sure there was a round in the chamber, Tish gave herself a second to breathe. Her heart was pounding in her ears, and she really needed it to stop so she could listen better. She should probably call the cops, or jump out a window, or...shit, what if it was Steven?

The realization it could be her brother and not someone there to burglarize her or worse...had hope rising, blocking out the flight-or-fight instinct she should be listening to. Determined to find out and still take precautions, Tish pulled on a pair of jeans.

With the gun gripped tight in both hands, she tiptoed out of her closet and moved to her bedroom door. It wasn't closed all the way, per usual, and she listened for a moment before opening it a little farther so she could peek out. There was barely enough light to see her own hand in front of her face. In hindsight, a nightlight would've been a good idea.

Tish took two steps into the dark hallway...and came face-to-face with her intruder.

She belted out a scream, scrambling backward, dropping one hand from the gun to grab the wall to keep from falling. "Get out! Right now, get out!"

"Fuck! Tishy, stop. It's me."

The sound of Steven's voice cut through her yelling, somehow. And then, after a little bit of what sounded like searching on the wall, he flipped on the hall light.

Tish blinked, squinting a little from the brightness. "Jesus fucking Christ, Steven! I could've killed you!"

"Holy shit! What the fuck are you doing with a gun?"

"I'm a woman who lives alone. What the hell do you think I'm doing with a gun? Stupid question." Tish brushed past him into her bedroom and put the gun away in her closet.

He sure did know how to make an entrance. Geez. Taking a breath, she pushed her hair out of her face. He'd been MIA for over a week, and she was beyond grateful he was alive, but still.

Ready to discuss what the hell was going on, Tish stepped back into her bedroom and found Steven going through her jewelry box on her dresser.

What is he... "Steven, what the hell are you doing?"

He ignored her and kept at it, pulling out a gold chain she'd had for forever and a bracelet that had a broken clasp. Was he seriously doing this?

Rage fueled by the hurt of this level of betrayal filled her veins, pulsing in time with her heartbeat. "Steven, don't do this. Please. You don't have to do this."

"You don't fucking get it." He glared at her, then went back to digging through her things. "It's too late for me. Just accept it."

A tear ran down her face. "You want me to accept my brother stealing from me?"

He pulled a ring from the bottom drawer of the box. It was the first piece of nice jewelry she'd ever bought herself. It meant a lot to her....

Steven shoved his bounty—her things—in his pockets and turned to face her. He raised his arms out to his sides. Based on his eyes, he was definitely loaded, and the expression on his face was somewhere between hate and sadness. "Accept my fate, Tish. You don't get it. You don't suffer this curse. Be glad you don't. I'm glad you don't." He shook his head. "I'm an addict. I'm going to die an addict. Stop trying to save what's already lost."

"You're not lost!"

Steven moved for the door, and Tish rushed to stop him.

She stood in the doorway, blocking his way. "Steven, stop, please?"

"You fucking stop! I swear to fuck, Tish, move or I *will* move you." He was barely a foot away from her, and that was when she realized how sweaty and fatigued he looked.

"Are you detoxing? How long?"

"Bitch, get off my dick! All you want to do is keep me here under lock and key and pretend you're some kind of savior. Telling you, I am *done* being controlled and manipulated by you. I'm tired of your fucking mind games, too."

Shit, he was completely delusional. Tish frowned. "Steven, that's not true. Honey, take a deep breath, please."

"Move!" He came nose-to-nose with her.

"No." Her response was barely a thread above a whisper. Fear zipped down her spine, but she held her ground. She'd never seen him like this before, but one thing she knew for sure, Steven would not hurt her. Not physically anyw—

"Fucking bitch!" The punch to the side of her head came out of nowhere.

As Tish stumbled to the side, stars burst behind her eyes and then she was shoved backward, hands slamming into her chest so hard it nearly knocked the wind out of her.

Tish hit the wall behind her, her head bouncing off the drywall, her teeth clacking together, before sliding down, her ass meeting laminate floor.

Trying to clear her vision, she watched Steven rush out of her bedroom, only to dig through her purse, taking her wallet before rushing out the front door. Tish sat on the floor for what felt like forever, her left ear ringing from where he'd hit her, her head throbbing from both him and the bounce against the wall.

And tears—sobbing, messy tears.

Steven, her precious brother, had done the unthinkable to her. Tish wiped her wet face. The brother *she* knew could *never* do something so horrible to her, not the Steven she grew up with and loved, anyway.

The same brother who suffered with her under their drunk and high parents. A child who suffered the same physical abuse she had, though he'd taken less because Tish would always run to protect him, take his blows as well as her own.

Hadn't that mattered at all?

More tears streamed down her cheeks, and she hugged her knees to her chest. Tish had been protecting Steven practically since the day he was born. And she was only two years older than him. The same brother she fought to stay with after they'd been removed from their parents' care, then later, running away from foster home after foster home to stay with him.

That person, her baby brother, Steven, would never raise a hand to her. Or steal from her. And yet he had—the man he was now, the person the drugs had turned him into, had done all of that.

And more, because he'd also broken her heart in two.

* * * *

Once Tish's tears finally gave it a rest, she got up off the floor and headed into the kitchen in search of some ibuprofen for her head. Second thing she had to do was report her credit cards and debit card lost. Dammit, she'd have to get a new license too.

Christ, Steven. What a pain in the ass this was going to be. Why did he have to do this to her? Clearly, the drugs had taken control of him, and the meth was causing all sorts of delusions, rather the *need* for more meth was causing them. He was probably coming down hard and needed what he stole from her to get more.

Popping two ibu's into her mouth, she swallowed them down with some water and glanced at the clock: 2:37 a.m. She sighed and moved out to the kitchen table. Third thing she had to do was call in sick to work.

An hour or so later, she'd gotten all calls made and crawled into her bed. For the first time in her life, she wished her brother didn't have a key to her place, because although she didn't think he'd be back—

Tish bolted upright, a thought coming to her.

"Shit." She jumped out of bed, ran out to the living room and grabbed her purse. Digging inside, she couldn't find what she was looking for. In a panic, she dumped the contents out onto the table.

No keys.

Fuck.

Tish ran out her door, then around the corner to the parking lot. Her assigned spot was empty. She looked around, her chest heaving with breaths...as if maybe she'd parked somewhere else when she got home tonight. As if that would be something she'd forget.

Fuuuuuck! She bent, resting her hands on her knees, trying to breathe and *not* have a panic attack. Goddammit.

He'd stolen her car.

Chapter 19

Tish paced her living room, staring at her cell phone, willing it to ring. The sun would be up soon, and she still couldn't decide what to do. She hadn't called the police yet, mostly because she knew if she reported the car stolen, then Steven would go back to jail for sure.

The idea that she'd be the one to put him there was far too unbearable to stomach. The last thing she wanted was to do something like that to her brother. Plus, maybe he'd read her text or listen to the message she'd left him and he'd come back and they could figure out what to do.

Maybe she should call Rayna and see what Derek suggested? Before she even finished the thought, she dismissed it. Tish was mortified enough as it was, she didn't want them to know about what Steven had done.

Tish paused, staring out the sliding glass window. Fatigue was like a wet blanket wrapped around her, weighing her down, and all she wanted to do was sleep, but she just couldn't. Not until she figured out what to do.

Giving in to the ache in her head and the weariness flooding her system, she took a seat on the couch. What a mess everything was. Worse, Jeff had been right. And God, she hated that.

It'd been more than a month since they'd had any contact. She'd purposely been avoiding meeting their friends out, knowing he'd be there, and conveniently using Steven as an excuse for why she couldn't hang out.

If she called Jeff for help, he'd have to keep it a secret, and although he'd probably never let her live it down, dealing with that was preferable to the mortification of Rayna and Derek knowing too.

With any luck, he could help her figure out what to do without getting Steven into trouble. Hoping this wasn't a mistake, she blew out a breath and dialed Jeff's cell. It rang several times before going to voicemail.

Tish disconnected and stared at the screen. It was close to five in the morning, an hour before he needed to be up for work. A pang of heartache beat through her at the memory of his schedule.

Maybe the no answer was a sign that she should let sleeping dogs lie. Calling Jeff would complicate the situation. Plus, she was emotional enough right now. Adding in the fact that her heart still ached for the man would just make things even harder to cope wi—

The phone rang in her hand, and she jumped, Jeff's contact info coming up on the caller ID. She pressed a shaking hand to her chest and answered. "Uhmm...hi."

"Hey. You okay?"

She pressed her palm to her forehead. "Yes and no. I'm sorry I woke you."

"It's fine. What's up?"

Tish stared out the glass door, the sky starting to lighten. "Something happened last night, and I don't know what to do."

"With Steven?"

"Yes." She bit her bottom lip.

"Is he okay?"

"I don't know."

"Okay, are you okay?"

"You asked me that already." She tried to laugh it off, but she knew he was going to read her like a book.

"Okay, I'm coming over."

"You don't—"

"You call me at five a.m. and you think I'm not going to come there to see for myself what you're not telling me? Come on, mami. You must have me confused with some other drop-dead yet very lovable gorgeous dude."

Tish rolled her eyes. Of course, he was being his typical goofy asshole self. Except the difference now was she knew his teasing came from a soft spot in his heart, his odd way of showing affection, she supposed. "No confusion, I know exactly who you are, Jeffrey Pearl."

"Good to know, Patrice Beck. Put the pot on. I'll be there in twenty."

"Okay." Tish disconnected the call and lowered her phone to her lap.

She really wasn't sure if she'd done the right thing or not, but there was no going back now.

Letting out a tired sigh, she forced herself off the couch and went to the kitchen to set the Keurig up and pull out two K-Cups. Unlike him, she didn't have a regular coffee pot.

But he knew that already, like he knew everything else about her.

* * * *

Jeff stood outside Tish's apartment door in full uniform, Rio by his side, suited up as well. He glanced down at his partner. "Stay cool, okay?"

Rio, panting because he was both excited to be going to work, but likely also excited to be at Tish's house, gave him a little moan/whine and then a sneeze.

"You don't have to remind me, dude. I know I gotta stay cool. Just let me do the talking."

The door opened, and Jeff snapped his attention to...the woman of his dreams.

As she always did, Tish took his breath away, and he just stared at her. He'd been starved for the sight of her, and having no idea when he'd get another chance, he needed to memorize every part of her.

The small mole she had high on her right cheekbone. The way her dark brown hair always looked pretty, even if she'd just woken up. Her crystal ice-blue eyes. The adorable dimples she had in each cheek when she smiled.

Jesus, she was a sight for sore eyes.

That was what he wanted to tell her too, but she beat him to the punch, sending them in a completely different direction.

She looked around him and down the corridor. "Are you...uh, having a conversation with the dog?"

Jeff shrugged. "Yeah, no biggie. We talk all day long. You know that."

She smoothed her lips together. "Okay, right. Guess I forgot. Well... come in, please." She stepped aside and held her arm out.

Forgot? Ouch. Okay, that felt *awesome*. He stepped inside and closed the door. She moved to the kitchen, and he followed. "So is your car in the shop, or does Steven have it?"

Her head snapped in his direction, and she visibly cringed, hissing as if she were in pain and raising her hand to her head.

Immediately, he moved to her, placing one hand on her upper back. "Hey, what's going on? Are you okay?"

"Sorry. Yes, I'll be fine."

He frowned, fear settling in his gut. What the hell? "Are you hurt? Tell me what's going on, please."

Tish sighed as if resigning herself to answering his question. "No. I'm fine. Just a headache. Let me get us coffee first, please? Then I promise, I'll tell you everything. I'm just so tired, Jeff."

Something was wrong, and whatever it was had the back of his neck tingling. He rubbed her back, not wanting to pull his hand away. "Okay, Tish."

"Thanks."

He nodded and had to force himself to step back and give her some space. "I'll grab the cream."

She gave him a small smile. "Sure."

Jeff did what he said and then watched her set the Keurig up and fill one cup, then the other. When they were both ready, he followed her to her small dining table and took a seat with her.

Jeff sipped his coffee and patiently waited for her to speak. With Tish, he'd learned to just give her the space she needed, and eventually she shared. That plan had always worked with her. But when she finally started speaking, nothing could have prepared him for what she was about to tell him.

As Tish laid out the story of what had been going on with her brother, and then what had happened that morning, how Steven had put his hands on her, every protective male instinct in Jeff's body was firing on overload.

If he got *his* hands on her brother, he'd probably beat him to a bloody pulp. Men who hit women were scum in his book as it was, but a man who touched Jeff's woman? God help him, brother or not, made no difference.

Drawing in a number of deep breaths to get his rage under wraps, Jeff got himself focused on next steps. She was hurting, physically and emotionally. The last thing she needed was him throwing a possessive male temper tantrum. "I know you're not going to like this, but you should report the assault, and also the car stolen. Even if it's found, you're likely going to need to make an insurance claim."

"I can't do that..." She shook her head. "Jeff, I...I don't want to report the assault." She blinked, her eyes filling with tears. "I just don't want him to get into more trouble."

Jeff sighed, frustration filling his veins. "Okay, what about the car?"

"Do I have to tell them Steven was the one who stole it?"

"Honestly, there's going to be a whole lot of questions you have to answer, and if you don't, you'll be lying to the cops. I don't think that's a good idea."

She nodded, staring down into her coffee cup. When the first tear streaked down her cheek, Jeff was on his feet, pulling her into his arms.

She cried for a while, up on her tiptoes, face buried against his neck, her arms around his neck as well. Jeff said nothing, simply held her, stroking her back while she broke down.

He hated that she was hurting and wanted desperately to make it better. She loved her brother, no doubt about it, but it was to her detriment.

Unfortunately, Steven had gone down the wrong road, yet again, and Tish was blaming it on herself.

He hated that she was doing that to herself, especially because it was in no way her fault, nor was it her responsibility. The situation was beyond common and something Jeff saw all too often in his line of work.

Unless someone was ready to get help, it didn't matter what their family or loved ones did to try to make them, it wouldn't work. That whole horse-and-water thing was exactly true.

Tish sniffled. "You know, hugging you is like trying to hug a brick wall."

He smirked. "Well, yeah, sorry about the vest."

She pulled back and gazed up at him. "I take that back, I think hugging a brick wall might be easier."

He laughed. "You want a tissue?"

"Yes, and sorry, I might've ruined your shirt." She glanced down and wiped her hand along his neck and his uniform collar.

Jeff cupped her cheek, and she focused on him again. He let his gaze roam over her features. So beautiful. "It's going to be okay, Tish. I promise you."

She nodded and touched her lips to his.

In that moment, even if he wasn't happy with her decisions, Jeff knew he was going to do everything he could to ensure that things really were going to be okay. Thank God he was able to temper his anger, shove it to the side and focus on her.

Nothing had changed for him. Jeff loved her, had always loved her... and God help him, he was more than prepared to do anything he needed to prove it to her.

No question, no doubt. He was never letting her go again.

Chapter 20

"Can't I just wait to report the car for a little while? I mean, he might bring it back. Technically, it's only 'stolen' if I say it is, right?"

"*Yeeah*, technically." Jeff shrugged a shoulder. "You have that option, sure."

"Okay, good. Good." Tish nodded, tension leaving her body immediately. "Can you..." Tish took a small step back. "Will you..."

Jeff tipped his face down, his brows going up. "Hmm?"

She fidgeted, trying to ignore the instincts roaring in her mind. "I know you're supposed to go to work, but do you think you can stay with me today?"

Stepping away from her briefly, Jeff grabbed a tissue from the box on her coffee table and then handed it to her. "I kind of have to. I mean, my uniform shirt is completely ruined. Can't go to work like this." He shrugged and glanced over at Rio. "Partner, looks like we're calling out for PTO."

Rio let out a low yip and lay down beside her kitchen table.

"Say what? What do you mean, I have to call? Okay, fine." Jeff pulled the various strips of Velcro free on his vest, removed it and set it on the couch. Looking back at Tish, he grinned. "He's really unfair wanting me to do all the administrative work."

Unable to hold it in, Tish let out a sharp giggle. "Maybe it's that whole no-opposable-thumbs thing?"

Jeff stepped close and circled her waist. "Don't go bringing that old excuse up. No thumbs, blah blah. Whatevs."

She placed her hands on his shoulders. "You are by far the goofiest man I have ever met, you know that?"

"I do." He nodded, a sexy smirk arching his lips.

"Do you also know that I missed you, and that until this moment, I didn't realize how much?" Tears welled again, and she blinked. Tish pressed closer, smoothing her hands to the back of his neck.

With his vest off, she could finally feel his body against hers. She let out a slow breath, more tension seeping from her body at the feel of being in his arms and close to him again. Gazing at him, she couldn't help but also realize she felt safe, like she could breathe. Even with all the drama Steven was causing.

His expression grew tender. "I didn't know that, no." He caught a tear as it escaped from the corner of her eye. "I missed you too, mami."

"Where do we go from here?"

Jeff stroked her cheek with his thumb. "Well, considering you look exhausted, I'm thinki—"

Tish gasped. "Wait, are you saying I'm not pretty?"

"—we get into your bed, you curl up in my arms and *you* get some sleep."

"Oh." Tish smiled.

"Yes. Oh." Jeff raised a single brow. "You do know that you're the most beautiful woman I've ever laid my eyes on, right?"

Tish felt that in her stomach. "No, I didn't know that."

"Right. Do you also know that every time I see you—Every. Single. Time—you take my breath away?"

Tish felt that from her head to her toes. "Didn't know that either."

"Right." He nodded, took her by the hand and walked them to her bedroom. "In you go."

"Okay." Tish tucked a hair behind her ear and glanced at Rio, who also came in the room and had already curled up on the floor at the foot of her bed.

Stepping into her closet, she stripped out of her jeans, leaving herself in her T-shirt and panties. Exhaustion was kicking in hard now, and the idea of being able to sleep with him next to her felt like a balm to her broken heart.

Returning to the bedroom, she climbed into bed and watched as Jeff stripped out of his uniform shirt, revealing the plain black T-shirt beneath it. He also removed his thick belt full of gear and his gun as well as his boots and pants.

Tish shifted over to what had once been "her" side of the bed, when they were together, and lay down.

Jeff got into bed beside her and lay down, holding an arm out for her. "Come on, babe."

Tish laid her head down on Jeff's chest, and he wrapped his arms around her. She drew in a deep breath, taking in his scent, and listened to his heart beating steady beneath her ear. It was amazing how easy it was to just fall back into their routine of how they slept together. Him on his back, her sleeping on his chest. It was even more amazing how safe and cared for it made her feel.

God, she'd missed this. How had she not realized how much she needed this, needed him? "Thank you, baby."

"No need for thanks, sweetheart." Jeff kissed the top of her head and stroked her back. "I'm right where I want to be."

Tish closed her eyes and cuddled closer. "Me too."

Chapter 21

"All right. See you soon." Jeff disconnected the call with Tish and poured two glasses of red blend and set them on a tray.

He had a plate of grapes, various cheeses, some preserves and crackers ready to go. When he finished getting it all arranged, he added it to the tray and carried it out to the living room, setting it down on the coffee table.

They hadn't made any formal plans for dinner, so he figured he'd just order something to be delivered, and in the meantime they could enjoy a snack.

It'd been about a week since the early morning he went to her apartment and they'd spent the day together in bed, sleeping. Well, she slept. He did a lot of holding her and catnapping on and off, refusing to get up and leave her side.

Before that day, they'd been apart over a month, and having no idea if he would ever have the chance again, Jeff stayed right where he was, soaking up as much of her as he could.

Since that day, which had turned into night, Jeff had been giving her space, only checking in once a day and waiting for her to reach out. She had been texting and calling, every day in fact.

With him worried that Steven might show up in the middle of the night, Jeff had come back over to her place a couple of times to spend the night, too. But they'd only held each other, nothing more.

As much as he didn't want to pressure her, he also really wanted to know where things were going between them. No denying she'd wrecked Jeff when she ended things between them. The last thing he wanted was to be hurt again.

But he also wasn't an asshole, so he wasn't going to walk away from her while she was still dealing with her brother and the unknown where the guy was concerned.

Jeff turned to go back into the kitchen to grab some napkins, and Rio caught his eye. The dog was sitting at attention, panting with his tongue hanging out and his eyes on the coffee table, specifically the food.

"*Nein.*" Jeff shook his head, chuckling. "That's not for you, young man. *Do not* even think about it."

Rio sneezed, gave him a whine, which turned into a yawn, and then slid his paws forward, landing in a lying down position.

"Good call." Jeff grabbed the napkins and silverware and then queued up some music on his phone and connected it to the Bluetooth speaker by the television. "All we need now is the girl."

Taking a seat on his couch, he waited for Tish.

A short time later, the doorbell rang. Rio scrambled to the door, and Jeff made his way there too. "Yeah, I know. It never gets old."

He opened the door, and just like always, lost his breath. She was still dressed in her work attire, which meant if he were a cartoon character, his eyes would be bugging out of his head and his tongue lying out on the ground.

Skirt, blouse, high heels... God, help him, the woman was so fine. So, so fine.

"What doesn't get old?" She smiled and stepped inside.

"You coming to visit." With a wide smile, he closed the door and pulled her into an embrace. Jeff buried his nose in her hair, breathing her in. "Glad to see you."

"Glad to see you too." She tickled the hairs at the base of his neck.

Jeff let her go and took a step back. But then grabbed her hand. "Come this way, my dear. I have snacks for us."

She laughed. "I thought we were ordering dinner."

He smiled back at her. "We are. This is pre-game."

"Oh, I see." She giggled and took a seat on the couch. "Looks delicious."

Jeff sat beside her and handed her a stemless glass of wine. She took it and nodded. Jeff grabbed his own. "What should we toast to?"

"To us." She smiled and clinked the edge of her glass to his.

He nodded. "I like the sound of that. To us."

They both drank, and he set his glass down. "You want me to set you up?"

"Sure." She crossed her legs.

Jeff prepared a little cracker, spreading one of the softer cheeses on it, then added a little raspberry jam. "Here you go, miss."

"Thank you, sir." She smiled and took the cracker and bit in.

Jeff made his own and then sat back, enjoying the moment. No need to rush into the "let's talk about our relationship" phase of the evening. After all, maybe they were on the same page. Possibly for the first time ever.

He wanted a life with this woman, the rest of his life, actually. A few more minutes wasn't going to kill him. Timing was everything.

* * * *

"I hope you know that I know what a big deal it is that you do things like this for me." Tish sipped her wine.

"What? Cut up meat and cheese and give you alcohol?"

She shook her head. "No, well...yes, but it's more." She giggled. "No seriously, it's that you set it up in this formal presentation. And it's all perfect and looks like something out of a magazine. It's this hidden talent I bet none of your friends even know you possess."

"Oh, that." Jeff smiled, his eyes crinkling at the corners.

"Yes, that." She moved her hair over one shoulder and played with the ends. He shrugged. "Well... Are you going to keep my secret?"

She sipped her wine. "Not a chance."

Jeff blurted a laugh, and Tish joined in, that familiar feeling of ease and comfort flowing through her.

Jesus, she had really missed the lightness of their usual tit-for-tat banter, hadn't realized how much she needed it. And at this point, she had every intention of ensuring she got to have it in her life going forward. It was high time to make some changes.

If the situation with Steven taught her anything, it was that she needed to start living her own life, at least a lot more than she had been.

It was horrible to realize how much she'd missed out on. Especially after she'd rearranged everything for her brother to move in with her, right down to ending the first real relationship she'd ever had. All of it had blown up in her face.

Plus, there was the debt she was saddled with, a debt she was in because of her failed attempts at helping him. Worse, at the end of the day, when he was getting loaded, Steven didn't really care what she was missing out on or how she was suffering. He sure didn't care if she was happy. Or if she was safe.

For fuck's sake, he'd stolen from her. And then assaulted her—though no one else besides Jeff knew that part, and she wasn't sure it was wise to dig that up now.

More than anything, she wanted her brother to be happy. But Jesus, she'd been so busy, so consumed with taking care of him all their lives, she'd never thought about taking care of herself first.

That whole "put the oxygen mask on yourself before helping others" airplane stuff really did make sense.

With everything that had happened, it was time to make some changes. Bottom line, until Steven wanted happiness for himself and actually *asked* for help, the real kind, which meant rehab and recovery, she was going to do her best to focus on her life, and more importantly, ignore the fear she had that he was going to end up back in jail—or worse, dead—and just live her life.

Being with Jeff again this week, though they hadn't done more than just sleep in the same bed, was a reminder that she deserved to be happy too. Hadn't she paid enough in her life to earn that? God, she hoped so.

"What's on your mind?"

Jeff's voice pulled Tish from her thoughts. She glanced up at him then back to her wineglass in her hand. "A lot of things." She took a sip. "You. Us."

He shifted in his seat, scooting back a little so he could face her. "What a coincidence. I was hoping maybe we could talk about us."

"Were you?"

"Yep. So—" He picked up a piece of pepperoni and placed it on a cracker. "You want to share your thoughts?"

She swirled the red wine in her glass. "I know that I want there to be an us. Do you still want there to be an us?"

He finished chewing and wiped his mouth with the napkin. "Are we renegotiating our contract?"

Tish laughed. "It wasn't a contract. They were guidelines!" She laughed again.

Chuckling, Jeff held his hands out to his side. "Potato, potahto."

Still laughing, Tish rolled her eyes. "Anyway, yes, I'm game for a renegotiation."

"Should I get the legal pad?"

"No." Tish laughed. "I think we can handle this without writing it down."

"All right. Hit me."

"Okay." She nodded and took another sip of wine. "Monogamous, committed relationship."

With raised brows, he tipped his chin down, staring at her. "You saying no more just 'casual'?"

Tish nodded. "I don't believe I stuttered."

"No, I don't believe you did." He pursed his lips. "Okay, I'm game."

"Good." Tish swirled the wine in her glass. "It's settl—"

"Not so fast." He balanced his elbow on the back of the couch, resting his temple on his fist. "What about friends?"

Tish blinked and then swallowed the last of her wine.

This was it, right? Game time. Do or die.

A small part of her still worried about everyone knowing and then having it blow up. Except, maybe it wouldn't? God, it would be such a mess if that happened. Outside of Steven, her friends were all she really had. Rayna in particular. Losing Rayna would be devastating.

But if she didn't let the light of day shine on her and Jeff's relationship, she was sure to lose him. And maybe this time for good.

"Well..." Tish took a deep breath and then blew it out, nice and slow. "That's part of the whole package, baby."

Jeff said nothing, just stared at her. There were so many emotions crossing his expression she could barely name them all, but for sure they were all positive. At least she hoped they were.

When the moment stretched, Tish's nerves started tingling the back of her neck to the point where if he didn't say something soon— "Oh, my God, this is killing me. Say something!"

Jeff straightened. "Killing you? Ugh, we've been over this, mami. The Heart song, remember?"

Tish laughed and set her wineglass down. Getting to her feet, she turned and held her hand out to him. "Let's get to it then."

Jeff jumped up, but instead of taking her hand, he bent and tossed her over his shoulder. Tish burst into a fit of giggles. As he jogged them down the hallway to his bedroom, she laughed harder, giving him a swat on the ass for good measure.

She was scared, yes, but at the same time, all of it felt right. And who knew, maybe things would work out for her and Jeff, and then eventually Steven would be okay too.

What a perfect world that would be...

Chapter 22

Jeff set Tish down on her feet at the side of his bed and stared down at her. His heart ached with all the unspoken feelings he had for her. The woman had no idea how much she meant to him, but he intended to spend the rest of his life, if he could, showing her.

Taking her face in his palms, he bent closer. "I missed you."

"I missed you too."

He smiled and brushed his nose over hers. "How about we spend the next couple hours showing each other how much?"

"I think that's a brilliant idea." Tish circled his neck with her arms. "You go first."

"If you insist." Jeff took her mouth, delving in with his tongue, giving her everything he'd been needing to give for weeks.

He broke the kiss long enough for her to take her shirt and bra off. He followed suit, tossing his T-shirt aside, and after she sat on the bed, she stripped out of her skirt and panties.

She slid backward to the pillows, and Jeff went for the top button of his jeans and then froze, completely enchanted by how fucking beautiful she looked in his bed, and still not even quite understanding how he got so lucky to have her there again.

"You okay?"

"I love you, Tish. I'm in love with you." He shook his head and raised his hand. "Don't say anything, please. You don't have to say it back. I know it might be too soon for you. That's okay. But...I just needed you to know."

Tish nodded and held her hand out. "Come to me, baby."

Jeff stripped off his pants and boxer briefs and then climbed onto the bed, lying along her side. Leaning on his elbow, he looked down at her and traced a line with his fingertip from her lips, down her chin, to the dip in her throat and then further to her breastbone.

As he continued exploring her skin, he ran his fingertip along the seam beneath one breast, and then over the curve to her nipple. Tish sucked in a breath, and he watched in awe as her areola drew up tight, the nipple becoming erect. "So sexy."

Unable to resist, Jeff bent forward and sucked the taut point between his lips.

Tish moaned again, this time arching, one hand landing on the back of his head, her fingers curling in his hair. "Baby..."

Jeff took his time, holding her full breast in his palm, giving it gentle squeezes, laving over her nipple. His cock was rod hard and rubbed against her thigh with each shift of their bodies.

He'd been dreaming of touching her like this. Hadn't thought he'd ever get to have it again. Losing Tish had been fucking devastating, and being close to her last week had already healed some of that devastation.

But being sexually intimate with her again took that healing to a whole other level.

Jeff smoothed his hand up her chest and then down her arm to her hand. Linking fingers, he rolled over her, raising her hand above her head and settling between her parted thighs.

Although they'd spent a few nights together since her brother took off, they hadn't had sex. Knowing it wasn't appropriate at the time, Jeff hadn't even tried to make a move, though he couldn't say it had been easy. Her soft body all curled against him. The scent of her skin and hair permeating his lungs and the deepest parts of his soul.

After arranging himself at her opening, Jeff took her other hand in his, raising it above her head like the other, and then took her mouth, thrusting his hips forward, pressing inside her tight core.

Tish whimpered, her knees squeezing his hips as he withdrew and slid back in. She rolled her pelvis, meeting his thrusts, and tangled her tongue with his, taking what he gave her and giving it right back to him.

Letting go of one hand, Jeff slid his palm down the curve of her side to her hip and then under to her ass. Taking hold of her bottom shifted their angle, and he thrust forward, grinding against her clit.

Tish gasped, moved her hands lower and raised her knees higher. "Jeff... Mmmclose, baby."

"Let me have it." The base of his spine tingled, his orgasm building too.

Tish must've planted a foot on the bed, because the next thing Jeff knew, they were rolling over and she was straddling him. Placing both hands on her hips, he grinned up at her. "Guess this is you letting me have it?"

She rocked her hips, grinning. "You know it."

Staring up at her, watching her ride him...Jeff nearly lost it. Her hair a sexy mess, her cheeks flushed and her perfect tits swaying in his face was enough to drive any man over the edge. Somehow he managed to hold it back, just long enough for her to come first—if she hurried.

"So, so good." She threw her head back, her pace increasing.

Jeff's cock jerked, and he pressed his thumb to her clit, rubbing it.

"Yes!" Tish bucked against him. Her orgasm hit, and she froze, his dick buried inside her, her tight sheath clenching down around his shaft in rapid spasms.

Jeff grabbed her hips and rolled his pelvis, grinding her back and forward on his cock. His climax hit hard, his semen shooting out of him, spurting over and over inside her.

Collapsing forward over his chest, Tish continued to ride him, slow and easy until she'd wrung him dry...and they were both completely spent.

He rolled them to the side and stroked her back.

"That was amazing." Tish curled against him.

"It was." He closed his eyes, not wanting the moment to end but also knowing that now it didn't have to.

"Then again, it always is, isn't it?" She pressed a kiss to his chest.

"Well, you know, when you think about it, we *are* like some sort of power couple." He gave her a squeeze. "I mean for realsies. People want to be us."

Tish started giggling against him.

"What? You don't agree?" Though she couldn't see his face, he was smiling like a fool. "Listen, we need to be sure we're on the same page here. Repeat after me: We are a badas—"

Tish tilted her head back, a grin on her face from ear to ear. "OhhhmyGod you are such a goofball!"

He laughed. "You love it."

"I will admit to nothing."

He rolled his eyes. "Okay, fine. It's okay, I know it's true. Anyway, how about food? Do you want food?"

She traced his bottom lip with her fingertip, her expression soft and full of feeling. "Yes, my sweet goofball. I would love food."

"Anything for you, mami." Jeff gave her a soft kiss before pulling away.

Yes, he was madly in love with her. Yes, he'd told her. No, she hadn't said it back, but that was okay. He was okay with her not saying it, because he knew she felt the same. He could see it in her eyes, in her body language and in her touch.

Every part of this felt different to him, felt new. It was a fresh and brand-new beginning for them.

Chapter 23

Tish woke with Jeff spooned up behind her. She pulled the blankets a little higher and burrowed a little deeper, loving the warmth and comfort she felt, had always felt, waking up with him.

They'd had a perfect night. Making love twice...both times mind-altering. The second being the half-asleep kind of sex couples had in the middle of the night when they found each other across the sheets.

There was something precious about that, the automatic way a couple knew exactly how to touch one another because they'd learned each other so perfectly.

Everything felt so much more intense, more intimate, too. Tish was sure that was because they'd made a full commitment to each other. Something Tish had never done before, with anyone.

And though she was nervous about what might lie ahead for them, she definitely felt freer, more at ease with Jeff than she'd ever been before, and she was looking forward to what else that would bring for them.

With things settled between them, Tish was now prepared to face what she'd been trying to ignore all week. She needed to report her car stolen. The idea of having to report Steven as the one who stole the car made her want to be sick, but what choice did she have?

She didn't want to lie, and a week had gone by and Steven hadn't shown back up, nor had he responded to any of her calls or texts. She didn't want her brother to get into more trouble, but she needed her car back too.

"What's wrong, babe?" Jeff's arm around her side tightened.

She sighed. "How did you know something was wrong?"

"Well—" He found her hand under the covers and linked his fingers with hers. "Your whole body got tense and your breathing changed."

"Huh. Interesting." She'd never realized that was something someone else might notice. Then again, she hadn't made a habit of sleeping in someone's arms like she was with Jeff, so she guessed that changed the game.

He kissed the back of her shoulder. "You want coffee?"

"Coffee sounds good."

"Cool. You can tell me over breakfast what's on your mind." Jeff rolled away.

"Okay." Tish rolled over and watched as he got out of bed and found his boxer briefs. "So what's for breakfast?"

"Whatever you want." He pulled two T-shirts out of his drawer and tossed her one of them. "I've got eggs, pancake mix, bread if you want French toast. Bagels and cream cheese too."

Tish couldn't help but grin. "The way you eat, I have no idea how you stay so in shape."

"We can go for a run later today if you want." He wagged his brows.

"Oooh, yeah, um no. I still kind of hate running. I do adore my yoga though. You want to do yoga with me?"

"Sure, mami. If that makes you happy, I'm down." He bent and gave her a closed-mouth kiss. "I saved your toothbrush for you." He smiled and sauntered into his bathroom.

Of course he had.

Warmth spread from her chest outward. How could something so benign as a toothbrush make her heart melt?

Tish looked down at the T-shirt he'd given her. It was a plain black shirt, faded from years of use. Probably one he wore with his uniform. She pressed the fabric to her nose and breathed in the clean scent of detergent.

Jeff appeared out of his bathroom, looking just as sexy as when he went in there. "Chop-chop, mami. Meet me in the kitchen." He snapped his fingers and headed out of the room.

"Coming!" She grinned, slipped the T-shirt on and climbed out of bed.

After brushing her teeth and trying her best to tame her wild mane, she gave up and went out to the kitchen.

Before she had a chance to sit at the island, Jeff pulled her into his arms and laid a toe-curling kiss on her.

Tish moaned, feeling arousal jump to life in her tummy.

He let her go and stepped back. "Morning, beautiful. Have a seat while the coffee brews."

"Good morning to you, too." Smiling, she pressed her fingertips to her lips. Doing as he said, Tish took a seat and waited for the coffee.

"I'm feeling like veggie omelets. You good with that?"

Tish linked her hands on the countertop. "Sounds awesome. Can I help?"

The coffee pot let out its last sputter. Jeff poured her a cup and brought it over to her. "Nope, just drink this, and then when you've had enough caffeine, tell me what's up?"

"I can't argue with that logic." Tish took the cup and the creamer he slid her way. After she'd gotten it to her liking, she took a careful sip. "Mmm. Perfect."

"Better cup of coffee than a Keurig." He cracked an egg and then another into a bowl. "Don't get me wrong, I get the allure, or the convenience rather."

Tish set her cup down. "I love my Keurig."

"You and everyone else." He set the bowl aside and started slicing up a green pepper. "I guess I'm just old-fashioned."

She took another sip. "I'll get you a percolator for Christmas."

"Now that would be awesome!" He grinned. "For realsies."

Tish shook her head, giggling. "You crack me up."

He winked at her and moved to the fridge. "You like spinach?"

"Yes." She watched as he pulled a few more ingredients out.

"Tomatoes?"

"Yes."

"Onions?"

She took a sip and swallowed. "Hard pass."

"I knew I liked you." Jeff chuckled and came back to the counter.

She leaned forward, resting her forearms on the counter. "Soooo..."

He paused mid-slice of a tomato and looked up at her. "I'm listening."

She drew in a breath. "I think it's time to report the car."

Jeff stopped cutting and set the knife down. "Are you going to report that your brother stole it?"

"Well, considering my boyfriend is a cop in the same city I need to report the theft in, I think it would not be a good idea for me to lie to the police."

Jeff nodded, his lips pursed, his eyes locked on hers.

Uh-oh. She'd never referred to him as her boyfriend before, and although she hadn't meant to shock him, it kind of looked like she had. "Jeff..."

"Sorry, just took me a minute, but I'm good. Actually, I'm more than good, and if we weren't about to eat a fab breakfast while you're about to talk about something very important, we would *so* be back in my bed right now with me showing you how much I appreciate that you just called me your boyfriend via several orgasms. That said, fair warning, I will be doing just that *after* we talk and eat."

Tish had started grinning about halfway through his declaration and hadn't stopped. "Is that a promise?"

"Damn straight it is." He gave her a wink and went back to slicing tomatoes.

Still smiling, Tish took another sip of coffee. She'd always struggled to be open with people. Even Rayna. Tish shared a lot with her best friend, but not all of it, not the true in-depth muddy and ugly stuff.

Jeff was whole different thing though. They'd had a rough start of course, more her fighting the nagging urge to be near him, but once that was out of the way, talking to him and opening up to him had happened without her having to push herself to do so.

Yes, she still had mounds of trust issues and commitment issues, abandonment issues and childhood trauma, but no one was perfect, right?

Here she was, just ready to tell the man damn near everything about her, or most of it anyway. He didn't need to know all the really dark shit from her childhood or teen years. No one did. That stuff needed to stay buried.

Point was, with Jeff, things were just simpler. Sure, it took time, but from the very beginning he just seemed to know what she needed, which was the freedom to share things when she was ready. On her terms. And the more that happened, the easier it got.

She brushed her hair over her shoulders. "I'm scared, you know? I don't want him to go back to jail, but I just don't see any way around it. I can't just write my car off and go get another one. Plus, I'm going to need to have the insurance cover the replacement if it's not found." She shook her head. "Maybe if he's caught, I won't press charges, and then maybe it won't be so bad?" She shrugged. "I don't know, I guess even if he has to go back to jail, at least I'll know where he is, and although he won't be in treatment, at least he wouldn't be getting high while he's in there."

"This is true." Jeff nodded and poured the beaten eggs into the pan. "I think for now, let's just take step one and report the car."

"First things first." She got up and refilled both of their coffees. "Step one is eat. Step two is file the report."

"You want to have an officer come here, or just go down to the precinct?"

She moved back to her stool at the island. "Is that an option? Going down there?"

"Yeah, of course." He smiled. "I can give you a tour."

"You going to parade me around to all your friends?"

"Pfft. What?" He pulled two plates down. "Of course."

Tish laughed. "Yeah, I thought so."

Jeff plated their breakfast and joined her on the other side of the island. They ate, talked, and joked around. She was about to go do something she didn't think she'd be capable of, and although she was nervous and afraid of what might happen, she knew Jeff would be by her side.

One way or another, she'd get through it. And Steven would get through whatever was going to happen, too. Until her brother was safe, Tish would worry, would always wonder and always want to try to help him.

But at least she didn't have to suffer and manage all those things alone anymore.

Chapter 24

Jeff parked the truck and looked at Tish. "You ready for this?"

"I was born ready, baby." She grinned.

He let out a laugh. "Yeah, sure. I bet you're nervous as hell."

"I am not! Why do you say that?"

He held up their joined hands. "Your hands are sweating like a kid who stole a piece of candy from the corner drug store."

She tugged her hand away and wiped it on her thigh. "Ew, Jeff. That's so gross."

He laughed again. "Mami, nothing about you is gross."

"Bet you there is. You're just blinded by the light." She opened the passenger door.

He got out of the driver's side. "Blinded by your light maybe."

She rolled her eyes and closed the door. He came around the front and caught her around her waist. "It's all right. I'm nervous too."

Tish blurted a laugh and put her hands on his shoulders. "You are not."

"Okay, you're right, I'm not."

"See!" Tish swatted his shoulder, chuckling. "Fine, I'm a little nervous, yes. It's just, they're all gonna go nuts, you know? Oh my God, and once we do this, come out in front of everyone, there's no going back. You realize that, right? I don't want it to change things for us. Or worse, what if things don—"

Jeff bent and took her lips, effectively silencing her. Rather than let her get herself all in a lather, worrying over things she didn't need to, he stroked his tongue over hers, intent on showing her exactly where he stood, where he'd always stood.

Things would change, yes, but not between them. What was between them was solid. It'd been a week since they were deemed an official couple. The next step in that was telling their friends, and Jeff couldn't be happier about that.

It'd been torture not being able to tell the world he had a woman. Not being able to share with Derek, and Rob too, about her, them, any of it, was fucking horrible. Jeff was so ready to leave all of that behind.

He and Tish had their second chance, and they were going to do it right this time.

Jeff broke the kiss.

With her eyes still closed, Tish licked her lips. "Mmm." She smiled and opened her eyes to stare at him, a dreamy expression on her face. "Okay, that worked. I'm good now."

"You're welcome." Jeff stepped away and took her hand.

"Thank you." She fanned herself.

Jeff chuckled and wound them through the other parked cars in the lot, making their way through the alley to head into the Whiskey Barrel.

All their friends were already there, and for the first time ever, he and Tish were going to walk into the bar together. Everyone would see and wonder. The plan was to let them wonder, but only for a short time before finally making their announcement.

Though, they hadn't planned that part out yet. They were going to just go with the flow and see how things went. Eventually, the opportunity would present itself, and boom, everyone would know.

Once that happened, well...yes, everything would change because there'd be no holding back for either of them anymore.

* * * *

Hands still linked, Tish shifted to walk directly behind Jeff as opposed to beside him as he stepped through the entrance to the bar.

Trace Adkins's "This Ain't No Love Song" was playing over the sound system above the buzz of the crowd. The band hadn't started yet, but as soon as they did, things would get even busier.

Jeff waved his free arm in the air, and Tish didn't have to look around him to know he'd spotted their group at one of the tables. As they weaved their way through the crowd, Tish followed, butterflies buzzing around her stomach. And dammit, her palms were sweating again too. Poor Jeff.

"What up, Shirley!" Jeff clasped fists with Derek.

Tish came around his left. "Hey, everyone."

Rayna's eyes went wide when she saw Tish, but she recovered quick. Hopping off the barstool, she gave Tish a hug. "I didn't even see you come in. Did you just get here at the same time as Jeff?"

"Yes, actually." Tish smiled and looked over at Heather. "Hey!" She made her way over to her. "What's up, lady? Good to see you."

Heather smiled, holding her arms out. "Good to see you too!"

Tish hugged her and pulled back. "You look awesome tonight, as usual. Cute top."

"Thanks. Rob took me shopping today."

"Aren't you just the good boyfriend." Jeff gave Rob a nudge.

"That's right. I'm going for boyfriend of the year."

Derek chuckled. "Sorry, dude, that's my title."

"Uh, aren't we the ones who get to be the judge of that?" Rayna rolled her eyes, laughing. "Y'all need to be taken down a peg or two, I'm tellin' ya."

Tish burst into giggles because, yes, Rayna was clearly a little buzzed, and there was a lot of country girl coming out of her, but also because her nerves were still kicking her ass, and she couldn't help it. How had they not noticed she and Jeff were holding hands?

"I'm ready for a drink. You want a shot, honeybun?"

Tish glanced at Jeff and she knew, right then and there, this was going to go down in a way that had everyone laughing as soon as they realized what was really going on.

Tish put a hand on her hip and raised a single brow. "Oh, now I'm honeybun? What happened to mami?"

"What's the problem, sugar lips? My vocabulary of endearment terms is growing. You should be happy about that."

"Jeff!" Rayna blurted a laugh. "Did you really just call her sugar lips?"

"I think he's trying to get slapped tonight. I should've brought popcorn." Heather crossed her legs and took a drink of her beer.

Tish made a show of placing her palm on her forehead, and then she moved closer to Jeff and crossed her arms. "Jeff, we've been over this. Have you learned nothing from all these months—"

"Years. It's been over a year, so years. Plur—"

She poked him in the chest. "And now you interrup—"

"But, snookums, I can't help it. You're just so pretty when you lecture me and then don't get the facts right."

"Lack of home training—"

"Punkin', your perfume is heavenly. What is it?"

Tish snapped her mouth closed and frowned, trying for all it was worth to look pissed, but the truth was, she was slowly losing the battle to keep from laughing her ass off. The gasps from their friends, combined with the bursts of laughter, plus the stupid shit Jeff was tossing her way was making it beyond hard to hold it together.

God, this man.

"How many slaps to the back of the head are you hoping this will earn you?"

Jeff placed his hands on her hips, a devilish grin arching his lips. "As many as you want to dish out, mami."

Tish drew in a deep breath, deciding her next move. She closed her eyes and gave a slight shake of her head, then gripped his jaw between her thumb and fingers. "Jeffrey Pearl, you are dead meat."

"Bring it."

As if they both closed the small distance between them at the same time, their mouths met in a clash of lips, teeth and tongue. Jeff wrapped his arms around Tish's waist, and she felt herself get lifted off her feet.

"Oh my God! What are you two..." Rayna trailed off.

Letting go of his face, Tish circled his neck and tipped her head to deepen the kiss.

One of the guys started laughing. "Holy shit, I fucking knew it."

And that was Derek, she thought. Not that it mattered. As always, the feel of Jeff against her, the taste of him, was all-consuming.

"Woo-hoooo!" Heather called out, laughing.

"'Bout damn time. Sheesh, I didn't think you two were *ever* going to get it together." That came from Kim; she must've just shown up.

Tish started giggling, and Jeff broke the kiss. With her forehead pressed to his, she whispered. "Guess the secret's out, huh?"

Jeff set her back on her feet. He smiled, his gaze roamed over her features, and then he brushed a strand of hair away from her eyes. "Looks that way."

"You two are in *sooo* much trouble!" Rayna said.

Tish looked at her best friend and grinned. "What can I say, he finally wore me down."

"Oh sure, blame it on me. Good thing I can take it." Jeff chuckled and gave her cheek a kiss before letting her go. "What can I say, I'm downright irresistible."

"All right, you two, start talking." Kim set her keys and pack of cigarettes down on the table. "I, for one, want to hear all the gory details."

Tish shook her head, unable to stop grinning. "I think we really need drinks. Like right now."

"That's what I'm talking about!" Heather jumped up. "I'll go find Bethany. Don't start talking until I'm back!" She pressed a kiss to Rob's lips and ran off.

Derek and Jeff found a couple more chairs so everyone had a seat, and when Heather got back, with Bethany in tow, they ordered a round of tequila shots for them all, a drink for Kim, and a couple of craft beers for her and Jeff.

"So what do you all want to toast to?" Tish raised her shot.

Jeff grinned. "I, for one, am completely out of ideas."

"That's a first." Derek shook his head. "How about we toast to you two finally pulling your heads out of your asses?"

"Sounds about right to me." Rob raised his glass.

Everyone clinked, then tossed the clear liquid back, and before Tish got her glass down on the table, everyone was chanting. "Kiss. Kiss. Kiss!"

Jeff pulled the lime from his mouth and turned to Tish.

"You big wimp. I knew you hated tequila." Laughing, she cupped his face in her hands and kissed him.

As he pulled away, Jeff brushed his nose over hers. "Yeah, but I'm your wimp."

"Oh my Lord, you two are so adorable! I can't stand it." Rayna jumped up and threw her arms around both of them. "I love you guys."

Tish giggled and wrapped an arm around Rayna while still holding on to Jeff. "We love you too, honey."

Tish's best friend let them go and returned to her seat. Jeff gave a kiss to Tish's forehead, and she felt her cheeks grow warm. Yeah, this was going to take some time to get used to, but it felt incredible just the same.

"All right, let's hear it." Kim winked and took a sip of her drink through her straw.

As Tish and Jeff launched into the story of how they finally came to be a couple, their friends listened as if they were telling the most important story in the world.

Instead of sitting, Jeff stood right beside her, his arm draped over her shoulder. Both of them going back and forth, letting them in on their little secret.

Rayna couldn't stop looking at them and grinning. Neither could Derek, for that matter. Everyone was beyond happy for them, which was excellent and not really surprising considering how they'd probably started a pool between them all on whether or not she and Jeff were together in secret.

But in spite of all the love and all the happiness going around, a small part of Tish couldn't help but feel bad, wishing her brother could be there too. Having Steven there would've made everything that much better.

Jeff pressed his lips to her ear. "They're playing our song, mami."

Tish listened for a moment as the band strummed the lead-in guitar of Kenny Chesney's "You and Tequila." She smiled. "Is this our song now?"

"First song we ever danced to together, anyway." He shrugged. "The first of many to come." With a sweet smile, he held out his hand. "Honor me?"

Tish's heart melted, and she extended her hand to his. "I'm all yours."

Chapter 25

Jeff pulled up in front of Tish's apartment building and put his police SUV in park. He glanced over his shoulder at Rio. "This is not how I thought our day was going to go, my man. You're definitely coming with me. She's going to need both of us for this."

Rio gave a low yip and then yawned, shaking his head out.

"Okay, let's get this over with." Jeff turned the ignition off and got out, then opened Rio's door and hooked his lead to his vest.

Rio jumped down to the pavement. When they got to her door, Jeff knocked.

After a few moments, Tish opened up with a smile. "Hey, are you off duty already?" She stepped back.

"Sort of, yeah." Jeff moved inside, wrapped an arm around her waist and gave her a soft kiss. Letting her go, he moved past her and unhooked Rio's lead.

Tish closed the door, and when she turned back, Rio went right to her, nosing her hand. She squatted and stroked over his white fur. "Hey, tough guy. You working hard?"

Jeff removed his vest, set it on the table, and then just watched her, a lump the size of a boulder in his throat.

She smiled up at him, still petting Rio. "And the vest is off!" She laughed. "So what's up? Everything okay?"

Jeff blew out a breath. "Honey, I think you should sit down."

She stared at him a moment, a look of confusion on her face, but then her eyes went wide, realization dawning. She straightened and moved to him. "Oh, God. What's wrong?"

Fuck, there was no way this was going to end in anything other than tears on her end. "Babe, let's sit—"

Her eyes flashed, and her face took on that "don't fuck with me" look. "No, I don't want to sit. Is it Steven? Did you find the car?"

Damn, his girl was stubborn. Something he loved about her, but he really wished at this moment she'd just do what he asked.

Jeff shook his head, trying to find the words he needed to say to her. No way to sugarcoat it, so he just laid it out. "There was a fatal accident. Steven was driving."

"Oh God, did he hurt someone? Wait, is he okay?"

Jeff shook his head. "There wasn't another car involved. Babe—"

"Wait, what? Wha...what are you saying?" She covered her nose and mouth with both hands and paced away from him and then turned to face him again. "Oh my God! Are you fucking kidding me? Jeff, is this a joke!"

He rushed to her and took her upper arms in his hands. "Tish—"

She pressed her palms to his chest, terror bouncing around her eyes. "Is he dead? Jeff! Oh my God, is Steven dead?"

Fuck, this was beyond horrible. "Yes, honey. He is. I'm so sorry."

"Are you sure?" Looking up at him, the expression of desperation and complete heartbreak on her face tore Jeff through and through. "How do you know? Did you see him?"

"No, I didn't see him. But the officers at the scene identified him with his picture in the system. I'm sure, sweetheart."

She pressed her lips together, chin quivering, staring up at him. The deep and raw pain in her eyes was something he couldn't even begin to fathom. He'd give anything to save her from this.

As his words sank in, tears ran down her cheeks. "I can't...I. No, no, no."

Her legs buckled, and Jeff pulled her against his chest. "I've got you, babe."

"*Nononononono!*" She sucked in a tear-strangled breath, shaking her head, her hands fisted in his shirt. "*Oh God, Steven! Nooooooo!*"

"I've got you." As her sobs echoed around the room, Jeff held her and guided them down to the floor. With the back of her head cupped in his hand, Jeff kept her tight against him, hoping like hell it'd be tight enough to keep her heart from splitting in two. "I've got you, Tish."

Chapter 26

Tish sat on her couch, glass of white wine in her hand, staring at the pretty mahogany box her brother's ashes were in.

Today was exactly two weeks from the day he died, and it still didn't feel real.

She'd had a small memorial service, and all her friends had come, but since she and Steven basically had no family, and Steven didn't really have any friends who weren't drug buddies, that was it.

So fucking sad, so pathetic.

Tish let out a sigh and sipped her wine.

The business of handling Steven's affairs had been nothing more than a matter of having him cremated and getting a copy of his death certificate from the state. She'd had an autopsy done, though. Cause of death was trauma from the car accident. He'd died instantly...but he'd had a shit-ton of crystal meth in his system, and his blood-alcohol level had been off the charts.

A knock sounded at her front door—Tish jumped and pressed her palm to her chest. "Dammit. Hate it when I do that."

She got to her feet, padded to the door and opened it.

"Hey, honey." Rayna stood smiling, holding a brown bag in her arms. "I brought Chinese."

Tish waved her in and shut the door. "I guess eating is a good idea."

"Always." Rayna set the bag down and pulled Tish into a hug, patting her back. "How're you, honey?"

"Just...you know." Tish pulled back and shrugged. "Two weeks today."

Rayna gave a little pout and squeezed Tish's shoulder. "Aw, sweetheart. I know. This is so hard."

Tish's eyes watered, and she did her best to blink the tears back. "It still doesn't feel real." She cleared her throat. "Anyway, you want wine with that?"

"Sounds good to me. You grab that, and I'll get plates and chopsticks." Rayna followed Tish into the kitchen.

With their plates full of sesame chicken, moo goo gai pan, and veggie lo mein, Tish and Rayna ate, staying quiet for the first several minutes. Since everything had happened, her lack of appetite had made eating difficult.

Tish was grateful for the silence. Talking served as a fabulous distraction as it was, and the first few bites were always hard to get down. But then the body did what it needed to, hunger kicking in, and it was easier from there.

Tish paused and wiped her mouth with her napkin, then took a sip of wine. "Thank you for this."

"That's what friends are for." Rayna smiled.

Tish smiled back. "You guys get everything unpacked?"

"Yes, thank goodness. Those boxes were making me crazy. Of course, the garage is packed full—we have a bunch of duplicate stuff. I'm thinking I might have a yard sale."

"That's a good problem to have. Do I get first pick at the sale?"

Rayna laughed. "Don't be ridiculous. You can have anything you want. You should come over next weekend and look through some stuff. You and Jeff can come for a cookout on Saturday or something."

"That sounds nice." She sipped her wine. "I'll ask him."

"You two doing okay through this?" Rayna wiped her mouth.

"He's been wonderful. Truly." Tish traced the rim of her wineglass. "It's me who's not doing okay. I feel like I'm not the best company right now, you know?"

"Well, yeah. I'm sure that's normal, though. Jeff gets that, right?"

Tish shrugged. "He gets it. I haven't sent him away or anything, haven't had to do that. Don't really want to either. He just..." Tish shrugged. "The good news is, he gives me the space I need. Doesn't press me to talk or anything like that."

"That sounds wonderful."

"He is wonderful." Tish picked at a piece of broccoli on her plate. "I don't know, Rayna. I'm still trying to wrap my head around losing Steven. How can he be gone? And then sometimes, it's like he was never here at all. How can that be?"

"I'm so sorry, honey." Rayna reached her hand across the table.

Tish clasped her friend's hand. "There is nothing to show for his life, nothing to show that he was here, and he was loved." Tish swallowed, feeling every emotion in her chest. "No one will ever know how wonderful he was. You'll never know. Jeff won't either. No one knows how smart he was or how funny—" Tears welled and ran down her cheeks, and a lump clogged her throat.

Rayna wiped her own tears away but stayed quiet. Instead, she held Tish's hand and let her cry, and cried with her.

Tish sniffled. "God... You have no idea the things we survived. It seems so unfair to make it out of all that and then lose him anyway." Tish shook her head. "I tried so hard, and nothing I did worked. Nothing. It's so fucking unfair."

"I know it is." Rayna got up and grabbed them some tissues. "Here you go. Blow."

"Thanks." Tish wiped her cheeks and eyes.

"Have you thought about going to grief therapy? Or even therapy for how you grew up? You've never really told me a lot, but from what you have shared, it does seem like you had a lot of trauma."

Tish shrugged. "I don't know. I mean, I guess that would be a good idea? I was always so focused on taking care of Steven, you know? I mean, I tried to get him to go to therapy plenty of times, and rehabs and twelve-step programs, but..." She shook her head and let out a groan. "I guess I never thought about it for me."

"Maybe now's the time to think about it." Rayna shrugged. "You owe it to yourself, honey."

"I guess." Tish took another sip of wine. "I'll give it some thought."

Her best friend was right, now was as good a time as any. Tish wasn't sure if she'd ever get over losing Steven, and the fact that she no longer had him to focus on, to worry about...she felt directionless.

Steven had always been where she put her energy. Putting it on herself hadn't been a priority.

Was she even ready to do this? All that shit they'd endured together, all the neglect and abuse, it was all locked in a box inside of herself, one she never opened. The idea of opening it now was terrifying. Jesus, what if she crumbled under the weight of all she'd been holding at bay?

"I'm scared, Rayna."

"I know, but don't you think Steven would want you to be happy? To find peace?"

Tish nodded, tears flowing again. "I hope so. I guess I have to try and believe that he's finally found peace, and yeah, maybe he wants that for me too."

Rayna got to her feet and came around the table to hug Tish. Tish stood and let Rayna wrap her arms around her. After a few minutes of tears and Rayna rubbing her back, Tish finally let go of her best friend.

Rayna smiled her soft smile and clasped both Tish's hands in hers. "Anything you need, just name it. I'm here."

"Thank you." Tish smiled and gave Rayna another hug.

It was time...time to take care of herself. Time to mourn. Time to work on healing what had broken so long ago.

And it was time to live.

Chapter 27

"Is there anyone here for their first, second, or third Al-Anon meeting?"

A few people in the big room—filled with at least fifty people—raised their hands, and since this was Tish's first meeting too, reluctantly, she raised hers.

"Wonderful! Welcome, everyone. Can we get your names again so we can get to know you better?" The person standing at the podium, who appeared to be running the group, focused on each person who'd raised their hand. Each responded, giving their names.

And then it was Tish's turn. "Hi, I'm Tish."

"Hi, Tish." The entire group said in unison. Then a few called out, "Welcome." And then, "Glad you're here."

Tish nodded, still unsure if she was in the right place.

As she'd committed to her best friend and herself, she'd started counseling about three months ago, right after Steven had died. Once she began unearthing the ugly details of her childhood, things had gotten harder.

The therapist had already been gently suggesting Al-Anon, but when all the traumas from her childhood started coming out, gently turned to strongly, and Tish had conceded to go.

In addition, Tish had started EMDR therapy, which was specifically for her to work on the many traumas she'd experienced as a child, of which there were plenty.

Between growing up with two alcoholic and addict parents, and then Steven being addicted to drugs the majority of his young teens and adult life, Tish had been (according to her therapist) severely affected by the family disease of alcoholism and drug addiction.

Tish had never considered the concept that drug addiction or alcoholism was a disease. But maybe these meetings would help her understand that idea better. To say she was skeptical was an understatement.

What good was this going to do her now? Steven was dead, and so was one if not both of their parents. However, her therapist said it didn't matter that they were gone, that Al-Anon was for Tish's recovery, and only Tish's recovery, not for them, even if they were all still here.

That said, in addition to coming in for her weekly sessions, her therapist wanted Tish to attend at least six Al-Anon meetings before she decided the program was for her or not. Tish had agreed, and now here she was, meeting number one.

Bottom line, the woman was convinced that Al-Anon was what Tish needed to help repair the damage that'd been done to her as a child and then as an adult. Hell, it wasn't like she had anything to lose by giving this deal a try.

Therapy wasn't easy, and Tish cried a lot. And she imagined whatever these twelve steps were wouldn't be easy either. But if that was what it took for her to find peace in her heart? To have better relationships in her life? And to be happy? She'd do it.

She'd absolutely, one hundred percent, do it.

* * * *

Jeff waited outside of the church where the Al-Anon meeting Tish was attending was being held. He'd found her car in the lot and parked near her. They had plans to grab some dinner afterward and then head to downtown Chandler to meet friends at the Whiskey Barrel.

Originally, she was going to head to his house after the meeting ended, and they'd head out from there. But Jeff decided to surprise her and be there when she got out.

He'd offered to go with her, but she hadn't wanted him to. He understood it was something she needed to do for herself, and the good news was, as usual, Jeff was still all good with letting Tish do things her way, and at her pace.

The last three months had been rough for her, but things between them were solid. That's not to say she wasn't grumpy, sensitive and difficult to deal with. At times she was so emotionally taxed with the stuff she was unearthing and talking about in therapy that all she did was fight with Jeff in between sessions.

It wasn't about him, and for the most part, he somehow managed to not take any of it personally. No easy task, a lot of biting his tongue, and a lot of walking out of the room to give her a few minutes to figure out she was being a dick.

As soon as she did, she'd come find him, wrap her arms around him and apologize, cry and apologize more. The good news was, after a blow-up, she'd open up and tell him all the things she was remembering and working through.

As of late, the blow-ups were less frequent, and instead, she was just sharing more and more with him. That was how he knew she would get through this, that their relationship would make it through this, too.

His girl was going to heal, and this meeting was just another step to doing that.

Jeff looked up as people started filing out of the long outdoor corridor that led to the meeting rooms at the church. After five minutes or so, he began to get a little worried, but then he saw Tish emerge. She was talking to a tall, red-haired woman and a petite blonde with a toddler on her hip.

She hadn't seen him yet, and that was all good. Jeff crossed his feet at the ankle, resting his ass against the tailgate of his truck, and waited for her.

Another ten minutes or so went by. Tish got hugs from the women talking to her and then made her way back toward her car. It was a matter of a few seconds before she saw him. Her ice-blue eyes widened, and her beautiful lips split into a big smile.

Jeff's heart skipped a beat, and as usual, he lost his breath. God, he loved this woman.

"Hi, baby." She moved right to him, wrapped her arms around his neck and gave his mouth a soft kiss. "I thought I was coming to meet you at your place. Did I get that wrong?"

Jeff circled her waist and shook his head. "Nope. Just figured I'd surprise you, and we could head out from here."

"You really are a romantic, aren't you?" She grinned.

Jeff winked. "To be honest, I prefer hopeless romantic."

Tish giggled. "Why hopeless?"

He gave her a gentle squeeze. "Basically, it means that for the rest of your life, I am never going to let you forget how loved you are." Tish gave a soft gasp, and he brushed his nose over hers. "It also means there's no hope for me. I'm all yours, mami, for as long as you'll have me."

Tish drew in a deep breath and cupped his cheek in her palm. "Jeffrey Shawn Pearl, what am I going to do with you?"

He turned his head and pressed a kiss to her palm. "Love me, I hope."

"I guess you're stuck with me too."

"Wouldn't want it any other way." He pressed a kiss to her forehead and let her go. "Let's head to dinner, and you can tell me all about the meeting."

Tish stepped back. "Sounds like a plan to me. Guess we can get my car later."

"You have the best ideas." Jeff grinned and walked around to the passenger side of his truck, unlocked and opened the door for her. "Hop in, honeybun."

Tish giggled and climbed into the cab of the truck. "Oh, God, don't start that again."

Jeff closed her door and came around to the driver's side. After getting in, he fired up the engine. "I think we should make a list of as many pet names as we can think of before we finish dinner and then use them on each other all night long at the Whiskey. It'll be hilarious."

Tish rolled her eyes, chuckling. "You're probably right."

"Oh yeah, I'm totally right." With a grin, Jeff backed out of the parking spot and proceeded out of the lot onto the street.

Tonight was going to be a blast. Ever since they'd revealed their relationship to their friends, the nights where they all got together were more fun than Jeff had ever had before. He and Tish had all the same banter they'd had before, except now it was also topped with a lot of PDA and a lot of dancing too.

In Jeff's mind, life was good. Life was damn near perfect. Tish was doing what she needed to do to get her heart, mind and soul sorted, and he was supporting her on that journey. Things between them could only get better and better.

She was all he'd ever wanted and would always want. Tish was everything.

Chapter 28

Tish sat on the couch at Karen's—her Al-Anon sponsor—and closed the notebook she'd been reading aloud from. The writing was Tish's fourth step inventory she'd been working on for a few months.

For the last four hours, Tish embarked on the fifth step, which consisted of Karen listening as Tish read each page. Every so often, they stopped and talked about a particular part Karen felt they should dive into deeper.

They'd laughed and cried, and now...it was all done. Tish had shared everything about herself. All of her past. The good, the bad and the ugly. And now, she felt lighter, freer, and...completely exhausted.

She wasn't done, though, not by any stretch. There was so much more to do. But what she'd learned in these last six months of therapy and Al-Anon meetings was that her counselor had been right, Tish was *severely* affected by the family disease.

The way she'd grown up had set in motion her reactions, thinking and behaviors. Those defense mechanisms and survival instincts she learned as a child did not serve her in adulthood. Of course, she had no idea about this and had unknowingly carried those negative "skills" into her adult life.

This shit blanketed every part of her life and every relationship she had. Which was why she had only a few of them. And the fact that she'd been solely focused on Steven allowed her to never have to look at herself.

She hadn't done any of it on purpose, but it had happened nonetheless. She'd hurt herself, and she'd hurt others. Hell, she'd even hurt Steven.

Tish did not want to live that way ever again. And because she was working with a sponsor, working the twelve steps, and had continued therapy, she knew she never had to.

For the first time in Tish Beck's life, she had hope. She had a desire to do so many things she could barely keep it all straight. And she had a man in her life she was madly in love with, and who she knew, deep in her bones, was madly in love with her too.

Who would've thought the goofy asshole who was also deadly good-looking would end up being her soul mate? The man gave her everything she needed and wanted and never dared to dream for.

Yes, Steven was gone, and although she was still mourning him, although she missed him every day, Tish knew deep in her heart that her brother was at peace. He'd struggled for so many years with his demons and addictions, and she'd struggled right along with him. There was no more of that now.

Now, there was only peace—for both of them.

Chapter 29

Sometime later...

"Hey, so...I finally looked up that damn Heart song." Tish hung her shirt up on her side of Jeff's closet...technically their closet now.

"What was that?" Jeff came to stand in the doorway of the walk-in.

Tish glanced over. "That song, 'All I Want To Do Is Make Love To You'? The one by Heart?"

Jeff chuckled. "What about it?"

"I looked it up."

"Mami, you telling me after all this time, you finally looked up the song?"

"Yep, finally did." Tish hung up another shirt.

He crossed his arms. "Well?"

Tish turned to face him and put a hand on her hip. "So basically all this time what you're really trying to tell me is you have another woman you're in love with, and you just want to knock me up so you can have a baby?"

Jeff burst out laughing, clapping his hands, throwing his head back.

Tish tapped her toe and somehow held back her own laughter. "Well?"

Still laughing, he stepped over to her and circled her waist. "No, wait, let me explain."

She raised both brows but let him pull her close to his body. "I'm all ears, cowboy."

Jeff started laughing again. Tish rolled her eyes. And after he got a grip on himself, he started singing the chorus.

Unable to hold it back any longer, Tish busted up laughing.

God, this man! She loved him; she really, really did. Or as Jeff would say, "For realsies."

* * *

Meet the Author

Dorothy F. Shaw lives in Arizona where the weather is hot and the sunsets are always beautiful. She spends her days in the corporate world and her nights with her Mac on her lap. Between her ever-open heart, her bright red hair, and her many colorful tattoos, she truly lives and loves in Technicolor! Dorothy welcomes emails at: dorothyfshaw@gmail.com. Or find her online at Facebook.com/AuthorDorothyFShaw and twitter.com/DorothyFShaw Newsletter sign up: http://bit.ly/DFSeNews.

Printed in the United States
by Baker & Taylor Publisher Services